BOSS EMPIRE

Boss #9

VICTORIA QUINN

CONTENTS

CHAPTER ONE

DIESEL

Tatum was off doing some networking at the trade show, and I lost track of her at some point. Thorn was nowhere to be seen and hadn't made an appearance at all that afternoon. I spotted Autumn at the bar, drinking a glass of scotch like it was ten in the evening rather than one in the afternoon. I didn't know the woman well and had barely exchanged more than a simple greeting with her, but I could tell the breakup with Thorn stung.

But she handled her pain with a lot more dignity than him.

I joined her at the bar and ordered a gin and tonic.

She watched me as she took a drink. "I've done so much chitchatting today that I needed a break..."

Tatum and Autumn hadn't given their presentation yet or revealed their new product. They were the last people to speak because they had generated the most buzz in the industry. In the meantime, they were dodging questions and making vague responses on their new launch. "Don't blame you." I stood beside her and glanced at the rest of the bar. A group of suits stood together, talking with their fingers wrapped around short glasses of liquor. Surprisingly, not too many engaged a conversation with me. Obviously, no one expected me to be there. I didn't participate in Tatum's other businesses except Stratosphere.

Autumn sipped her drink again, a lipstick smear appearing on the glass. She was in a pencil skirt and a teal blouse, her hair in big curls. Both she and Tatum looked like models rather than astute business professionals. Every time a man passed, he immediately glanced at Autumn's backside.

Didn't make a difference to me. But if this were Tatum...heads would be rolling.

"Thorn is pretty miserable too."

Her cheeks immediately reddened with embarrassment, and her eyes flicked away. "We don't need to talk about that..."

"It's the reason I came over here."

"Well, it's unprofessional."

"And you think Tatum and I are professional?" I asked with a smirk.

She couldn't fight the smile that formed on her lips. "You guys are different."

"But we don't have to be."

She turned back to me, her eyes narrowing and her

smile fading. "Thorn and I want different things...and that's perfectly fine. He was honest with me from the beginning, so I can't pretend to be surprised. But being with him was a lot more difficult than I anticipated. It makes me realize I want all of him instead of settling for some of him."

"He feels the same way."

"Trust me, he doesn't," she said with a scoff.

"I haven't known Thorn as long as Tatum has, but she's never seen him this way before. He looked like he got hit by a bus."

"I got hit by that same bus..."

"There's more hope than you think. He'll come around."

"I don't know about that..."

"Start seeing someone, and see what happens."

"Go out with another guy right now?" she asked incredulously.

I nodded. "Or just flirt with someone. It'll drive him insane."

"I'm sure it would, but that doesn't mean he'd change his mind. He's set in his ways. And that's okay. I don't judge him for it. I wish I could keep seeing him in a meaningless way. But I'm far too attached to him already."

"I understand. If Tatum didn't want me, I'd have a hard time too."

She chuckled. "That woman is so in love with you..."

I grinned. "Yeah, she is. Pretty pathetic, if you ask me."

She smiled because she knew I was kidding.

"I really think Thorn will come around. He's just an idiot who needs to figure this out on his own. So there's still hope."

"I'm not in love with him or anything... I just want more."

I had all of Tatum, but I still wanted more.

"I hope Titan doesn't think less of me because of all this."

I hated hearing people call her that, but since she wasn't my wife yet, there was nothing I could do about it. "She doesn't. When we worked together on Stratosphere, we weren't professional at all...trust me. She likes you and wants this to happen for Thorn. She wants him to be happy."

"She's an incredible person. She's stern when she needs to be, but compassionate too."

"You're right."

The men huddled to the left burst with a unanimous laugh. Their voices trailed over as they grew louder, and the sound was a stark interruption to our conversation. I tried to ignore them until I heard someone mention Titan.

"Less than two months after being shot, she's back in the game." A middle-aged man with glasses spoke to his colleagues, oblivious to my presence because they all stood in a circle. I was slightly behind Autumn with my head angled toward the bar. "Pretty incredible."

"You know what's more incredible?" a man in a gray

suit asked. "That after being shot, her ass is still plump like a juicy peach."

They all laughed like they'd never heard anything funnier.

I slammed down my glass, spilling the gin across the counter.

"Ignore them," Autumn whispered. "It's just how——"

I was already gone.

I approached their circle in my finest suit, my heart pumping blood to my already flexed muscles. If we were standing in the middle of a bar on a Saturday night, I would throw a punch to every single man standing there. Now that we stood in a room full of the wealthiest people in the country, asking for a lawsuit was stupid.

But that didn't mean I wouldn't make them shit their pants.

I shoved my shoulder into the guy in the gray, knocking him sideways so he splashed his drink on the front of his suit.

"Hey, watch what you're——" He shut his mouth when he recognized the rage on my face.

I came face-to-face with him, looking down at him because I was nearly a foot taller than him. His drink was still in his hand, so I snatched it and dumped it on his head. The amber liquid seeped down his front and stained the quality material of his collared shirt and tie. He closed his eyes to fight the burn as the rivulets trailed down. "I should bruise your face like a peach."

None of his friends came to his aid, choosing to be dead silent and avoid eye contact.

I kept standing there, staring down at him and making him grow more uncomfortable by the second. I could do this all day, intimidate a man until he nearly shit his pants. I inched closer and closer, until my nose was almost touching his.

He finally caved and stepped back.

"You just made a lifelong enemy. Congratulations." I walked past him and avoided his shoulder so I wouldn't stain my own suit. The men didn't hustle away immediately, standing there like they didn't know what else to do.

I walked back to the bar where Autumn was waiting and picked up my glass. "What were you saying?"

She turned around and saw the man dab at his clothes with cocktail napkins, not that it would do anything other than get the liquor out of his eyes. She turned back to me, unable to stop smiling. "Don't mess with Diesel Hunt."

"No," I said coldly. "Don't mess with the future Mrs. Hunt."

————

I sat in the dark in the presidential suite. My ankle rested on the opposite knee, and I wore my black boxers as I blended in with the darkness. I helped myself to the extensive bar and made myself an Old Fashioned—an extra one for my guest.

Tatum had a meeting with a potential client, so she had a late dinner.

I wasn't allowed to go.

Maybe that was for the best because I'd almost punched someone in the face just a few hours ago.

The doorway clicked as she swiped her key in the machine. The knob turned and she stepped inside, her heels clicking against the hardwood floor. She stepped into the room then moved to the wall where the light switch was.

"No."

She flinched at the sound of my voice. She turned her neck my way slowly until she spotted me sitting in the large armchair next to the window. She set her folder on the table and crossed her arms over her chest.

"Strip."

She didn't comply, staring me down.

I snapped my fingers.

Her features were difficult to see in the dark, but I was certain her eyes narrowed in resistance. But she didn't dare disobey me. The articles of clothing slowly came off, starting with her blouse and then her bra. Her skirt fell to her ankles before she peeled her panties down her long legs. Once she was just in her heels, she placed her hands on her hips. "I had an interesting conversation this evening..."

"You can tell me later." I nodded to the bed. "Put that on. Now."

After a brief pause of resistance, she walked to the bed

and picked up the glittering lingerie I'd picked up from Versace. With the diamonds and the fabric, it cost me fifty grand. But my woman wouldn't be dressed in anything but the finest. She examined it before she pulled it over her head and adjusted it around her petite figure.

There were no panties because she didn't need any.

She turned back to me, her heels clapping as she moved.

I eyed her with greed, considering how I would take her. The world watched her with fascination because she was the most remarkable woman on the planet. She had it all...beauty, brains, and so much money. But they didn't get to see her like this, obedient and sexy.

I could get her to do anything.

That made me the most powerful man in the world.

I conquered Tatum Titan.

And now she would be a Hunt.

"On your knees."

She lowered herself to the floor, her knees hitting the hardwood.

I pushed my boxers down and let my cock spring from his restraints. "Eyes on me."

She settled between my thighs and sucked my dick, her eyes shifting up and looking into mine. Her fingers massaged my balls delicately, touching me the way I liked. She sucked my tip hard then pushed me deep down her throat. Tears sprang into her eyes and streaked down her face.

My arms rested on the armrests, and I watched her,

feeling like a king while my queen obeyed my every command. The lingerie fit her body perfectly, and the diamonds reflected the light from the city outside the window. Her hair was pushed to the side so it wouldn't get in the way of sucking my dick. I usually held it in my hand, but this time, I let her do all the work.

I liked watching her work.

She pushed me into her throat again, saliva pooling at the corners of her mouth.

A more beautiful woman had never sucked my cock.

I wanted her to keep going, to edge myself so I could make it last all night. But naturally, once I shoved my dick in one place, I wanted to shove it somewhere else. I wanted to push her own salvia back into her pussy. I wanted her to feel how hard she made me. I wanted to squirt my come onto her belly, but I also wanted to pump it into her pussy.

I wanted to give it to her everywhere.

I fisted her hair then pulled her mouth away from my length. A trail of saliva stretched between the corner of her mouth and the head of my cock. "I'm fucking you in the ass tonight." The men had talked about the similarities between her ass and a juicy peach, but I was the only one who knew firsthand. And I was going to fuck her deep and hard, knowing every other man in the world would give anything to be me.

She didn't argue.

"Get on the bed."

She crawled on the mattress on all fours, the fabric

bunched up around her hips. Her glistening pussy was on display for me to enjoy. I grabbed the butt plug with the diamond tip and a bottle of lube from my bag. I tossed it on the bed before I positioned myself behind her, my dick slathered in her spit. I shoved myself inside her pussy with one swift move, greeted by her overwhelming slickness.

She moaned as she lurched forward, her pussy tightening around me harshly.

I gripped her hips and pumped into her hard, fucking her like she was a whore I'd bought for the night. I clutched the back of her neck and held on as I pumped, sliding through her cream and building up the slickness at the base of my cock.

She was already going to come. I could feel it.

I slowed down and coated the butt plug with lube before I inserted it into her relaxed behind. It fit without resistance, the sparkling jewel shining back at me. It was five carats of real diamond, because her gorgeous ass only deserved the finer things in life—including my dick.

She moaned at the fullness of my cock and the jeweled plug.

"Not yet." My hands wrapped around her body and squeezed her tits as I pounded into her, feeling the diamond press against me as I thrust. I hit her in the right spot every time, bringing her to the beginning of a climax.

She clenched the sheets and moaned as she felt the

explosion. She started to writhe as she lost the fight, her back arching deeper and deeper.

"No."

She growled in response.

"You want my dick in your ass, baby?"

"Please."

I was a man with a big dick, so I knew it hurt. Titan hadn't been fucked that way too often, so she wasn't used to it. Well, she'd better get used to it because it was going to happen a lot more often now. I pulled the plug out of her ass and then inched my dick inside her.

She stiffened at my entry, her breathing changing as she took the pain with patience. Her nails dug into the sheets, and she moaned as more of my dick slid inside her. I stretched her wide apart, filling her with my massive size. I kept going until she inched away from me, unable to take the last few inches.

She was gonna take them.

I held her hips and gave a quick thrust.

She moaned as she lurched forward.

I gripped her neck and leaned over her. "That's all of it, baby."

She reached between her legs and rubbed her clit.

"You want to come?"

"Yes, Boss Man..." She rubbed herself harder.

I settled back on the balls of my feet and held her hips. I yanked her toward me as I thrust deep, hitting her hard with my entire length. Her ass was even tighter than her pussy, and the slickness from her slit was enough for me to move deep inside her easily. I stared at her gorgeous ass as it shook, knowing this gorgeous woman was mine forever.

I was the only one who got to fuck her like this.

She reached behind her and gripped both of my wrists with her hands, her face pressed into the sheets. She moaned louder as I fucked her harder. Her pussy still glistened with arousal, and her ass tightened around me as I moved in deeper. "Diesel…"

"Yes, you can come."

Her nails cut into my forearms as she came with a scream. I hoped her yells were loud enough for our neighbors to hear. Tatum Titan was only fucked by one man— me. Her screams were muffled by the pillows, and her hips started to buck instinctively.

This wouldn't be a night for multiple orgasms. When I stared at my dick in her gorgeous ass, I couldn't restrain myself. I clutched her hips and shoved myself as deeply as I could go and came with a grunt.

I came deep inside her ass.

"Fuck…"

I gripped her neck as I finished, the wave of pleasure coming over me. It seemed to stretch on forever, aligning with hers. I didn't notice the sweat that had collected on my body until that moment. I didn't feel the exertion of my muscles until I was finished. But now that I was done, I felt like a man who had just conquered the world.

A king who had just conquered a queen.

———

When we were finished, I immediately got into the shower and rinsed off the sweat. My fingers massaged the shampoo into my hair before I dipped my head and rinsed. After a good fuck, I was exhausted. I could have just rolled over and gone to sleep.

The door opened behind me, and Tatum joined me.

I grinned before I turned around. "Another round, baby?"

Now that the fun was over, a glare had returned to her face. "I had dinner with Roger Thompson and some colleagues."

No idea who that was.

She stared at me like that should mean something to me.

"And...?"

"He said you dumped his glass of scotch on his head."

Now I knew exactly who she was talking about.

"Is that true?"

"Probably. I did dump booze on some guy's head this afternoon..."

Her eyes narrowed to slits. "What the hell were you thinking? Roger Thompson is one of the biggest names in energy. I can manufacture most of my supplies at half the cost with him. And now you pissed him off."

"You think I give a damn?"

She dragged her hands down her face. "Diesel..."

"Did he mention why I dumped that booze on his head?"

Now her makeup was smeared because of her fingertips. "Said you misheard him say something."

I laughed because it was ridiculous. "No, there was no misunderstanding. I know exactly what he said—and Autumn can back me up."

"What did he say?"

Now I didn't want to tell her. "Something insulting."

"Why do you care what he thinks of you? I thought you were a man so secure in himself that it didn't matter what anyone thought?"

I sighed and shook my head. "You think I would snap like that because he insulted me? Take a minute and think about it..."

It took her less than a minute. "He said something about me."

"Yes. He said he's surprised your ass is still juicy like a peach even after you've been shot." I remembered the sound of the guy's voice like I'd just heard it five minutes ago. Pissed me off all over again. The strongest person in the world was reduced to a woman with a nice ass. She survived an attack, and instead of being revered as a man would be, she was a joke. It was bullshit.

Tatum hid her anger far better than I did. She was used to comments like those, so they didn't bother her anymore.

I didn't know if that was sad or impressive.

"You think I care what he thinks of my ass?" she asked

calmly. "This ass has made me the richest woman in the world. I've busted this ass for everything that I have. He can admire it all he wants."

I grinned, surprised she would take something like this so well.

"He says he won't work with me unless you apologize."

The laugh that escaped my throat actually hurt my ears. "Baby, you know that's not going to happen."

"Yes...I know."

"You don't need him. You can figure this out on your own. I have some contacts, so I can make it happen too."

"Fine. But you could not make enemies with people too."

"He made enemies with me." I stepped out from under the water to get closer to her. She was naked and beautiful, and I felt my cock slowly twitch to life even though I'd just had her. "If you think I'm gonna hear someone talk about my wife like that and just look the other way...then you're going to be disappointed."

"I'm not your wife, Diesel."

"I've committed to you for the rest of my life—same fucking difference. If I ever hear anyone slight you in any way, you bet that peach of an ass they're gonna get what's coming to them. If I want to make lifelong enemies with someone, that's my choice. There's no better way to spend my time. Now you need to tell him that if he wants the best business partner in the world, he can fucking apologize to me."

CHAPTER TWO

Autumn

Lance Palmberg and I sat together at a table in the bar of the hotel. The festivities for the day had died down, and now everyone was enjoying their evening. People tended to network after the conference ended, and when I ran into Lance, we decided to get a drink. He'd stopped by my office a few times in an attempt to recruit me to work for his company. It was a lot smaller than mine, but at the same time, it was a chief competitor.

"So now you are partners with Tatum Titan." He shook his head and didn't touch his beer. The bubbles continued to rise to the surface, and the foam remained on top. "Pretty incredible accomplishment. How did that happen?"

"She offered to buy me out. I said no."

"And then asked to partner with you?" he asked in surprise.

"No. I asked her. I told her I wouldn't sell for any price."

"Wow," he said with a chuckle. "She obviously thinks your company is the real deal."

I spent all of my time in the lab, constantly reworking numbers and improving projects as I worked on them. I didn't just want to produce something for the world to consume. I wanted to make the best possible innovation. I wanted my name to be revered, just the way Titan's was. "I think she values my work."

"Of course, she does. You're the most brilliant student out of MIT."

"I dropped out after the first semester." I couldn't take credit for an education I never received. To be accepted at such a prestigious university was a compliment, and a lot of people thought I was crazy for dropping out.

"Oh, that's right. I remember." Lance was young, an apprentice at his father's company. He'd slowly moved up in the ranks, and now he was in the process of heading the company.

It was unfortunate because it would be out of business in the next five years.

"So I'm guessing there's no chance for me to recruit you anymore?"

"No, I'm sorry."

"And there's no price?" he asked. "Because I can pay anything."

I shook my head. "It's not about the money."

"Now that you're working with Tatum, money is the last thing on your mind."

"You want my advice?"

"Advice on what?" He finally took a sip of his beer.

"If I were you, I'd break into another niche while you still can. Titan and I are going to break into this space and monopolize it. There are a lot of other specialties you could focus on. I would improve solar energy for houses since Tatum and I are more focused on commercial progress...just an idea."

"I'll consider that."

"Or, if you're going to sell...do it now. Don't wait until we go public in a few weeks."

"My dad is pretty stubborn. He's been working in energy since he was young. It's not something he can just walk away from."

"Well...you need to adapt or die." It was the cold and hard truth, but that was how it was. Sometimes you had to take the deal you didn't want to take just to survive. But that was how the world worked.

He gave a slight nod. "I suppose."

"You're young. You have a lot of time to figure out your place. Don't be discouraged."

"That means a lot coming from a genius like you," he said with a smile.

I hated being reduced like that. People labeled me based on my intelligence, but I was more than just a scientist. I was a woman with hobbies and a nice laugh. I was someone who enjoyed sports and a brisk jog in the park. But that wasn't what people saw. They wrote off all my difficult decisions as easy because I was so intelligent...but no amount of intelligence could make things easy. "How are the wedding plans?"

"Easy."

I chuckled. "Then your fiancée must be doing everything."

"Exactly," he said. "That's why it's easy."

I looked past Lance's shoulder and spotted a man step into the lobby from the elevator. In dark jeans and a long-sleeved black shirt, he displayed a chiseled, muscular form. With dirty-blond hair and blue eyes, he was a beautiful man. Tall and rigid, he had a lean, athletic build just like a soccer player.

My heart immediately began to race. Even at this distance, I knew exactly who it was. I wished my stomach didn't tighten with butterflies. I wished my thighs wouldn't press together so tightly. My cheeks flushed with heat, and I suddenly felt his kiss without touching his lips. That man had reduced me to a woman desperate for passion—desperate for him. I'd never felt the shake in my hands like I did with him. I'd loved Max with all my heart, but he never made me tremble the way Thorn did. With Thorn, I felt like the most beautiful woman in the world —even if he didn't say it.

It was smart to walk away from him when I did. If I stayed any longer, I would have drowned. Right now, I was still hurting like someone punctured one of my lungs. I tossed and turned when I slept because he wasn't beside me. In a short amount of time, I'd become attached to a man I'd vowed to never fall for her.

I broke that promise.

Flings were fun. Getting dressed up and having dinner with a pretty man was always a good time. Hot and meaningless sex was always great too. There was no meaning behind it, but that's what made it so wonderful.

But fucking Thorn was never meaningless.

I wished we were still fucking.

"Ms. Alexander?"

I stopped staring at Thorn and returned my look to Lance. "I'm sorry...I just remembered something."

"I have to make a call real quick. Do you mind if I step outside?"

"Of course not."

"Be right back." He smiled before he walked to the other side of the lobby.

I turned my gaze back to Thorn, who was walking this way. He was dressed casually, my favorite way to see him. He filled out his suits like a model on a billboard, but his body looked the best in t-shirts. His body stretched the fabric in all the right places. His arms stretched the sleeves until they nearly ripped. He was all muscle and no fat—dreamy.

He walked toward the bar, obviously not seeing me yet. He looked just as irritated as he had earlier that morning. His hair was combed now, but he still wore a pissed look in his eyes. Diesel told me Thorn was miserable too, and now that I stared at his depression, I actually felt bad for him.

Even though I felt a million times worse.

His eyes snapped in my direction, and he couldn't contain the surprise on his face. He slowed down his pace, taking me in a little longer. We hadn't said more than a few words to each other since we saw each other that morning. It wasn't awkward to be together.

It was just painful.

Our last night together kept coming to mind. I enjoyed it so much that I didn't want to go in the morning. I had to force myself to leave, to walk out of his penthouse with dignity.

But I was getting tired of holding on to my dignity.

He considered just walking by, but something pulled him in my direction. He walked up to my table then noticed the nearly full glass of beer beside me. I was drinking scotch, so he knew I was with someone else. "Hey."

"Hey." Just saying a single word to him hurt. I wanted to return to a normal relationship, but that didn't seem possible anymore. Thorn was such a beautiful man that I couldn't look at him without feeling my entire body float in midair. Ever since the first time I'd laid eyes on him, I'd thought he was *the* sexiest man in the world—not one of the sexiest. Sleeping with him was like being with my celebrity crush. I thought I would get him out of my system, but I found myself wanting him more. "Lance Palmberg and I were talking

about work. He had to step away to talk to his fiancée."
Truth be told, I had no idea who he was talking to, but I
didn't want Thorn to think I was on a date or something. Diesel recommended trying to make Thorn jealous, but I didn't want to do that. Playing games wasn't
my style.

He glanced over his shoulder and saw Lance talking
away in the corner, pacing back and forth. He slowly
turned back to me, his hands sliding into his pockets.
"Still working, huh?"

"Lance and I have a history."

"What kind of history?" he asked.

"He tried to recruit me to work for his company a few
years ago. That was before my company took off. Now
we're talking about my working relationship with Titan,
and I'm giving him advice about what to do about his
father's company. I don't think they'll last with the
competition, and I'm not just saying that out of arrogance. They're a good, family company, and I don't want
to see them lose everything."

"That's nice of you. People in business are a lot more
cutthroat than that."

"Money isn't everything," I said quietly. "I know Titan
would have done the same thing."

"She adheres to a different code of ethics than the rest
of us."

"And I wonder where she learned it..." I took a drink
to cover up my nerves. He always made me nervous. I
wondered if he'd ever noticed before. Keeping my confi-

dence was always important when I felt intimidated, but I wasn't sure how effective I was.

"Not me. I'm ruthless."

"You're full of it."

He gripped the chair he stood behind and continued to stare at me. His angry look slowly morphed into an expression of sorrow. The second he walked me out of his penthouse, he seemed morose. Now he was still in the same state of sadness.

I crossed my legs just so I had something to do.

Thorn didn't walk away even though our conversation had died away. Now we had nothing to talk about. We didn't always have much to say, but when we were alone together, it was okay not to talk.

We usually did other things.

"Are you going out?" I asked, unable to find a better conversation starter.

"Not sure. I've been in my room for a while and wanted to stretch my legs. What about you?"

"When we're done with our drink, I'll probably go to bed."

He nodded, his blue eyes locked on mine.

The second I mentioned bed, I thought of sharing it with him. "Are you going to visit your parents?"

"Tomorrow."

"Good. You told them you were here?"

"Yeah. Mom is all excited…"

I smiled, imagining a woman with blond hair and blue eyes. "That's cute."

"Titan is coming along because she's close with my family, so she's bringing Diesel too. They want to meet him."

"That's nice."

He stared at me for another moment, the silence becoming tense. "Would you like to come?"

To meet his parents? That sounded like a terrible idea. "That's nice of you to offer, but that's okay."

"My mom is a great cook. And Titan insists they're both great company. We could have some fun...you should come."

It was the second time he'd asked me, and now it didn't seem like he was doing it out of politeness. Maybe he really wanted me there. I would love to see his parents, to see where he came from. He was an incredible man, so he must come from a wonderful family. "Okay, I'll come."

"Great. My brother will be there, so just ignore him."

"Why would I ignore him?"

"Because he'll think you're hot and try to land you."

"Really?" I asked in surprise.

"He's a bigger manwhore than I am, if you can believe it."

"I can't, actually."

He grinned then looked away. "I guess I'll let you get back to your conversation."

I didn't want him to leave. "Alright. Have a great night."

"I'll try...but I'm sure it'll be boring." He held on to the back of the chair as he stared at me. His knuckles turned white from gripping it so hard. A quiet sigh escaped his lips, and he finally released the chair. "Good night, Autumn." The last time he'd said my name, it didn't sound right. Now it didn't sound right again. I was used to hearing him call me baby. Knowing he would never call me that again brought on another wave of sadness.

"Good night, Thorn."

He finally walked away, turning his back on me. His muscles shifted under his t-shirt, and his jeans were tight on his ass. He was a powerhouse of a man, beautiful from head to toe.

I stared at him until he was gone from sight. When I couldn't see him anymore, I let out a sigh...dreading going to bed alone later that night.

CHAPTER THREE

Titan

Diesel was still in a terrible mood the next morning.

When he woke up, he moved on top of me and gave me a quick fuck that was just about getting off. He was barely awake, and his hands grabbed at me aggressively, pulling my hair and gripping my neck. He came inside me with a grunt, like he was claiming me in a way that everyone would notice at the conference.

Because he was a psychopath.

I got ready then left without waiting for him. Whenever he was pissed off, the mood lasted days. Even when he didn't say anything, I could feel his rage through his silence. People made sexist comments about me all the time, even some of the most respectable men. No matter what I did or how successful I was, I was still defined by the perkiness of my ass. My appearance would always be more important than my work ethic, unfortunately. I'd come to terms with that a long time ago, and I didn't waste my time being upset about it. Diesel still had to learn that, and it was taking him a while to catch on. If he fought every person who insulted me, he would have no time left to do anything else.

I walked into the conference and spotted Roger Thompson speaking with some of his colleagues. I pretended I didn't see him and walked to the coffee table. I hadn't had a chance to enjoy my morning joe because I was too focused on getting away from Diesel. Once he got out of the shower and realized I was gone, he'd get pissed off all over again.

"Morning, Titan." Autumn appeared at my side, a cup of coffee in her hand. Her black hair was straight and shiny, and she wore a black dress with five-inch heels. Her striking green eyes stood out against the darkness of her hair. She appeared to be younger than me, but she possessed the grace of someone who had lived much longer.

"Morning, Autumn. How are you?"

"Good." She wore a smile that was so convincing I almost believed it. But since I knew she and Thorn were no longer an item, I understood that smile was just a cover-up for the pain throbbing beneath the surface. I'd never spoken to her about it because it didn't seem professional. I didn't know her on a personal level. "Hope everything with Diesel is alright."

"We're fine," I said. "He's just driving me crazy."

She chuckled. "I thought what he did was sweet...he loves you."

"I know he does." It was impossible for me to say that without smiling. "But he needs to understand I don't need a man to defend my honor. People are going to say some very cruel things. He needs to learn to ignore them."

"That's not gonna happen, and you know it," she said with a chuckle. "Not only does he love you, but you're going to be a Hunt. You'll be family to him. And if someone said something about his family, you know fists would be flying."

When she put it that way, it made perfect sense. "Yes, but if he fights off all my attackers, he'll never have time to do anything else."

"I don't think he wants time to do anything else."

Diesel was like the fiercest guard dog I'd ever had. He growled, barked, and bit on command. He circled me like a shark, ready to take a piece out of anyone who crossed me. He understood I could fight my own battles easily, but that didn't stop him from wanting to intervene. I'd shot a man in the neck and the face just to survive.

I certainly didn't need someone to protect me.

Roger Thompson noticed me and moved in, adjusting his navy blue tie with a hint of arrogance. He was livid when he spoke to me. Diesel had embarrassed him in a room full of his peers, and he couldn't let the slight go. Now he refused to work with me until he got a public apology.

Like that would ever happen.

"Titan." He stopped in front of me, just as hostile as he was yesterday.

"Roger." I sipped my coffee. "How are you?"

"Am I going to get that apology today?"

I sipped my coffee again so I wouldn't laugh. "Sorry, Roger. That's not going to happen." There was nothing I could do to change Diesel's mind, and I wouldn't want Diesel to cave anyway. It would be ridiculous to apologize for defending your fiancée. I didn't need his business that much.

"He's not?" he asked coldly. "Well, you can kiss our arrangement goodbye. I could do everything you need for half the cost, but now the competition is going to eat you alive. Your margins will take the biggest hit."

I wore a professional smile. "Mr. Thompson, in just a week, I'm going to be the richest person in the world. You think I give a damn about margins?"

Autumn couldn't hide the smile on her face.

Roger's cheeks turned red.

"Diesel is the best business partner I'm ever going to find, and I would much rather have him by my side than a sexist little swine like you. Remember what happened to the last man who insulted me?"

The redness faded, and he turned white as snow.

"You won't be getting an apology from Diesel Hunt. But if you want to stay in business for another decade, I suggest you apologize to him. He's a very vengeful man." I turned away, taking Autumn with me. I had nowhere to be specifically, but I walked at a slow pace like I had all the time in the world.

When we were out of earshot, Autumn chuckled. "Oh, that was priceless."

I couldn't keep the smile off my face.

"Fucking asshole got what he deserved."

Thorn joined our group, his face etched with lines of concern. "Everything alright? Looked like you and Roger were having a deep conversation." In a navy blue suit with his hand in one pocket, Thorn looked like a business tycoon and a billboard model. His dirty-blond hair was styled for a photoshoot, and his cleanly shaven jaw showed the hard lines of his masculine mouth.

Autumn's smile immediately dropped once Thorn joined us.

"Everything is fine," I said. "Roger and Diesel have some beef now. I tried to bury it, but I think I may have made it worse."

"No, you put that bitch in his place," Autumn said.

Thorn's eyes moved to her face, and they hovered there for a few extra seconds before he spoke again. "What happened?"

"Apparently, Diesel overheard him make an inappropriate comment about my ass."

Thorn's head immediately snapped in Roger's direction, and the threat in his eyes was unmistakable. His jaw tightened, and his hands formed fists. "I'll make his face look like his ass..." He moved to the other side of the room.

I grabbed his arm and yanked him back. "What's gotten into you?"

"No one talks about you like that," he snapped. "That's what. Come on, you were just shot. That's all people have to talk about?"

I whispered, "Lower your voice."

Thorn shut up, but he looked like he wanted to scream.

"I just got Diesel under control," I said. "Don't make me do the same with you."

Autumn moved her hand to his bicep. "Titan already put him in his place."

As if she had superpowers, the second he felt her touch, he released his anger. A deep breath filled his lungs, and the icy expression in his gaze faded away. He relaxed like a flower in the sun, suddenly at peace. It was the quickest I'd ever seen him come down from a rage. It was almost instantaneous, like her touch placed a spell over his being.

I'd never seen Thorn react that way to anyone before.

Autumn continued to massage his arm. "She reminded him exactly who he's messing with...the richest couple in the world. And the woman who killed her attacker. So there's nothing left for you to do." Her hand slid down until it fell from his arm.

The second her touch was gone, the calmness in his eyes disappeared. He seemed to be angry as soon as her touch was withdrawn. Thorn had never been a moody kind of guy. He was always pragmatic and logical, but once Autumn was in the mix, he was all over the place.

The more I watched them together, the more I realized this wasn't just some fling.

It was something more.

And I wasn't going to let Thorn throw it away. He would never let Diesel slip out of my grasp, and I would do the same for him.

"Diesel is here." Autumn spotted him across the room.

I thought I felt a dark cloud block out all the light. I watched him step into the conference room, a large man in a black suit. He parted the crowd on either side of him, his presence as tangible as a hand on your shoulder. With arms by his sides, an open chest with shoulders back, he was unmistakably confident. His dark eyes scanned the room as he searched for me. While he was looking for me, everyone else was looking at him.

"And I'm sure he's looking for you," Autumn added.

"He's always looking for me..." My sarcasm made it sound like a joke, but there was nothing funny about it. His hand was constantly on my waist, even when we weren't in the same room.

His eyes landed on me, and his gaze became a million times more intense. The look was packed with so much heat, it almost seemed like he hated me. He began his path toward me, ignoring anyone who approached him for a conversation. He treated everyone like they didn't matter when it came to me. Until he greeted me first, no one seemed important.

It made me hate him, but love him at the same time.

When he reached our group, he circled his arm around my waist and pulled me in for a kiss that was completely inappropriate for a room full of colleagues and professionals, but I didn't dare pull away because I knew he wouldn't have allowed it. He spoke against my mouth. "You left without saying goodbye this morning."

"I had somewhere to be."

"The only place you should be is in my bed, unless I say otherwise." He dropped his hand from my waist and stepped away so he wouldn't smother me anymore. He finally greeted Autumn and Thorn with a simple nod. "Morning."

"Titan just told off Roger," Autumn said. "And it was awesome."

"Did she now?" He turned to me, a ghost of a smile on his lips. "And what did she say?"

"That he shouldn't fuck with the richest couple in the world," Autumn said. "And she reminded him what happened to the last man who crossed her."

Diesel's grin widened, and there was more pride in his eyes than my father ever showed for me—and he had always been so proud of everything I did. "That's my woman—fucking badass." He gripped my ass as he kissed me on the corner of my mouth. "She's gonna make an excellent Hunt." He patted my ass before he walked away and

joined a group of suits he knew. Taller than almost everyone
in the room, he stuck out noticeably. A lot of the women
nearby couldn't help but turn their gazes in his direction to
check out the perfect man that filled out his suit so well.

I didn't give a damn how much they looked. He was
marrying me, not them. Staring was as close as they were
going to get. Drool all you want, ladies. In just a week, I
would be Mrs. Hunt.

Thorn drifted away too, joining Diesel and the group
of suits he was speaking to.

Autumn's gaze lingered on Thorn a little longer than it
should before she turned back to me. "You're very lucky.
I'm not jealous you have Diesel. But I'm jealous you have
a man who loves you more than life itself. Love like that is
hard to find..."

I glanced at Thorn before I turned my gaze back to
her. "It's not as hard as you think."

She looked down into her mug before taking another
drink of her coffee. "Thorn invited me to his parents' for
dinner tonight."

Why wasn't I surprised? "Good. His parents are
very sweet."

"I thought so. He's a great guy, so it makes sense."

I enjoyed listening to her speak so highly of him. "I
know this is none of my business and I should butt out...
but I can't. Please be patient with Thorn. I know he'll
come around."

She smiled at my bluntness. "We don't need to talk

about this. I'm here for the trade show. I don't want you to think all I care about is Thorn."

"All I care about is Diesel, but it doesn't interfere with my work." I didn't judge a woman for loving a man. If a man claimed he loved someone, he was considered romantic and brave. But if a woman did it, she was obsessive and pitiful. It was ridiculous. "Please be patient with him. I know he'll come around."

"Honestly, waiting around for a guy to treat me right isn't the best way to utilize my time," she said with a sigh. "I'm not the kind of woman who waits around for anyone. I would judge myself if I did."

I completely understood that and didn't disagree. No woman should wait for a guy to be ready. They should find someone who treated them right from the beginning.

But I knew Thorn would come around. I knew he would realize Autumn was someone he had to take a risk on. "Do you love him?"

She nearly did a double take at my question. "Uh..."

"I'm sorry. I know that's personal."

"I...I think I could love him. That's what scares me. I was with this guy a few years ago, and I thought we would get married. But then he left me for someone else...it hurt pretty bad. So the idea of being with a guy who doesn't know what he wants right off the bat isn't appealing to me."

"Understandable."

"That's why I decided to end things before they could

get any worse. An easy hookup is impossible when it comes to Thorn...because I actually like him."

Women like Autumn were as rare as flawless diamonds. If you ever came across one, you should snatch it while it was still there—otherwise, someone else would. I knew Thorn felt something for her. That couldn't be denied. But if he dragged his feet for too long, he would lose her for good.

I couldn't let that happen to my friend.

He wouldn't let it happen to me.

———

Thorn left a conversation with a group of men and headed into the hallway toward the restroom. Autumn was on the other side of the room catching up with acquaintances, so she was preoccupied. I walked over to Thorn and intercepted him before he could reach the restroom. "I need to talk to you."

"Everything alright?" He smoothed out the front of his tie, his bright blue eyes narrowing in concern. He wore a serious expression most of the time. It was rare to see him smile, but I suspected he did it around Autumn all the time.

"No." I grabbed his arm and directed him to the other side of the hotel, where they had a different restaurant and bar area, away from prying eyes at the conference. It would be less than a minute before Diesel realized I'd left the room.

"Can I pee first?"

"No." I took a seat at the table and ordered scotch for both of us.

"Did Roger say something to you?"

"I don't give a shit about Roger. I want to talk about Autumn."

His eyes immediately fell in irritation. "We talked about her in the car."

"We're talking about her again."

His heavy frame thudded against the chair when he leaned back. He ignored his scotch and didn't make eye contact with me.

"The second she touched you, you were a different man."

"I always act that way when a beautiful woman touches me."

I called him out on his bullshit with just a look.

"I like it when she touches me...obviously."

"Thorn, someone else is going to take her if you don't swoop in now. That woman is insanely intelligent, gorgeous, and just awesome. I don't want you to regret losing her for the rest of your life. She's hung up on you just as badly as you're hung up on her. End this life of permanent solitude and be with her."

He shook his head slightly. "I'll just hurt her."

"Then don't hurt her."

"Not so easy. She's already had her heart broken, and I don't want that to happen again."

"Then make sure you never break it. Take care of it."

He sighed. "Titan—"

"You miss all the shots you never take."

He rolled his eyes. "Stop acting like a motivational poster."

"It's cheesy, but it's true. If you do nothing, then you definitely will lose her. But if you at least try, you might keep her forever."

"We both know I'm not a one-woman kind of guy." He adjusted his Omega watch on his wrist, the shiny metal reflecting the fluorescent lights. "In the ten years you've known me, have I ever been with the same woman for more than a few weeks?"

"No."

"Have I ever even mentioned a woman I'm seeing to you?"

"No."

"Then I rest my case."

"Actually, no." I leaned forward and lowered my voice. "Everything you've said is true...but none of that applies to Autumn. You've been seeing her for a month. You're still obsessed with her. You're miserable without her. For the past ten years, there's never been a woman who's ever meant anything to you...until now. Doesn't that tell you something?"

He bowed his head.

"It means she's the one, Thorn. She's the one woman you've been waiting for."

He still wouldn't look at me.

"Diesel hasn't loved any other woman but me. And he

didn't meet me until he was thirty-five. Sometimes it takes a long time before we meet that special person. Autumn is your special person, Thorn. Be a man and fight for her."

He raised his head slowly and looked at me. "Maybe you're right. But I'll still hurt her. I can't do that... I'll kill myself if I hurt her."

"The fact that you don't want to tells me you never will."

He clenched his jaw as he stared at his scotch. "When she told me her ex left her for someone else...I was so angry. The guy must be an idiot to think he found someone better than Autumn. There is no one better."

How could he say that to me and not fight for her?

"And turning her down makes me feel like an idiot."

"You are," I said honestly.

"But it doesn't change anything. I'm afraid I'll do the same shit and break her heart. I'm afraid I'll hurt her even more than that asshole did. I've spent the last thirty years of my life as a single man. Can I really change?"

I'd known Thorn for a decade, and I considered myself to be the closest person to him. He'd never been so down, so vulnerable, as he was right now. Only someone special could make him that way. "We can get your answer."

"How?"

"By answering this question. Do you want to see other women?"

He stared at me in silence.

"If you can picture yourself with someone else, then you have your answer. But if the only woman taking up every inch of your brain is Autumn, then you have your answer. You'll never want to be single again if she's the only woman you want. That's your answer, plain and simple."

———

I touched up my makeup then clasped the gold necklace around my throat. I wore skinny black jeans with black booties and a long-sleeved gold cardigan. It was cold in Chicago with snow everywhere since they just had a storm blow through.

Diesel stepped into the bathroom in the same suit he'd been wearing all day. He came up behind me and moved his hands to my hips. His face was reflected in the mirror, but he didn't make eye contact with me in the glass. He stared down at me instead, his lips at my hairline.

His hands snaked around to the front of my jeans, and he undid the top button.

"We're leaving for dinner soon."

He nibbled on my earlobe. "You think I give a damn?" He pulled down the zipper next.

I shouldn't succumb to his touch, but it was impossible when the man was so unbelievably handsome. With a strong jaw and chocolate eyes, he was exactly the fantasy I would touch myself to.

He pushed my jeans down. "Guess who apologized to me." He moved to his knees and yanked my jeans down until they were off my feet.

"Roger?"

He got them over my heels then rose to his feet again, this time dropping his slacks and boxers. "Yep. Looks like he came to his senses." He grabbed the back of my knee and pinned it against my chest, opening me wide in front of the bathroom mirror. He guided his cock to my entrance and pushed his massive girth inside, stretching me before my body had a chance to even take him.

I gripped the sink for balance, moans escaping my throat.

Diesel thrust hard, hitting me deep as he pounded into me. He grabbed a fistful of hair and shoved his massive dick inside me over and over. "Watch me fuck you, baby."

I kept my eyes on the mirror, watching the intense expression in his eyes. He didn't just fuck me, but possessed me. He made me entirely his, filling my small pussy with his enormous length. He pushed deep and hard, sliding through my wetness.

My phone started to ring on the counter, and Thorn's name appeared on the screen.

They were probably waiting for us in the lobby.

I didn't dare touch the phone.

Because Diesel never would have allowed me to.

CHAPTER FOUR

Thorn

When I arrived in the lobby, Autumn was the first one there. She was dressed in a long-sleeved shirt and skintight denim jeans, and all of her lovely curves were amplified. She wore short booties and had her hair pulled back in a sleek ponytail. Most of the time when I saw her, her hair was down and perfectly framed her face. This was the first time I'd seen it back, revealing her slender neck and clearly displaying all of her beautiful features.

I liked it.

She hadn't noticed me yet, so I took advantage of the moment just to stare at her. Titan made her opinion about the matter perfectly clear, that Autumn meant something to me, and it would be stupid to let her go.

It would be stupid.

And she did mean something to me.

But I cared about her so much that I wanted to protect her.

From myself.

But watching her stand there alone made me wonder if I was protecting her at all. By refusing to give her what she wanted, I was just hurting her anyway. I was hurting too.

She turned slightly and noticed me out of the corner of her eye. She pivoted more, her eyes locking on to mine in intense connection. She didn't smile the way she used to. Now we just shared constant memories back and forth, swapping them in our silent expressions.

I walked across the lobby and joined her. My eyes raked over her body, seeing the way the fabric hugged her beautiful figure perfectly. Her eye shadow was different this time. She wore a single band on her right hand. Her hair was in a high ponytail, off her neck so she could show off all of her natural qualities. I didn't say hello or make small talk. "I like your hair..." It was a stupid thing to lead with, but it was the best I could do. I'd always felt intimidated by her sexiness. How could a woman be so perfect?

"Thanks. You look nice too. I like it when you wear t-shirts like that."

I looked down at myself because I couldn't recall what I was wearing. "Thanks."

She looked at her watch then glanced at the painting on the wall. "Not sure where Titan and Diesel are."

I had a good idea. "They'll be here soon." When I looked out the front window, I saw the black SUV with tinted windows. A man stood on the sidewalk in a suit, and I assumed he was our driver ready to take us to dinner. "Thanks for coming."

"Of course. I can't say no to a home-cooked meal."

I smiled when I remembered the one time I cooked for her. She seemed to have enjoyed it. "My mom is pretty good around the kitchen."

"I can imagine, since you learned from her."

I slid my hands into my pockets so I wouldn't touch her. Now the urge to grab her was even stronger than before. I loved it when she smiled at me. Made me feel like the luckiest guy in the room. I wished I wasn't sleeping alone in a hotel room this weekend. I wished I was making love to her on every piece of furniture in the place.

I wished I was sleeping beside her tonight.

"Are you enjoying the conference?"

"For the most part. There's a lot of arrogance swirling around when you have so many suits in one room."

"True."

"And drama seems to follow Titan wherever she goes."

"As long as there are sexist assholes in the world, that will always be the case."

"But I made some good connections and spread the word about our new company. I think people are excited to see our presentation tomorrow. Titan will blow them out of the water."

"As will you." I wouldn't even pay attention to Titan. I'd heard her speak hundreds of times, and I tried not to fall asleep during her presentations. Not because they were boring, but I just didn't care all that much. But if Autumn were on a stage, I'd watch every move she made. I'd memorize every single word.

"You're sweet."

"I'm not trying to be."

Her eyes softened, and she crossed her arms over her chest, trying to keep her hands to herself just the way I was doing. She cocked her head to the side and released a sigh.

It was so hard to be this close to her without touching her.

I missed her—bad.

Titan and Diesel finally joined us. "Sorry we're late," she said. "My meeting ran long."

Diesel walked slightly behind her and shook his head.

Autumn's face bunched up, and she tried not to laugh.

A meeting, my ass. "We're all adults here, Titan. You can just say you were getting laid."

Titan turned around and flashed Diesel a glare.

He shrugged and didn't wipe away his grin.

We headed outside and got into the SUV. Titan and Diesel sat in the front, so Autumn and I sat in the back. A seat was in between us, but it wasn't enough space. I felt like I was sitting too close to her, so close I could smell her perfume. Vanilla and summer mixed together in the intoxicating smell. I missed that scent on my sheets. Now my bed just smelled like me...and it was the smell of loneliness.

Diesel wrapped his arm around Titan's shoulders and scooted close to her, his face pressed into hers. They shared whispers and kisses on the drive, in love and oblivious to everything else.

I had to watch Diesel love Titan.

And I was jealous. Not jealous he had Titan, but jealous I couldn't even grab Autumn's hand.

We left the center of Chicago and receded to the outside of the city center. After twenty minutes, we started to reach the quiet suburbs, where there were more fields than houses. Snow was caked on either side of the road, and the fields of white made the world looked like it was covered in a single blanket.

I tried not to stare at Autumn.

Now we were just five miles away from the house. My mom would be bustling in the kitchen, my dad would be watching TV in his favorite armchair, and my brother would probably be texting a new woman he'd picked up.

Autumn stared out the other window, careful to avoid my gaze.

Now I couldn't help it. I turned my gaze and stared at her. I pictured my hand running through the strands of her ponytail and then latching on to it. I pictured her swollen lips after a long night of sucking face. I imagined how her pussy tasted on my tongue. There were so many things I wanted to do with her. Just sitting in the car with my arm wrapped around her shoulders would make me happy.

But I didn't have that.

Now there was a seat between us, but it felt like a mile. I kept the distance between us on purpose even though I could have her whenever I wanted her. By keeping my restraint, I protected both of us. But one day, some charming guy would grow the balls to sweep her off her feet.

She wouldn't even remember my name.

I'd be in my penthouse with some woman I wouldn't remember. The sex would be good but not memorable.

She'd get married and start a family.

I might be lucky enough to find a woman who was willing to have a partnership rather than a marriage.

Her life would be full.

Mine would be empty.

Without my even realizing it, we pulled up to the roundabout driveway of my parents' three-story mansion in the countryside. White with green shutters and a big blue door, it was a dream house. Tall pillars established the large porch that had a perfect view of the horizon.

We came to a stop, and the doors opened.

Diesel and Titan got out first.

Then Autumn went.

I stayed back for a second, my mind overrun with endless thoughts. I wasn't sure what I was thinking because I was thinking so many things at once. I finally got out of the vehicle and saw Titan and Diesel admiring the house.

Autumn had her hands in her pockets to stay warm, and she was looking up at the house. "Wow, it's beautiful."

I didn't care about the house. Now I was only staring at her.

Diesel and Titan walked up the stairs to the porch. "This place is nice, Thorn," Diesel said. "I like it."

I ignored him. My heart was beating so hard I felt winded. My heart and lungs couldn't work at the same time. I had to choose one or the other, but I needed both to survive. Just as I needed Autumn to survive.

She walked up to the house.

My mom opened the door and screamed when she saw Titan. "Oh, honey. It's so nice to see you." She wrapped her in her arms and hugged her. "And who is this you brought with you?"

I quickened my pace to catch up to Autumn. My mom was too busy paying attention to Titan and Diesel to notice her right away, so I still had time. I jogged slightly then reached her at the bottom of the stairs.

I pulled her hand out of her pocket and placed it in mine.

She looked down at our joined hands, confusion on her face.

I squeezed her fingers and pulled her with me.

She didn't pull away despite how confused she was.

I had been confused the entire drive here, but now I wasn't.

Titan and Diesel stepped out of the way so I could greet my mother.

"Thorn! My baby—" She stopped when she saw my hand joined with Autumn's. Her jaw was practically on the ground, and her hands were pressed against her chest.

"Mom, this is my girlfriend, Autumn."

The look on Autumn's face was priceless. Her eyes softened in a way they never had before. She squeezed my hand back, a beautiful smile on her face. Her cheeks didn't redden like they usually would, probably because it was freezing outside.

Titan grinned wider than anyone as she hugged Diesel's arm. "Aww..."

"Girlfriend?" Mom asked. "I had no idea..."

"I wanted it to be a surprise." I turned to Autumn. "This is my mom, Liv Cutler."

Autumn shook her hand. "It's nice to meet you, Mrs. Cutler."

Mom pulled her into a hug instead. "Sweetheart, you're so beautiful. Please call me Liv."

"Okay," Autumn said with a chuckle. "I will."

"And this is Thorn's father, Thomas."

"Pleasure to meet you." Autumn couldn't stop smiling, probably because of the stunt I had just pulled.

"Let's get out of the freezing cold and inside." Mom ushered us inside and helped us with our coats. "Dinner is almost ready. Take a seat at the table. Titan, can I make you a drink? Scotch or whiskey?"

Titan and Diesel moved with her into the kitchen.

Autumn and I were finally alone, and she stared at me, clearly speechless.

I grabbed both of her hands and brought them to my

lips, kissing each knuckle. I released them then placed my forehead against hers. "I can't make any promises...but I want to try."

"I want to try too," she whispered.

"Because I don't want to be with anyone else...and I don't want to lose you."

"I don't want to lose you either."

I kissed her forehead then pulled away. "I'm sorry I dropped that bomb on you."

"No, it's okay," she said with a smile. "It was a nice surprise."

A whistle erupted from the hallway, and Tyler appeared from nowhere. "Wow. My brother sure knows how—"

"Mine." My brother and I got along well enough, and we teased each other a lot. He knew I had an extensive sex life, as did he. The women never meant anything to me, so I didn't care what he said about them. But Autumn was different, and that needed to be established right from the start.

Tyler dropped his smile then stepped forward. "Plea-sure to meet you, Autumn." He extended his hand and turned into the polite man I expected him to be. "I can't say that my brother has mentioned you, but judging by his pissed-off expression, I better not cross you. That can only mean one thing—you must be special." He shook her hand.

"Nice to meet you too."

"I'm Tyler, Thorn's younger brother."

"Hi, Tyler," she said. "Your parents have a lovely home."

"Thanks. It was definitely a chick magnet when we were growing up." He winked then joined everyone else in the kitchen.

I turned back to her, calm now that the introduction was over.

"You and your brother don't get along?" she asked with a chuckle.

"We do. I just want him to understand you're off-limits."

"Off-limits, huh?"

"Yeah." My arm encircled her waist, and I pulled her into me.

"You and your brother trade women often?"

"We have."

"Have you brought them to the house before?"

"No...you're the first."

Her eyes softened.

"And I wanted to make sure my brother realized that." I pulled her into my side and kissed her on the mouth, kissing her in a way I'd never kissed anyone before. It felt different from the last time because this kiss was full of hope, not full of goodbye. It was the first time I wasn't anxious to get naked. I looked forward to a regular evening with my family, talking over wine and gourmet food. I looked forward to just being with her.

My girlfriend.

———

Mom thought Autumn was the most interesting person in the world. "So you started this company all on your own?" My mom had hardly eaten the dinner she'd made because she'd been more involved in the conversation. It started off as a general question about what Autumn did in her free time, and it turned into a biography.

"Well, that wasn't my intention at the time," Autumn said. "I was just passionate about my idea, and I wanted to devote all of my time to it. So I got the biggest storage facility I could find and got to work because there wasn't room at home...and that's where it began."

"That's fascinating." Mom's eyes were wide open, like she couldn't believe everything she was listening to. "Good for you. Reminds me of Titan. It's so wonderful to hear about women making their own companies. When I was young, that's not how things were. And I'm so glad my son has excellent taste in women."

I shouldn't feel the warmth in my body when my mom said she was proud of me, but I couldn't help it. I'd always been a mama's boy. Tyler teased me about it, but I didn't give a damn. "I never dated Titan, so I really only have great taste in one woman...just to get that out there." I drank my wine to cover the awkwardness that statement must have caused.

"But Titan's your best friend, isn't she?" Mom pressed.

"Of course," I answered.

"And our choices in friendships mean a great deal too." Mom rested her hand on Titan's and gave her a smile.

It seemed like my mom loved both of the women in my life, Autumn and Titan. I was glad Titan was still a part of my family even though it didn't work out between us. It wouldn't be the same without her.

"You guys raised the bar pretty high," Tyler said. "Chicks like that are slim pickings..."

"You're gonna have to step it up," I teased. "Women aren't attracted to lawyers..."

He tore off a piece of bread and chucked it at my face.

I caught it with my mouth and chewed it.

My dad tapped his fork against his glass to get our attention. "Settle down."

My brother and I tried not to laugh when Dad acted like we were still five.

"Thorn." Mom turned to me. "Why didn't you tell me about Autumn when we spoke on the phone yesterday?"

Mom and I talked every day, usually right after lunchtime. If I didn't call her, she would call me. So I chose to be proactive about it. Thankfully, Mom didn't stay on the phone longer than fifteen minutes, so it wasn't a pain. I actually enjoyed talking to her. Dad and I had never been as close, not that we had a poor relationship. "It never came up."

"How could this perfect woman not come up?" she asked incredulously.

I grinned and turned to Autumn. "The second you're out of the room, my mom is gonna grill me hard."

"I'll grill you now," Mom said.

"I guess I wanted it to be a surprise," I said with a shrug. "Come on, you love surprises."

She smiled before she sipped her wine. "Very true."

Dodged that bullet.

"How long has this been going on?" Mom asked.

"Honey." Dad chimed in, his tone clipped. "Now you're just interrogating him."

"It's okay if you wanna embarrass me, Ma," I said. "Just do it when my lady is in the bathroom or something."

We finished the meal by talking about Titan and Diesel. My parents were interested in their love story as much as they were interested in mine. Titan was like a daughter to them, even though I would never marry her. Diesel was always pleasant company, now that I knew he wasn't out to sabotage our every move.

"I have to admit, your father is my celebrity crush," my mom said.

Diesel smiled, but it was full of awkwardness.

"He's so handsome. He aged so phenomenally well."

Dad glared at her. "Hon, I'm right here."

"Don't act like you don't have a celebrity crush too," she countered.

"But I don't talk about it in front of our guests," he countered. "Let alone mention it to her son."

"It's okay," Diesel said with a chuckle. "I understand that he's an appealing man."

"He is handsome." Titan rubbed Diesel's forearm. "If

Diesel looks anything like him at that age, I'll be a very happy lady."

Diesel rolled his eyes. "Baby, please don't tell me you have the hots for my dad."

"I don't," she said. "But I see where you get your good looks from."

I turned to Autumn and lowered my voice to a whisper. "You don't think my dad is hot, right?"

She laughed and never answered.

When we were finished, Mom collected the plates and brought them into the kitchen. "Thorn, you wanna help me with the dishes?"

"Sure." I set my napkin down and joined her in the kitchen. The dishes were stacked and ready to be washed. Whenever we had people over, it had always been my job to wash the dishes while she saved the leftovers. Tyler was supposed to take care of the dessert and take out the trash. Anytime we visited, we were still expected to do these chores. Tyler and I could probably object, but we both refused to deny our mom anything.

I started to rinse the dishes and stack them in the dishwasher.

"Please tell me this one is genuine."

I looked over my shoulder and saw Mom putting the leftovers in plastic containers. "It's real."

"Oh, thank god. You aren't just saying that to me to keep up the façade?"

"No, Ma." I grabbed the next plate and rinsed it off. "I'm serious."

"Good. I'm glad you found someone—and not just anyone. She seems like a lovely woman. Very successful, bright, and beautiful. Sometimes I worry a woman will only like you for your wealth, but a woman of her talents doesn't need you for anything. That's how you know it's the real deal."

"She definitely doesn't need me for anything. She's out of my league."

"Honey, that's not true at all." She came up behind me and rubbed my back. "Don't ever think otherwise."

I tried not to laugh at my mom's inflated opinion of me. "I'm glad you like her."

"And I'm glad you changed your mind about finding someone."

"I didn't change my mind...she changed it for me."

"Aww..." She grabbed the dishes I had rinsed and set them in the dishwasher. "I hope I live long enough to see both of my sons get married. Nothing would make me happier."

"Mom, you aren't old. You've got plenty of time."

"You're so sweet to me..."

I finished doing the dishes, and she packed up the food. Then she brought out dessert, and Tyler came into the kitchen to help her serve the slices of pie.

I sat beside Autumn again. "Need anything?"

"No." She kept grinning.

"Why are you smiling at me like that?"

"I walked by the kitchen on the way to the bathroom..."

"And...?"

"I heard you talking to your mom."

God, the truth was out. "So?"

"I think it's sweet you're so close to your mom."

"Told you I was a mama's boy. Said that in the beginning, so this isn't brand-new information."

"I know you did." She leaned into me and kissed me on the cheek. "I think it's cute."

A kiss on the cheek was below my interests, but when she did it, it made me feel special. "Yeah?"

"Yeah." She took a piece of pumpkin pie from Tyler, her gaze distracted from me.

Titan was staring at me across the table. She wore an arrogant smirk and an even more arrogant gaze. She mouthed, "You're welcome, asshole."

I grinned then mouthed back. "Thank you. I owe you."

CHAPTER FIVE

AUTUMN

Thorn placed his arm around my shoulders on the drive back to the hotel. Now there wasn't an empty seat between us. There wasn't even air between us because his body was pressed to mine. His hand wrapped around my arm as he pulled me closer to him, ignoring the seat belt that stretched across my chest. His face was angled toward mine in a silent embrace, his lips teasing me.

Now we looked like Titan and Diesel, cuddled in the back and oblivious to everything else going on around us. His nose rubbed against mine in a tantalizing dance. His eyes sparkled in their own way, crystal blue and beautiful. I knew he was teasing me on purpose, withholding his incredible kiss until we were behind closed doors.

"So, I'm your girlfriend, huh?" My hand stretched across his thigh, feeling the muscles through his dark jeans.

"My first girlfriend."

"You've never had a girlfriend?" I asked incredulously. "Even when you were young?"

He shook his head. "There were girls...but not girl-friends."

"Wow, I'm special."

"Damn right, you are." He moved his lips against my hairline but still didn't give me a kiss.

"Your parents are cute."

"They're alright," he said with a chuckle.

Titan and Diesel had their heads pressed together the way ours were. They were whispering to each other, and when they weren't talking, their lips were locked together. We had our privacy since they seemed more absorbed in each other than us.

"They're more than alright," I said. "They're adorable."

"Pshaw, I'm the adorable one."

I gripped his thigh. "No, you're the sexiest one."

He smirked. "Yeah, I like that better."

"You and your brother look a lot alike."

"Don't get any ideas," he said immediately. "I don't share my woman."

I tried not to smile. "Jealous, much?"

"I know my brother is a good-looking guy. We compete for woman all the time."

"Well, there's no contest. I'm already yours."

"I like the sound of that." His fingers started at my knee and slowly moved up my thigh. His strong fingers pressed into my jeans, feeling my warm skin through the fabric. "So, I'm your boyfriend...that's an interesting thing to say."

"I like the way it sounds."

"I don't have a lot of experience in this area, so try to be patient with me."

"You'll do fine. I know you will." I pressed my mouth to his, taking a kiss because I was tired of waiting for one.

He kissed me back, and slowly moved his hand into my hair, and he cupped the back of my head. Like we were two teenagers making out on the ride home from the movies, our lips moved together then broke apart. Thorn's cologne and natural scent filled my sinuses, making my fingers dig into him a little harder. My hand slid up his arm until I reached his corded neck. I cupped the skin and felt his strong heartbeat as I kissed him.

His kisses moved along my jaw to my ear. "I'm gonna make love to you when we get back." His hand moved up my thigh to my ass. "All night long."

Goose bumps erupted across my flesh, and I squeezed my thighs together. I wanted him buried between my legs with his come sitting inside me. I wanted to feel that weight every single night, the weight of his seed.

He moved back to my mouth and kissed me again, his fingers exploring everything from the waist down. His tongue delved into my mouth, and I felt the temperature increase more and more, our writhing bodies fogging up the back windows. It was too intense for a car ride with other people, so I pushed my hand against his chest and broke apart—as much as I didn't want to.

He squeezed my thigh and stared at my lips with aggression, like he might move in and keep kissing me anyway.

"We're almost there," I whispered.

"That's not soon enough."

A few minutes later, the Escalade pulled up to the roundabout, and we exited the car.

Diesel scooped Titan into his arms and carried her into the lobby.

"What are you doing?" Titan asked with a laugh.

"Those heels are killing your feet," Diesel responded.

"Are not," she said. "Put me down."

"No. I like carrying you like this." He rubbed his nose against hers. "It's practice for our big day next week."

They both forgot about us completely as they disappeared into the elevator.

"Want a lift?" Thorn asked me.

"I only want you to pick me up if you're about to throw me on a bed."

He hooked his arm around my waist and escorted me to the elevators. "That can be arranged." The elevator doors closed, and he kissed me, his mouth locked on mine as we rode the elevator to the top floor. It was a long ride, allowing the embrace to intensify as each floor was reached. His hand groped my tit over my shirt, and his other hand squeezed my ass.

I was going to come right then and there.

The elevator beeped when we reached our floor, and we were forced to break apart. I never asked whose room we were going to enjoy for the night, but I assumed we were headed to his. My room was on a completely different floor.

He pulled me into the room and got right down to business. His hand was in my hair, and his lips were on mine. There was no restraint like there was in the car and the elevator. With no more need for propriety, he pushed me against the wall and devoured me like a starving man in a buffet. He peeled my clothes off and took breaks in between to squeeze my tits. His hot breath filled my mouth, and his tongue danced with mine.

I pushed his clothes off until his chiseled physique was revealed, tanned skin with gorgeous muscles. His dirty-blond hair was in disarray now that I'd fingered it, and my nipples chafed against his rock-hard chest as he moved against me.

When we were both naked, his hard dick was pressing against my stomach, the crown already wet with his arousal. It stuck to my skin and smeared over my rib cage. His throbbing dick was searingly hot, visibly aching to be buried deep inside me.

It made me feel more beautiful than I ever had. It made me feel wanted, like Thorn would never want someone else over me. The pain I carried from Max didn't stick to my skin anymore. I felt like I belonged somewhere, like I'd always belonged somewhere.

His hand fisted my hair as he guided me to the bed.

"I've never wanted you more than I do right now..." He maneuvered me onto the bed, our bodies perpendicular to the headboard. His muscled thighs parted mine, and he widened my legs so he could fit right against me. He folded me underneath him, getting our bodies as close to each other as possible. "This is my first time." He pressed his face to mine then guided his crown inside my entrance. He'd been inside me more times than I could count, but it felt different. He was a little thicker, a little slicker. He pushed inside me and stretched me wide, making the rest of my body tighten a little. I gasped at his girth, feeling the incredible stretch his dick gave me. "Fuck, did you get tighter?"

I hooked my arms around his shoulders and pulled him into me. "You just got bigger."

He sank inside me until he was buried deep inside my warmth. "Baby...this is all mine." He rubbed his nose against mine before he started to thrust inside me. He didn't take me roughly like he usually did. His pace was slow and steady, giving it to me without racing to the finish line.

"And you're all mine."

He kissed me as he moved inside me, his lips concentrating on my mouth while his cock focused on my soaked pussy. His thrusts became deeper, but he never quickened his pace. He purposely tried to make it last as long as possible. His arms pressed into the mattress on either side of me and shook my whole body as he pounded into me.

Just like every other time, he made me come within the first few minutes. "I'm gonna come, babe…"

His hand fisted my hair, and he locked his gaze on to mine, his cock still sliding deep inside me. "Babe…I like that." He tilted his hips and hit me at a different angle, his hard body sliding right over my clit. He grinded into me, stimulating me until I was on fire.

My hands gripped his solid ass, and I pulled him harder into me. "Yes…" I closed my eyes and bit my bottom lip.

"I love that face…"

My head rolled back, and I was reduced to a woman riding her hormones. My moans turned to screams, and my nails sliced his back like a knife diced a zucchini. It was so good, so explosive. I hadn't had him in almost a week, and that was too long of a drought for me to stand. Feeling that big cock buried between my legs every night was exactly what I wanted. And I wanted Thorn to be the one to give it to me.

I buried my face in his neck and dug my teeth into his skin as I soared on the high, feeling my pussy constrict around him until it finally let go. I listened to Thorn breathe directly into my ear canal, and I was right on the verge of coming. My hands slipped against the sweat that coated his skin. I tried to hold on to him harder, but my fingers couldn't grip his tight muscles.

He gave his final pumps as he pushed me into the mattress, his groans becoming louder and louder. When he reached the peak of his orgasm, he thrust hard inside me and released with a moan. His hand cradled my head, and he moaned directly into my ear, his deep voice setting me on fire all over again. His come stuffed me good, his dick still stretching me and his seed filling me. I could feel his satisfaction, feel his moan all the way down to his bones. The baritone of his voice was always sexy, especially when he was enjoying me.

His dick eventually started to soften, but he remained on top of me, his heavy size sinking me back into the mattress. He kissed the corner of my mouth then sucked my bottom lip. His gentle embraces slowly picked up speed, and before either of us knew it, we were kissing just as hard as we were before we made love. My hands dug into his hair, and he breathed into my mouth with restrained intensity. His dick hardened again, filling me even more than before. My pussy was stuffed, but it was about to be stuffed again.

"Babe, make love to me again."

He started to thrust, his mouth against mine. "I'd love to, baby."

———

I closed my eyes and drifted off for a bit as Thorn lay beside me. His perfect physique was outlined with grooves of muscles, and his chiseled forearms were covered in veins. There was a cord in his neck that stuck out no matter how relaxed he was.

My hand rested across his happy trail, a small line of

hair that rubbed against my fingertips. I slowly migrated up, feeling my hand rise and fall over his abs. Even when he was relaxed, his muscles were still tight. With flawless skin and a perfect complexion, he had the looks of a Greek god.

And he was all mine.

He stirred beside me slightly, his throat clearing. "Can't keep your hands off me, huh?" He kept his eyes closed, but a grin stretched his lips.

"Not when you're this sexy."

He opened his eyes, and his grin widened. "Good answer."

My hand migrated up his chest until I felt the slab of muscles of his pectorals. "You're a beautiful man."

"And you're the most beautiful woman." He turned on his side and snuggled close to me, pulling my leg over his hip. His warm cock was hardening and slowly expanding against my clit.

I hadn't showered after sex, so Thorn's seed was still sitting inside me. Some had streaked onto the sheets, and the smell of come filled his hotel room.

"Beautiful tits." He palmed my left breast. "Beautiful skin." He dragged his fingers down my arm. "Beautiful curves." He rubbed his palm against my belly. "And a very beautiful face." His hand cupped my cheek, and he leaned in to kiss me at the corner of my mouth.

Butterflies soared in my stomach, and I felt my guard slowly slip down as this man pulled me under. When I'd first met Thorn, my walls were higher than the sky. Slowly, he broke them down, making his way into my heart just as he made his way between my legs. "You can be very romantic sometimes."

"Sometimes," he whispered. "But don't get used to it."

"I already have." When he'd grabbed my hand in front of his parents' house, it was the most romantic moment of my life. He didn't want to introduce me as a friend. He wanted his parents to know I meant something to him. For a man who was interested in being alone, he seemed to want me close.

"Damn. I guess I have to keep up the charade, then."

"It's not a charade." I kept touching his chest, my favorite feature of his. It was like a weight on my body when he was on top of me. I liked the pressure. I liked the way he sank my back into whatever I was pressed against. He was heavy like a man should be.

He rubbed his nose against mine. "You caught me."

I propped myself up and looked at the time on the nightstand. When I saw how late it was, I sighed. "You'll never guess what time it is."

"One?"

"No."

He shrugged. "One-thirty?"

"Three."

He cringed. "We've gotta get up in a few hours."

"Yeah..."

"But I'm not sure if I can sleep anyway. I've got a gorgeous woman beside me...and she's all mine." He pressed a kiss to my hairline.

For a man who didn't want to be committed, he knew exactly how to treat a woman. He made me feel special, made me feel loved. "What changed your mind about all of this?" I should probably just leave it alone and enjoy it, but I wanted to know what I was getting myself into. Thorn had the power to crush my heart with his bare hands. It was a scary thought.

Instead of looking away in discomfort, he held my gaze. "Titan talked to me a few times."

She'd told me to be patient with him. Diesel said the same thing. I guess they were both right.

"She told me you were special to me. And instead of figuring that out the hard way, she told me I had to try to make this work. If I didn't, I'd have to watch you find someone else, and by then, it would be too late for me. The thought terrified me. And when it did, I knew she was right. I don't want to lose you, Autumn." His hand trailed over my hip and along my waistline. "My whole life has been spent in solitude. Women come and go. I never let them stick around longer than a week. I dominate them, satisfy my needs, and then stop calling. That's been the last decade of my life. It's never bothered me. I've never felt lonely. But the idea of going back to that sounds depressing. I don't want to fuck anyone else. I only want to fuck you."

He said it in such a crass way, but it was still touching.

"I told Titan I didn't want to hurt you. After what you've been through, I couldn't stand to see you get hurt again—especially if I was the one responsible. I thought breaking things off would protect you, but Titan made me realize I was only hurting both of us. The last thing I want to do is break your heart, so I'll do everything I possibly can to make sure that doesn't happen. But I can't promise you much else."

The fact that he cared at all made him a wonderful man. He truly cared about my feelings. He truly wanted to protect my heart from further damage. "Unfortunately, there's no way to stop a heart from getting broken. We're so deep into this now that there's nothing that can be done. But I appreciate the fact that you care so much."

"I do care," he whispered.

"Then just be honest with me. If you get tired of me, all you have to do is tell me."

Thorn opened his mouth to say something, but he abruptly closed it again. He probably wanted to say he would never get tired of me, but then he realized he couldn't make a promise like that.

I appreciated that he didn't. "So, you and me?"

"You and me. No one else...especially Connor fucking Suede."

A chuckle escaped my throat. "I don't want Connor. I only want you."

"Good. I only want you." He moved his hand into my hair, and he kissed me, a soft embrace that was filled with passion.

I rolled him onto his back then straddled his hips with my knees. I felt his hard cock underneath me, ready for another round. He was already oozing from the tip, his lubrication ready to meet mine.

"I can't promise you forever," he whispered against my mouth. "But I promise everything I can give."

"I know, Thorn." I directed his thick crown inside my entrance. "That's more than enough."

CHAPTER SIX

DIESEL

My baby never showed weakness.

She stared in the mirror and finished her makeup with the same calm she always possessed, but now she seemed even more certain of herself. Her spine was a little straighter, her shoulders were back farther. She looked herself in the eye with the same respect every woman should show herself on a regular basis.

But now that I knew her better than anyone, I knew it was just a mask.

The stronger she seemed, the more vulnerable she was. She tried to compensate for the nerves by pretending they didn't exist at all. The only reason I knew that was because I knew her better than anyone now —even Thorn.

I came up behind her and smacked my large palm against her perky ass in her skirt. My lips moved to her ear, and I stared at her reflection in the mirror, seeing the way she stiffened at my touch. She held my gaze with the same intensity I showed. "A queen has no reason to be nervous. All the peasants in that room should be nervous." I gripped her ass harder before I let go.

"I'm not nervous."

"Let's not lie to each other. Not now and not ever." My hands moved to her waistline, my fingers resting right under the curves of her tits in her black blouse. I felt her body expand with every breath she took, and I could feel her erratic heartbeat too. Sometimes it raced because of me. But now I knew it was racing for an entirely different reason.

Her hand glided across my forearm, my mother ring's sitting on her left hand.

I wanted to lift her leg onto the counter and fuck her against the bathroom sink, but I knew she was short on time.

When it came to making love, I didn't like to be rushed.

"Alright," she whispered. "No lies."

"Tell me why you're nervous."

"I always get nervous with big crowds. The more impressive I am, the more people despise me. The taller you stand, the more people look up to stare at you. The more eyes on you, the more problems. It's just how it is. When a man stands up there and dominates, he inspires people. But when a woman does it...people question whether she deserves it."

"I know you deserve it," I whispered against her ear. "And so do a lot of people. Don't concentrate on the assholes. It's the quickest way to live an unhappy life. You're better than them, so who cares what they think. You know the truth." I squeezed the area around her ribs slightly. "Now, don't be nervous. Pretend I'm the only one out there."

The corner of her mouth rose in a smile. "Can I pretend you're naked?"

I pressed a kiss to her neck. "Pretend all you want. But I want you to see the real thing as soon as you're finished."

"You've got yourself a very perverted deal."

"Well, you are a pervert." I smacked her ass again before I walked away.

————

I sat beside Thorn in the second row. He looked well rested despite the night he must have had. He wore gray slacks with a black collared shirt, dressed casually but not informally. I flattened my tie against my chest and caught a blond woman staring at me from the end of the row.

My engagement to Tatum was public information now, so I didn't understand why eyes lingered on me longer than they should. Perhaps they didn't take it seriously, or perhaps my commitment to a woman made them wonder if they could get that same commitment from me. Whatever the reason, it annoyed me.

I hoped men didn't stare at her so much anymore—with that big rock on her finger.

"How's it going?" I rested my ankle on my opposite knee then glanced at my watch.

"No complaints." His grin indicated there was a much bigger story behind his words.

"That's all you're gonna give me?"

He chuckled. "I'm a gentleman."

"Since when?"

"Since I found the right lady to turn me into a gentleman."

"Fair enough. So things are good?"

"Oh yeah." He gave a nod. "Let's just say we haven't gone to bed yet. Well...we haven't gone to sleep yet."

I'd never seen Thorn smile so many times in a single interaction. He was usually serious to the point of boredom. But now his body was relaxed, his grin was constant, and he had the look of true happiness in his eyes. "I'm glad to hear that."

"Autumn is incredible. I know I'd be miserable picking up some random woman somewhere else...so I thought I would give it a try. And if she were with some other guy, it would drive me absolutely insane."

If a man even looked at Titan wrong, I'd bite his head off. "I think you made the right call."

"I'm not single anymore...it's strange."

"You'll get used to it." I'd lived the single life for my entire adulthood, and once Tatum came into my world, I knew those days were over. I hung up my former self and

said goodbye to those days for ｧ
back once. "It's a new kind of ha
need...when you're ready to acce

"Responsibility?" he asked.

"Yeah. It's your job to
twenty-four seven."

"You're thinking of marriage."

"No," I corrected. "If she's your woman, she's your responsibility."

"I guess that's true," he said in agreement. "I want to make her happy, so I guess I don't mind."

"And that's how you know you've found the one."

His eyes shifted away as he thought to himself. His face hardened once more, the smile gone and the seriousness set in place. "When did you know Titan was the one?"

There wasn't a specific memory that came to mind. We screwed for a while before feelings began to develop. But right from the beginning, I respected her in a way I hardly respected anyone. She was an admirable woman, always taking the high road, even when other people tried to cut her down. She earned the respect of her peers with her poise and success. She was the smartest person I'd ever met, and that was obvious the first time we spoke. My obsession started at the same time. I pursued her relentlessly, unsure what I even wanted at the time. "I guess the first time I met her."

He cocked an eyebrow. "Not possible. You didn't know anything about her."

think I needed to know anything. I just knew
one-of-a-kind. It takes a lot to earn my respect,
he did it instantly. Not too many people can
that."

"Respecting someone and loving them are two different things."

"But you need to respect someone before you love them. What drew you to Autumn in the first place?" I didn't know Autumn very well, but I knew her allure was her intelligence and success. Thorn responded to it because he was impressed by it. "She's playing with the big boys and kicking ass. She earned your respect the first time you met her. And that's why you're head over heels and stupid in love."

"I never said I was in love with her," he said quietly.

"You aren't?" I challenged.

Thorn looked away this time, avoiding my gaze like the answer was written in his eyes. He focused on the stage, and as if luck was on his side, the presentation began. Tatum and Autumn walked to the podium, possessing the elegance of two world leaders and the beauty of two models. With perfect poise, professional smiles, and enough confidence to make everyone else in the room feel unsure of themselves, they started right away.

I got comfortable and watched my fiancée rock the room.

And I was hard the entire time.

Once the presentation was over and people swarmed Tatum to introduce themselves or pick her brain about her new product launch, she was swallowed up the attention she'd been anticipating. Autumn was in the same position, being pulled in different directions as people battled for a moment of her time.

I wasn't going to wait until everyone else was done to talk to my woman.

I walked right up to her, ignored the suit she was talking to, and wrapped my arm around her waist. "You did great, baby." With fifty pairs of eyes on us, I leaned down and kissed her on the mouth.

She immediately kissed me back, despite the conversation she was in the middle of having. "Thank you."

I moved my lips to ear. "Your legs make me hard."

She smiled at the comment and brushed it off. "Thanks for letting me know."

"I'm going to get a drink. Join me when you're finished."

"Alright."

I kissed her on the cheek before I let her go. Now that I was finished with her, people could have her attention. But since I was the man marrying her, I got to have her attention anytime I wanted it.

Thorn came to my side at the bar. "Aren't our ladies sexy? People are hanging all over them right now."

I ordered my scotch then turned to look at them.

They were both swarmed by people at the massive gathering. Autumn and Tatum weren't standing together, so they drew two individual crowds together. "Very."

"No one even cares about us," he said with a chuckle. "Kinda nice."

"I guess we'll both have to get used to sharing the spotlight."

"I don't mind in the least," Thorn said. "The spotlight is overrated."

"True."

We enjoyed our drinks, watching our ladies control the room and everyone in it.

"I forgot to tell you..." Thorn set his drink on the bar. "There hasn't been time, and I didn't want Titan to know about it."

"That doesn't sound good." I sighed as I stared at my drink.

"Bridget came by my office a few days ago."

I'd hoped Bridget would only make the one appearance before she faded away. Tatum didn't want anything to do with her, and I wasn't sure what Bridget wanted. Tatum had already been through a lot, and I didn't want to stack anything else on her plate. "What did she say?"

"She was looking for Titan."

I pivoted my body toward him, my back facing Tatum and Autumn in the center of the conference room. "What does she want?" After what Bruce did to my woman, I'd become a very paranoid man. Everyone seemed to be a threat.

"She said Titan's near-death experience made her realize she wanted a relationship with her. She wanted the opportunity to apologize and possibly start over. She wants to know Titan..."

All of that sounded nice on paper, but Tatum wasn't as sympathetic. She didn't need a relationship with her long-lost mother because she was a grown woman who didn't need anything anymore. She was still connected to her father's spirit, hallucinating about him under anesthesia. She'd never felt empty because her mother walked out on her. "Do you believe her?"

"I told her she wouldn't get a dime from Titan. She said she wasn't looking for money, that she has plenty of it. You never really know when it comes to stuff like that...and I can't read her. She seems genuine, but you never know what someone's intentions are."

"This was the second time she tried to speak to her. There will probably be a third."

"Maybe."

Tatum did everything she could to bring my father and me back together. My father did a lot of terrible things, but now I didn't think about his sins anymore. When I looked at my father, I saw a man I admired— and loved. Love was the most powerful thing in this world, and it could nullify even the worst crimes. I wondered if I should do the same for Tatum, to make her reunite with the one parent she still had left. But the situations were different. My father never abandoned me. My mother died, and he did the best he could without her. Bridget took off and left. "I'm not sure what to do."

"Me neither."

"I think they should sit down together and talk."

"Really?" Thorn asked in surprise.

"If Bridget is just going to keep coming by the office unannounced, it seems inevitable. At least we can do this on our terms if we plan for it."

"I guess." He drank from his glass then licked his lips. "But Titan will never go for it."

"I'll talk to her."

"Titan won't agree even to make this woman go away. She doesn't negotiate with anyone, and after what happened with Bruce Carol, she'll be even more stubborn about it—which I respect her for."

"This is different. It's her mother."

Thorn shook his head. "That's not how she sees it. This woman isn't her mother. She's just someone who shares her DNA."

"And she has two brothers. I'd want to know if I had a brother."

"But since she doesn't see Bridget as her mother, I doubt she'll view them as brothers."

"Maybe," I said. "But I know Titan understands Bridget's the only family she has. Other than you and me, she's completely alone. If she were to get to know her mother and her two brothers...she wouldn't be the last of her line."

"I don't know..." He shook his head. "Titan has never needed anyone."

"Bullshit. She needs you and me."

"That's different," he said. "We've earned her trust. This woman walks back into Titan's life almost thirty years after she left her. You don't just get to do that. She left, so she forfeited her right to stop by Titan's office whenever she feels like it."

"Yeah, I know," I said. "But I keep thinking about my relationship with my father. Tatum put us back together, and now I'm so grateful she did. I was so angry with him. I even hated him. And now...I'm grateful he's in my life again. Tatum may feel angry or indifferent about her mother. But if she really could start a relationship with her, it might make her happy."

"It might...but it might not too."

Now that Tatum was going to be my wife, I viewed our relationship differently. Like a guardian, I tried to decide what was best for her. I respected her decisions, but sometimes I felt the pressure to override her to do the right thing. Was reconnecting with her mother the right thing to do? Or was Tatum right not to care? Should I just leave it alone? Or should I jump in?

"What are you going to do?" Thorn stared at me, knowing I was thinking about it deeply.

"Not sure yet." I dragged my finger around the rim of my glass.

"Whatever it is, you should wait until after the wedding."

"Definitely."

"Can you believe you're gonna be a married man in a week?" Thorn asked incredulously. "Did you ever think that would happen?"

"Not once." I thought I would be a permanent bachelor. I'd never been against relationships, but I'd never met a woman I wanted to spend more than a week with. And then I met Tatum, the hardest woman I'd ever met. She fascinated me right from the beginning...and I never looked back.

"Nervous?"

"About?"

He shrugged. "Marriage in general."

"Marriage in general makes me nervous. Marriage to Tatum does not."

The corner of his mouth rose in a smile. "Not a single doubt?"

"Nope." Tatum was the one. I didn't believe in the *one* until I met mine. She was the only woman I would ever give my name to. She was the only woman strong enough to wear it. The fact that she agreed to take it despite her stubbornness was a torch of her love for me.

"You sound pretty certain."

"Come on, it's Tatum Titan. A lot of guys would kill to be in my shoes."

He nodded in agreement. "Very true."

I wasn't referring to Thorn specifically when I said that, but he didn't seem to take my words offensively.

"So, did you guys decide how you're combining this

empire? Prenup? How are you handling your businesses that are in competition? Is she selling her place, or are you selling yours?"

Thorn spoke about the legal ramifications of a lifetime so casually. "Don't know."

"You don't know?" he asked in disbelief. "You're getting married in seven days. You should figure it out."

I'd been dreading the conversation, and since Tatum hadn't brought it up, I knew she was too. She was constantly focused on important matters, so her disregard for our legal union was clearly on purpose. "I realize that." I shook my glass then downed the rest of it.

"Any couple with money always has a prenup," Thorn said. "It makes sense for the two of you."

"I suppose."

"It's not like Titan will get upset about it. She has an entire empire to protect, so do you. If you got divorced, she would technically get alimony because you make a few billion more than she does, but she would never take it. She's a very proud woman like that."

The word *divorce* hurt my stomach. I'd lost her once, and I never got over it. And when I almost lost her again...it nearly killed me. Divorce was a word that should be prohibited from our marriage. I never wanted to hear it out of her mouth, and I'd never let it fly out of my mind.

"I'm sure you have a good lawyer for the prenup, but I know a great guy if you need one."

I didn't have anyone in mind, but I didn't ask for the contact.

Thorn drank from his glass then eyed me. "Everything alright?"

"Yeah...I just don't like thinking about these things."

"Trust me, Titan won't get upset. I promise you, she wants a prenup. You aren't gonna offend her."

"She said that to you?"

"No, not technically. We agreed to have one in ours."

That was a different situation. "That's not why I don't want to bring it up."

"Then what's the problem?"

I wanted to spend my life with Tatum because I was madly in love with her. Her money didn't mean anything to me, but the work she did to earn it turned me on. She was independent and fierce, but underneath that hardness, she was so soft—for me. I wanted to be the man to take care of her, to be the powerhouse partner she needed. Only a strong man could handle such a capable woman. "I don't want a prenup."

―――――

We returned to New York late that night. Thorn's driver took Autumn and him home, and Tatum's took us back to her penthouse. We hadn't discussed where we would live as husband and wife, but it didn't make a difference to me. Our penthouses were about the same size, and they both had extraordinary views. The only reason we were at her place most of the time because she had been recovering from her injuries.

But I'd live wherever she wanted.

I carried the bags into the bedroom and peeled off my jacket. Too tired to put it where it belonged, I tossed it over one of the armchairs in the small living space in front of the TV.

She immediately kicked off her heels and left them on the floor. She was a neat freak, so her abandonment obviously meant she was just as exhausted. She disappeared into the bathroom and washed her face.

I tossed my clothes on the floor and looked at my watch before I set it on the dresser. It was two in the morning, and we both had to go into the office in a few hours. As the owners of our respective companies, we could do whatever we wanted. But having the right kind of discipline was what got us here in the first place.

I got into bed and set my alarm on my phone. My eyes were heavy with exhaustion, but I didn't close them just yet.

Titan came out of the bathroom after her nightly routine. She washed her face, used a special microdermabrasion machine to cleanse her face, and then she had a line of creams that she applied to different areas of her face, like the corners of her eyes, her eyelids, and her cheeks. It must be her secret to radiant and young skin because she looked just as beautiful without makeup as she did when she had it on.

In one of my t-shirts, she crawled into bed beside me.

A sigh escaped her lips as she moved to the center of the bed, soaking in my body heat the second she was against me. She closed her eyes and rested her hand on my chest.

I rolled her onto her back and moved on top of her.

"Diesel, I'm so tired...and I washed off my makeup."

"You think I care if you're tired?" I sank her into the mattress with my size and widened her thighs with my knees. "And you look fucking beautiful without makeup." I held myself on my forearms and shoved myself inside her. She wasn't as wet as she normally was, but after a few seconds, it would be there. I started to thrust, our bodies moving together with momentum due to my size. It was a lazy fuck, about getting off as quickly as possible before bed. It would be easy to skip sex and just go to sleep, but now that I'd almost lost her, I didn't take anything for granted.

I loved her like it was the last chance I had.

She got into it after a few minutes, her fingers yanking on my hair. She rocked her hips back with me, taking my dick with the same enthusiasm as she received it. Her pants filled the room, the sexy sounds that filled my fantasies. It took her longer to come than usual, but her orgasm was just as explosive as all the others. "Diesel..."

I didn't drag it out because I'd completed my mission. I came inside her, filling my woman with as much seed as she could get. I kissed her neck and pressed my teeth against her collarbone. The most amazing woman in the world was underneath me, and I would be the only man who got to be on top of her for the rest of her life.

We would be just like this—forever.

———

I left the office, and my driver took me to Illuminance, where Tatum's main office was.

I sat in the back seat with my phone pressed to my ear. My father had called on my way out the door.

"How'd the conference go?"

"Tatum killed it."

"Not surprised."

"She owned that room," I said proudly. "People say whatever they want to say about her behind her back, but once she's on that stage, they shut their mouths. They know she's the queen—and they're just fucking peasants."

My father paused over the line. "Something happen?"

"Some asshole made a comment about her ass... I didn't appreciate it."

"Did you do something about it?"

"Fuck yes, I did. I poured his drink over his head and told him to fuck off."

"Good," my father said proudly. "Humiliate him, don't hit him."

"He eventually apologized to me. I knew it was just because he understood he was missing a great opportunity with Tatum, but whatever."

"At least he apologized."

"Tatum threatened not to work with him unless he did."

He chuckled. "That woman doesn't even need you, Diesel. She can handle her own."

"And I can handle everyone else that crosses her when she's not looking."

"That's what a man's purpose is. Other than that, how did it go?"

"It was alright. They're all the same after a while."

"But this was the first one where you and Tatum were together."

"That was a nice change." People watched us the entire time, and when they saw me talking to Thorn, they were probably confused. But none of us gave a damn. "How are you?"

"Pretty good. I was hoping the three of us could have dinner this week. Something I want to talk to you about."

"You know I'm getting married on Saturday, right?" I didn't need any extra bullshit this week.

"It's nothing bad. Just want to tell you in person."

"Alright. Tomorrow?"

"Tomorrow it is. I'll talk to you later, son."

"Bye, Dad."

When I hung up the phone, the car was pulling up to the building. I got inside then rode the elevator all the way to the top floor. It was near the end of the afternoon, so Tatum would be leaving soon. I thought I would catch her and escort her home. If she knew I was doing it on purpose, she would tell me to take a hike. So I pretended I just wanted to see her. It was partially true, at least.

I walked past her assistants and headed right to her

office. I didn't even need to knock on the door. I just stepped inside.

She was sitting at her white desk reading a folder of papers. Her face was tilted down, and the light hit her features in the most exquisite way. If her doors weren't constructed of glass, I'd fuck her right on her desk.

My heavy footfalls against the hardwood floor announced my presence.

She looked up, probably assuming it was me since I was the only one who had the right to step inside her office like that. "Hey."

"Hey, baby." I came around the desk and leaned down to kiss her.

She abandoned what she was working on and kissed me back, her lips enthusiastic. "What brings you here?" Her mouth moved against mine.

I kissed her again, giving a slight tug on her bottom lip. "You."

"That's all you're going to give me?"

I righted myself then took a seat in the chair facing her desk. I unbuttoned the front of my jacket before I sat down and rested my ankle on the opposite knee. My slacks rose slightly, revealing my black socks underneath. "I don't need a reason."

The corner of her lip rose in a smile before she shut the folder and placed it in the drawer. "I suppose not."

"My father wants to have dinner with us tomorrow night. Said he has something to tell us."

"Ooh...I think I know what it is." Her smile widened.

"I told him to give Scarlet Blackwood a real chance. I hope he listened to me."

"Who's Scarlet Blackwood?"

"Editor in chief of *Platform*. Your father met her when she interviewed him."

Tatum had mentioned it, but I didn't get involved in my father's personal life. It was none of my business. He didn't stick his nose in mine either. "I see." I rested the side of my face against my fingertips, my eyes glued to the woman who would be my wife on Saturday. I never pictured what I wanted in a wife when I was growing up, but I imagined if I had, this was how she would look. I just didn't think I'd ever be lucky enough to score a woman like her. Sexy, smart, and with a splash of ruthlessness, she was perfect. She was the kind of woman who knew what she wanted—and wasn't afraid to take it. "Since we're getting married in six days, I thought we should have a talk. You know what I'm talking about." Discussing it in someone's office was better than doing it in our personal space. At least we could leave our anger at the door if it came down to it.

Her smile slowly faded away. "You're right. We should." She brought her hands together on the desk, her fingers interlocking together. As if this were a business meeting, she turned stern. The playful affection was no longer in her eyes.

It reminded me of our first negotiation, when we were both trying to get what we wanted. Neither one of us was willing to let the other have the upper hand. We were constantly trying to outsmart each other.

I didn't want to repeat that.

Tatum still didn't speak.

I didn't say anything either.

The silence stretched on, our eyes locked on each other.

Neither one of us wanted to go first without knowing what the other was thinking.

She finally cleared her throat. "Perhaps we should treat this as a business arrangement. That's pretty much what a marriage is."

"Maybe your marriage to Thorn. But certainly not ours." The only reason I was marrying her was for love, because I couldn't live without her.

"That's not how I meant it, Diesel. You know that."

We were already off to a rough start.

"We both have a lot of personal wealth. We have our own businesses. I say we operate the same way we always have. You take care of your stuff, and I handle mine. When we leave the office, we go home to each other and have our personal time."

"But we aren't utilizing each other's potential. There are a lot of things I can do for you, Tatum. And there are certainly a lot of things you can do for me. If we truly merge everything together, we could have a completely different kind of empire."

"Yes...but it could get complicated."

"We're both very logical people."

"Even so...we're both very independent. We like having our own space."

"I never said we couldn't have our own space," I said quietly. "But keeping everything rigidly separate seems unrealistic."

She crossed her arms over her chest and leaned back in her chair, her feelings stoically hidden.

"We're a team, baby. We should act like it."

"I'm not saying we shouldn't. We both have so many projects. Merging together would just take—"

"And we have a lifetime to do it."

She sighed quietly, her painted lips pressing hard together. "It'll make the prenup extremely complicated."

So she did want a prenup.

I swallowed the burn all the way down to my stomach. It was just a piece of paper, a precaution that kept everything organized. It was an easy escape plan if our life together fell apart. It crossed the t's and dotted the i's. I shouldn't take it so personally, but I did. "I don't want a prenup."

Her features remained exactly the same, but slowly, her hard expression softened. "It's just a precaution—"

"I don't need a precaution, baby." I held her gaze, ignoring the throbbing pain in my chest. "I'm coming into this knowing it's going to last forever. If you don't feel the same—"

"I do, Diesel. But from a business standpoint, it's just a smart thing to do. It's not any different from getting a trust. You probably won't get hit by a bus, but it's good to have plans laid out just in case you do."

I understood her opinion because I knew her thought process so well. But when it came to Tatum, I thought emotionally rather than logically. That was what this woman did to me. Almost losing her made me hold on to her even tighter. We'd been given a second chance, and I didn't want to waste it. "If you really want a prenup, I'll do it. But I'd rather do something else."

"What did you have in mind?"

There was no other form of legal protection besides a prenup. My idea was something else entirely. "When you wanted to have our arrangement, you wanted to have our own contract and an NDA."

"Yes."

"Let's make our own contract."

She raised an eyebrow. "I don't know if that would hold up in a court of law."

"Our marriage has nothing to do with the law." I respected Titan's logic. She built an empire all on her own, and she had to protect it. But I was the one who had more to lose, and I was willing to gamble it all—because I knew we would win. "Our contract outlines the parameters of our relationship. It binds us together, and it ensures that we stay together. It's not any different from when you wanted to marry me for convenience."

Her expression didn't change. "Diesel, I still don't understand."

I propped my elbow on the armrest and rubbed the pads of my fingers against my thumb. "It's a document that binds us together. Whenever we hit a rough patch, we turn back to it and the promises we made to each other. It's like wedding vows, but different. For instance, I promise to always remain faithful to you—no matter what. I also promise to never lie to you—not ever. I expect the same from you, as a business partner. If we have issues, we have to talk about them—no matter how painful they are. If you find yourself falling out of love with me, we need to talk about it and fix whatever problems we have. Same goes for me. The bottom line is, divorce is not an option."

She considered it quietly, her eyebrow slowly falling. "So it's the opposite of a prenup?"

"Exactly. I don't want an escape plan. I want a plan to make this work. No, it's not legally binding in court, but if we have certain rules, we should never get to that point. It's a business contract just like anything else."

"I suppose we can talk about it more."

So she was still considering the prenup. "Tatum."

Her eyes shifted back to mine.

"I want all of you, not some of you. If you want to marry me, then no prenup."

"So, you're giving me an ultimatum?"

"I'm asking you to put everything on the line, just as I am. We're in this together."

She dropped her gaze again, staring at her pen as she considered it. The silence filled the space between us, the tension heavy. Two bosses fought for dominion, and one of us had to give in. "Alright."

————

We finished dinner, and our glasses of wine remained behind at the dinner table. I already had the contract typed up, so I had two copies on the surface along with two pens. I pushed one copy toward her and watched her eyes glance over the words.

Her hair was pulled over one shoulder, and her eyelashes were thick and long from her mascara. Her tight blouse hugged the swell of her tits perfectly. The idea of their being swollen with pregnancy turned me on. I was excited to see Tatum waddle around the house because she was pregnant with my child. Nothing sexier.

She turned her gaze back to me. "Ready?"

"Yeah." I turned to the first paragraph. "Cheating and unfaithfulness are completely disallowed. In the event there's serious temptation, we need to speak to each other about it. But the act is outlawed. No exceptions whatsoever. By signing down below, we both promise to give each other that level of commitment."

She read it over again before she added her signature.

I did the same.

"What happens if one of us tells the other they're struggling to remain faithful?"

"We figure out the best course of action. Whether that's marriage counseling, the removal of the person we're attracted to, or we discuss having an open relationship. Whatever it may be, we need to talk about it openly. No cheating or lying."

"I can't see either one of us cheating..."

It was the first time she said something that cured the ache in my chest. "Me neither, baby. But these rules will ensure nothing ever happens. Divorce is something we can never allow to happen. If we're both committed to avoiding that under any circumstance, we'll be together forever."

"You're right," she whispered.

We moved to the next paragraph. "In the event one of us falls out of love..." This section hurt even more than the previous one. I couldn't imagine ever not loving Tatum the way I did now. The only way it would change was if I loved her more, not less. The idea of her not looking at me the way she did every single day killed me. "We talk about it and resume a business marriage. We renegotiate our terms, whether that's marriage counseling or an open relationship. But splitting up isn't an option. We still have a powerful alliance that we can't lose. We need each other."

She signed the line.

I did the same.

"This is why the prenup would be easier," she whispered. "We don't have to talk about the things we don't want to think about..."

"It's painful, but I'd rather make sure I never lose you."

"Diesel, I can't see myself cheating or falling out of love with you." She shook her head. "I tried to get over you once, but I just ended up falling for you harder—and I thought you were a lying cheater at the time."

"I can't see that happening with me either, baby. I'm sure we'll have a long and happy life together. But now we have some reassurance that we'll always make it work—no matter what gets thrown our way."

We made our way farther down the list until we got to the section about kids.

"We always keep our relationship issues separate from them," I said. "Whether we're fighting or struggling, they're never included in that. If we decide to have an open relationship, they're never to find out about it. And whatever happens between us, we always treat each other with respect when we're around them. We're role models to them, and they need to be exposed to a healthy relationship, even if we aren't in love anymore."

She signed.

I did the same. "That's it." The two-page contract was complete. "I'll make a copy for you." I gathered the papers then set them off to the side.

"Thanks."

"All this talk of divorce has made me a bit depressed."

"Not divorce. We'll never get divorced, baby."

"You know what I mean."

I reached out my hand and grabbed hers. My thumb stroked her knuckles. "We're going to be together forever —and we're going to be happy. I just love you so much that I want to make sure I never lose you. I couldn't be married to you and lose you. It would kill me." I brought her hand to my lips and kissed it.

"I couldn't lose you either, Diesel. I would never get over it."

"Then let's choose to be happy and in love. Let's live our lives like we'll never be apart. I won't look at another woman as long as you're my wife, and I know you won't look at another man as long as I'm your husband."

She smiled. "I like the sound of that."

I pushed the papers away then rose to my feet. There was only one thing to do after a conversation like that. I wanted to erase the painful thoughts and the aches in our chest. I wanted to do something that reminded both of us of the connection between our souls. I wanted to feel her love and shower her with mine.

I lifted her onto the dining table and yanked her skirt up to her waist. Her panties were peeled off and dropped on the floor. I pushed my slacks and boxers down so my dick could be free, and I shoved my massive size inside her with a single thrust.

She moaned and dug her fingers into my arms at the exact same time. "God…"

I laid her back against the cherry wood and adjusted her hips perfectly against me. Her stilettos were still on her feet, so I pressed them against my chest, bending her knees underneath me. Instead of fucking her slow and steady, I fucked her hard. I gave it to her good and deep, ramming her with my entire length. Her tightness slowly decreased as she got used to me, but her moans became louder and louder.

She broke her thighs apart and pulled me on top of her, making my face float above hers. She looked into my eyes as she screamed and moaned for me, getting off to a monster cock inside her. "Diesel..." Her fingers ran up my collared shirt, her nails sharp enough to give me deep pressure. "I want you for all my life."

When her moments of vulnerability came out, I truly felt like a man. Not only did I conquer an unconquerable woman, but I made her trust me. I made her fall so deeply for me that she didn't hide a single emotion. She wasn't scared I would hurt her. She trusted me with her heart, trusted me with everything.

That was worth more than the billions sitting in my bank account. It was worth more than my penthouse, my private jet, and my collection of luxury cars. Having the love of Tatum Titan gave me more wealth than all of that put together.

And the love of Tatum Hunt would be even better.

———

Tatum had the same bedtime routine every night. She did it with perfect precision, going through the motions the exact same way every time. She put on different face masks to take care of her skin, and she applied a heavy lotion around her face to keep it hydrated and radiant.

Instead of it being a turn-off, I thought she looked beautiful.

Not too many women could look as beautiful without makeup as they could with it.

The best part was when she opened my drawer and pulled out one of my t-shirts. She did it every single night, picking whatever one was on top and sliding it over her petite body. My shirt was at least three sizes too big for her, so it reached her knees.

That was when she looked the most beautiful.

She walked to her nightstand and set her alarm on her phone.

I was already in bed, my hand behind my head as I watched her.

She turned off the lamp and got into bed beside me. The second her body hit the sheets, she was on my side of the bed, her leg hooked around mine and her arm wrapped around my waist. "Diesel?"

"Yes, baby?" My fingers moved through her hair slowly, touching the soft strands I loved to caress.

"I have a doctor's appointment tomorrow."

My fingers halted when I heard what she said. At her last checkup, the doctor said she was completely healed and ready to return to ordinary life. "Everything alright?"

"Yeah. I was going to get my IUD removed." She propped herself on her elbow and looked down at me. "They say it usually takes a few months for my body to be able to conceive, so I thought I would do it now. But it's possible I can get pregnant immediately."

All the stress left my body when I heard what she said.

"Do you still want to do this? Or do you want to wait a while?"

That was what I was looking forward to the most for the honeymoon, knocking her up. "I'm sure, baby. I'm going to have so much fun getting you pregnant. And you're gonna look damn sexy pregnant."

She chuckled. "I don't know about the second part."

"I do." My hand moved over her belly on top of the t-shirt. "Little Hunt."

She moved her hand over mine. "Then, you are sure?"

"Yes. Are you?"

She nodded. "I've been looking forward to being a mom for a long time now. I was so close with my father, and I want to have that relationship again, just with me as the parent. And I don't have anyone in the world I'm actually related to...but now I will."

"What do you want first? Boy or girl?"

"I don't care. As long as they're healthy."

"I hope we have one of each. Never had a sister, so I kinda have always wanted a girl. But I also want to have a son."

"We can keep trying until we get one of each."

I smiled. "Sounds fun to me."

She rose on her knees and peeled her panties off. "Want to start practicing now?"

My grin widened because it was always sexy to see Tatum want me. "Yes. I need as much practice as I can get."

CHAPTER SEVEN

Vincent

The elevator doors opened to Tatum's penthouse, and I stepped inside to see Diesel sitting on the couch while Tatum set the table.

"Hey, Dad." Diesel met me in the doorway and gave me a hug.

I hugged him back, grateful I got to have these moments with him. It seemed so casual on the surface, but deep down inside, I lived for these embraces. I lived for the moments when he called me Dad. "Hey, son. How are you?"

"Good. Can I take your coat?"

"Sure." I peeled it off and handed it to him.

He placed it on the coatrack. "We're having wine with dinner. Is that okay, or do you want something else?"

"That's perfect."

"Dinner is ready." Tatum had the table set with three

plates, a bottle of wine, and a fresh basket of bread. Three white candles burned in the center along with a vase of pink roses. She walked up to me and hugged me, a smile on her face that would make anyone melt. "Thanks for coming. We're so glad to have you."

Tatum was such a gift to Diesel that it hurt to know Isabella would never have the chance to meet her. She would never know that her son met a woman who would always take care of him. She loved him enough to put his best interests before her own. It was because of her that I had a relationship with Diesel. I could never thank her enough for that. "I'm very happy to be here."

Diesel poured the wine then took a seat beside Tatum.

"How was your weekend?" I asked as I sat across from him.

"Good," Diesel answered. "Tatum and Autumn killed it. By the end of the day, the company had more preorders than they can even fulfill. Now Tatum and Autumn are trying to figure out how to manage it."

"And it'll also be Thorn's problem when I'm gone for two weeks," Titan said as she cut into her food.

"It's nice that Thorn is helping you so much," I answered. "He's a good man. I like him."

"I like him too," Diesel said. "And when he needs to step away from his business, we'll be there to cover for him."

"That sounds fair." I took a few bites of my food and ignored the basket of bread on the table. "Tatum, this is delicious. Where did you learn to cook?"

"YouTube," she said with a chuckle.

"Whatever works." I asked them about the wedding plans and if there was anything I could do to help, but since it was such a small wedding, it didn't seem like there was much to do anyway.

Tatum talked about her wedding dress for a bit before she changed the subject. "So, what did you want to discuss, Vincent?" Judging by the smile on her face, she knew exactly what I wanted to share with them. I hadn't said much to Diesel about Scarlet, but I'd poured out my heart to Tatum.

Diesel was a grown man who always thought rationally, but the idea of my being with someone else besides his mother must bother him. Alessia and the others were meaningless flings. Anyone who paid attention deduced that. But I'd never been with a woman I actually cared about...until now. "I've been seeing Scarlet Blackwood for about a month now, and it's gotten serious." I sipped my wine before I turned to Diesel. "I know this is difficult, but I hope I have your support."

Diesel smirked and held back a laugh. "Dad, come on. I want you to be happy. I'm thirty-five years old. I understand how the real world works. Mom would want you to move on and be happy."

Hearing my son's approval meant a lot to me. If he rejected my relationship with Scarlet, I would probably stop seeing her. My sons were everything to me. They were gifts Isabella gave to me, and I wouldn't squander them. "Thanks...I appreciate it."

"So, she's the editor of *Platform*?" Diesel asked.

So Titan did mention her. "Yes. She loves her job. Frankly, she's good at it." I saw the way she worked with her employees. They respected her direction and did whatever they could to earn her approval. She handled multiple tasks so fluidly. Only someone with high intelligence could do that with such obvious grace.

"What's she like?" Diesel asked.

I would have brought her to dinner, but I thought it would be too soon. "She's very smart. Very pretty. For someone working in fashion, she's very laid-back. She's funny...makes me laugh. I like how easygoing she is. When I talk to her, it's not difficult. I'm a man of few words, but that doesn't seem to bother her. She accepts me for how I am. I told her how much I still love my wife, and she doesn't have a problem with it. She's very understanding."

"She sounds great," Diesel said. "Maybe we can meet her soon."

"You'd want to?" I asked in surprise.

"Absolutely," Tatum said. "You can bring her to the wedding as a plus-one."

That option wasn't even on the table. "That wouldn't be appropriate. I'd rather go by myself." I couldn't go to my son's wedding with someone other than Isabella. I was happy for my son and it was a day to celebrate, but without his mother there, it was also a sad moment for me. She wasn't there to enjoy a day she'd have given anything to experience.

"Dad, it's really okay," Diesel said. "I don't mind if you bring your girlfriend."

I guessed Scarlet was my girlfriend. It was weird to think about. "I know, but I'd rather go by myself."

Tatum dropped her smile, and Diesel didn't press the argument any longer. It was awkward for a while, and I knew that was my fault.

"We should get together sometime after the wedding," Titan said. "Maybe the four of us could have dinner."

"Yeah, maybe," I said noncommittally.

"Is Jax happy for you?" Diesel asked.

"I haven't told him yet. I will sometime this week."

"Well, I'm sure he'll be fine with it," Diesel said. "Does Scarlet have children?"

"One daughter," I answered. "She's in nursing school right now."

"Have you met her?" Tatum asked.

"No," I answered. "We're still in the beginning of our relationship."

"Was she ever married?" Diesel asked.

"Yes," I said. "She's been divorced for about ten years now. Never remarried. From the way she talks about it, sounds like the guy was an ass. But she's never told me more, even though I've asked a few times." I wanted to know exactly what happened between them, but it was really none of my business. She didn't ask a bunch of questions about Isabella.

"She got it right this time, though," Tatum said with a smile. "Judging by that article she wrote…"

"Yeah, Dad," Diesel said. "She's got it bad."

I tried not to smile at the way they teased me. The fact that it was true only made me feel good. She was twelve years younger than me, beautiful and smart, but she seemed to only want me. She was patient with me in a way no one else would ever be, so that must mean something. "She does put up with a lot..."

"She's a keeper," Tatum said. "You want a partner who's understanding. You want a partner who wants you so much, they'll settle for only half your heart. That's exactly what you need, Vincent. And she needs a man to protect her."

"She's not the kind of woman who's looking for protection." She could handle herself perfectly fine. She held herself with grace and walked down the sidewalk like she owned it. She was smart and calculating, conquering the fashion world easily.

"All women want a man who can protect them...even if they say they don't." Her hand moved to Diesel's forearm on the table.

The only time I saw Tatum show vulnerability was when it came to my son. The rest of the time, she was as cold as an ice cube. "She used to be a model in her younger years. When she turned thirty, she retired because she was forced to. She was told to get plastic surgery, but she refused. So then she started working at the magazine and moved up to her position."

"Too old?" Titan asked incredulously. "Plastic surgery? Forget that. That's ridiculous."

"I couldn't agree more," I said. "Scarlet is a very beautiful woman. I wouldn't change anything about her." She had a beautiful body, flawless skin, and the wrinkles on her face were hardly noticeable. "She's one of the most beautiful women I've ever seen."

Tatum smiled. "Now I'm even more excited to meet her."

"Me too," Diesel said.

I understood just how lucky I was. They were doing everything they could to make this transition easy for me. It didn't seem to be an act. They truly wanted me to have someone in my life, even Diesel. He must know how much I loved his mother and how much I wished she were still here, so it wasn't a betrayal of her memory.

She'd want me to fall in love again.

———

I hadn't seen Scarlet in a few days, so I called her after my workout. I usually used my own personal gym so people wouldn't stare at me and take pictures on their phones. I wasn't a celebrity, but judging by the actions of the people who recognized me, I felt like one.

I got out of the shower with a towel wrapped around my waist. The phone rang in my ear several times before she answered.

"Vincent, how are you?" Unsuppressed happiness was in her voice. I could hear it loud and clear. Her smile was probably wide, and it formed the instant she saw my name on the screen.

"Good." She was the easiest person to talk to, but since she was so easy, it was simple not to say anything at all. That was how comfortable I was. I pulled out a pair of boxers from my drawer then tossed them on the bed. "You?"

"Well. But I'm better now that I'm talking to you."

I smiled when she flirted with me. "Have dinner with me tonight."

"I'd love to. How about I cook dinner at my place?"

A home-cooked meal sounded wonderful. "That sounds great."

"I'll text you my address. Be here in forty-five minutes."

"See you then."

I put on dark jeans and an olive green t-shirt with a black leather jacket. My driver took me to her place on the other side of town. She lived in a nice building in a good area, still a wealthy district most people couldn't afford. It wasn't anything like my penthouse, but it was certainly lovely.

I took the elevator to her floor then knocked.

"It's open."

I stepped inside to the smell of Italian cuisine and *Jeopardy* on TV.

Her apartment was small but cozy. It was decorated with classy style, blue couches with a white coffee table. Pictures were everywhere, and there was a pink rug on the hardwood floor. I spotted a picture hanging on the wall, and a young brunette was in the image.

I recognized her daughter.

Photos of her were everywhere, the obvious joy in her life.

Scarlet came out of the kitchen in a gray sweater that hung off one shoulder. It showed her tanned skin and a few freckles that sprinkled the surface. Her straight hair was pulled over one shoulder, and she had on black leggings that fit her sculpted legs. Her casual attire somehow made me feel more at ease.

But also made me more attracted to her.

I could make out the curve of her body even better. I saw the enormous dip in the small of her back, the slenderness in her neck. Her legs were even longer than I realized. She was barefoot, and even the sight of that was erotic to me.

Not getting laid in months was starting to get to me.

"You look handsome." Her eyes roamed over my body, taking in my wide chest and powerful shoulders. She had to rise on her tiptoes to bring her face level to mine, and even then, she fell short. She went right for a kiss, giving me a quick peck on the lips.

My hands immediately gripped her hips, and I squeezed. "Thank you. You look beautiful—as always."

She smiled as she flattened her feet. "Always such a gentleman." She pushed my leather jacket off my shoulders. "I can take this."

I peeled it off and let her take it.

She hung it on the coatrack. "I know you're a picky eater, so I tried to make something good without carbs... which is nearly impossible."

I chuckled. "You're right."

"So, I made chicken Marsala with a salad. Boring, but good."

"I'm sure anything you make will be fantastic."

She smiled. "You always say the right thing." She took my hand in hers and guided me to her kitchen table, which was part of her living room. In New York City, this was a killer apartment despite its size. It still must cost a small fortune to live there, especially with the nice plaster on the walls, perfectly conditioned hardwood floors, and the brand-new appliances. "Wine?"

"Sure."

She opened a bottle and poured two glasses before she set the table.

A plate of hot chicken slathered in a thick sauce with mushrooms stared back at me, along with a medium-size salad full of chicken, nuts, fruits, and kale. I grabbed my fork and dug in. "Thank for cooking. This is incredible."

"Thanks." She smiled then sat across from me, eating slowly. "Do you cook when you're at home?"

"Sometimes. But most of the time, Betty makes dinner for me."

"Betty?" she asked.

"My maid. She's the other woman in my life."

Scarlet chuckled. "Looks like I have competition."

"Actually, you don't. You're a better cook."

"You're just saying that...but I appreciate it." She placed her hand over mine and gave me a gentle squeeze.

I liked it when she touched me. It made me feel good inside. When Alessia or another woman touched me, I felt a spike of arousal and sex came into my mind. But when Scarlet touched me, it felt a lot different. It didn't feel just sexual, but affectionate as well.

When her touch was withdrawn, I immediately missed it. "You like *Jeopardy?*"

"I love it. I've been watching it every day since... forever. Do you watch it?"

"If it's on," I said. "But I don't record it or anything."

"It's a classic. I like it."

I thought it was cute that she enjoyed a trivia show. "How was work?"

"A nightmare," she said. "I won't bore you with the details, but items were supposed to be delivered for a shoot but were actually never ordered, so I had to throw something together. In the end, everything was fine. But it was still a pain."

"At least you averted the crisis."

"I love being the editor because I love the magazine and I love fashion, but sometimes, it's overwhelming. I miss being a model sometimes. It was a lot simpler. Someone else dealt with the difficult stuff, and I just got to put on pretty clothes and smile."

"You could still be a model."

She laughed. "You're too sweet sometimes."

"I'm being serious." I'd never been more serious in my life.

"We went over this, Vincent. I'm too old. I'm forty-two. No one wants to see a forty-two-year-old model showing off clothes."

"I disagree." I couldn't wait to see her with her clothes off. "There will always be women in their thirties and forties. They tend to be financially stable, so they have the income to spend on clothes. If anything, they should be the main demographic advertisers aim for. If you had a line of clothes and a magazine geared toward those women, I promise you it would be successful. All this bullshit about being too old and needing plastic surgery to be beautiful is stupid. Look at you. I've been with models in their twenties, and they don't hold a candle to you, Scarlet. You're a bombshell."

The look she gave me was priceless. She didn't smile, but her eyes showed a million different reactions. She was obviously touched because she stopped eating. "Vincent..." Speechless, she turned quiet.

"Just my thoughts." I brought my voice down, knowing I'd gotten overly passionate with what I said. "I know business better than anyone, and I'm telling you, women everywhere would go for that. You could start a movement."

She tilted her head toward her plate. "Maybe."

Our conversation died away, and I hoped I hadn't made it too uncomfortable to continue. I could be overly aggressive without realizing it sometimes. In my world, that was the only way to get anything done—by being more aggressive than my competitor. "How's your daughter?"

Her smile formed again. "She's good. She went on a date last weekend and seems to really like the guy. He sounds nice."

The girl looked just like Scarlet, a very beautiful young woman. If the guy wasn't a complete idiot, he wouldn't let her slip away. "That's good."

"I'm not in a hurry to be a grandmother, but I am looking forward to grandkids."

"So am I."

"Are Diesel and Titan planning on having a family right away?"

"Not sure," I answered. "I think Titan is in a hurry, but I'm not sure what they decided."

"Hopefully, that will happen soon. I'm excited to have a baby around again, but a baby that isn't mine. I get to play with it and spoil it before I hand it back and go back to my quiet apartment." She chuckled then took another bite.

"I'm not interested in having children either." I'd never specifically told her that, so I was relieved we were on the same page.

"I actually had my tubes tied a few years ago. I didn't want to take birth control anymore, and I'm not interested in having more kids."

That worked out well for us. I didn't have the energy to have a kid in diapers again. I finished all of my food until my plate was just as clean as it was before she placed the food on it.

"Wow, you were hungry."

"No, it was just that good."

She cleared the table and dumped the dishes in the sink.

I came to her side and started to wash them.

"Vincent, no." She shut the faucet off. "You're my guest. Don't worry about it."

"You cooked, so I should clean."

"Not in this house." She grabbed my bicep and guided me back into the living room. "I'll do them later."

I let her guide me to the couch. *Jeopardy* had ended, and now a different game show was on.

She sat beside me and crossed her legs. "What do you want to watch?"

I rested my arm over the back of the couch. "Whatever you want."

"Well, I honestly don't want to watch anything." She changed it to ESPN and turned on the game.

My brain focused on her words and the obvious implications.

She moved into me and glided her hand up my chest. She inched closer then kissed my neck, her soft lips feeling incredible against my warm skin. Her breaths fell across my ear, the gentle sound of her mouth arousing. Her lips moved to my jawline next, and she slowly approached my mouth.

I turned into her kiss and dug my hand into her hair. I

kissed her aggressively for the first time, letting my body do exactly what I wanted to do. My mouth sucked her bottom lip hard, and I breathed deep into her lungs. I pulled on her soft hair before I felt her bare shoulder. Like a caveman, I gripped the back of her head and turned her face away so I could kiss her neck.

Her hands clawed at me, scratching my skin. She yanked on my body and pulled me down into the couch, situating me on top of her. Her thighs were spread, and she locked her ankles around my waist.

It was the most intimate we'd ever been.

It felt good. It felt right.

Her lips were on mine again, and she kissed me with tongue, her passion increasing as she squeezed her thighs around my waist.

After a few minutes, I was hard.

Harder than I'd been in a long time.

She slowly grinded against me, feeling my cock right against her clit in her leggings. "Vincent..." She reached for my shirt and slowly pulled it up. She got it over my head and tossed it on the coffee table. Her hands explored my rock-hard chest and my abdominals. She felt the grooves and valleys then explored my back. She paused our kiss to look at me. "Jesus...you're ripped."

Now she knew why I didn't eat carbs. I could barely eat anything to look like this. It was all protein and no sugar or carbs. The more I aged, the more difficult it was to maintain this physique. But watching Scarlet devour me with her eyes made it all worth it.

She panted into my mouth, slowly grinding her body against me. Her nails dug harder and her moans deepened. I could hear her fall apart underneath me, feel her lips tremble against my mouth. "Vincent, you're gonna make me come..."

All the muscles in my back tightened. My hips dug deeper into her, pressing my cock through my jeans against her sensitive nub. I'd been with insatiable women before, women in their twenties who just wanted more and more. But I'd never wanted to please any of them the way I wanted to please her.

My hand fisted her hair, and I ground my hard cock perfectly against her throbbing clit.

"Yes..." Her head rolled back, and her hair stretched across the cushion. She bucked against me automatically, her sexy moans filling the apartment. She clawed at my back with the ferocity of a wildcat. She hit her peak then slowly came down, floating like a feather on the wind. Slowly, reality came back to her, and she stopped grinding against me with the same intensity. "God, I can't remember the last time a man made me feel that good..."

I gave her a final kiss before I pulled away, my ego much bigger now than it was when I walked in the door. It was probably the reason I got so hard, watching this woman want me so badly. She loved my body and worshiped it with her hands.

Her hands moved to my jeans, and she popped the button.

As much as I enjoyed this, it suddenly felt like too

much. I actually liked this woman, so I didn't want to rush into anything. I already felt connected to her, and that connection scared me. As much as I wanted to make love to her, it seemed too soon. "Not yet." I grabbed her wrist and steadied it, feeling like an ass for telling this beautiful woman no. "I'm just...not ready."

"I know," she whispered. "But let me make you feel just as good as you made me feel."

Her words were verbal sex right against my ear. I was still hard and eager. The idea of getting naked and sweaty with her in bed sounded like the best thing in the world right now. But I didn't want to cross the line unless I was ready.

"Trust me." She looked at me with those pretty green eyes and made me forget reason. She slowly pushed me back to the couch until I was sitting upright again.

Then she moved to her knees on the floor.

Fuck.

My jeans were undone, and my boxers were yanked down along with the top of my pants. Seeing Scarlet on her knees with eager eyes made all the muscles in my body tighten. I pictured that wet mouth around my dick and felt a shiver down my spine. I couldn't remember the last time I was this turned on.

Scarlet eyed my dick like it was fucking candy. She was obviously impressed by my size because she couldn't wipe away the surprise on her face. She gazed at it like a picture in an art gallery before she scooted closer to me and grabbed me by the base. "Wow..." She directed my dick to the ceiling before she licked the crown.

Fuck.

I closed my eyes, and both of my hands formed fists.

She kissed and licked the tip before she slowly lowered her throat down my length. She could only get halfway, but that was more than enough to make my balls tighten. She used both hands to massage my length, to jerk up and down as she swiped her tongue across my tip, gathering the lubricant I was already producing.

Jesus Christ.

Scarlet had never looked so sexy. She used her tongue with precision and sucked me off like she was really enjoying it.

I wanted to last longer, but I couldn't. I hadn't gotten action in a long time, and I just couldn't control myself the way I used to when I was younger. When I had sex on a daily basis, it was much easier. But now that I'd found a woman I actually cared about, her touch was a million times more deadly. I could stop myself from blowing my load with Alessia but not with Scarlet.

No fucking way.

"I'm gonna come, sweetheart." My hand fisted her hair, keeping it out of her face as she continued to suck me off. If she wanted to pull away and let me come on myself, now was the time to move. But she kept going, sucking harder and jerking her hand quicker.

"Fuck..." My voice came out deeper than usual, and I forgot to breathe. A tidal wave of pleasure swept over me, and I came inside her mouth, hitting her in the back of the throat and the top of her tongue. I thrust into her mouth slightly, giving her the last few drops I released. I knew I came a lot, but she took it like a pro.

She sucked my crown before she licked her lips.

For not being on a date in a year, she knew how to give head pretty damn well.

"Fuck...that was incredible." I felt like an ass for cursing in front of her, but it slipped out. It was just felt so good that I couldn't think straight.

"It was... I liked it." She wiped her thumb along her mouth. "And I've never enjoyed doing that before."

This woman was driving me crazy. She made me feel like the only man she'd ever really given a damn about. Maybe I was. The possibility made me light in the head. "Well, you can do that all you like."

"I definitely plan on doing it again." She moved between my thighs and kissed my softening cock.

The touch made my chest tighten. My fingers moved into hair, and I couldn't stop myself from grabbing her. The beast inside me was slowly emerging, the sexual man that I kept at bay. I wanted to possess her in a way I had never possessed the others. I purposely kept a wall between us so neither one of us would cross it.

But that wall suddenly got lower.

CHAPTER EIGHT

DIESEL

The young man behind the desk looked up when I approached him. "Yes?"

No one spoke to me like that, so this young guy obviously had no idea who I was. "Diesel Hunt for Scarlet Blackwood."

He cocked an eyebrow. "You aren't on the schedule."

"Obviously. I would have mentioned it if I were."

His eyes narrowed with the same hostility I expressed on my face. "If you don't have an appointment, then you can't see her. She's very busy. The editor in chief of *Platform* magazine is extremely busy."

"I bet she's not too busy for me. Tell her I'm here."

He didn't move.

I narrowed my eyes. "Trust me, you don't want to go there." I walked to the couch and took a seat.

He pressed the phone to his ear then made the call.

When he glared at me and hung up, I knew she'd told him to send me in. "She'll see you now." He didn't get up to walk me.

Fine by me. I walked past him and entered the double doors that led to her office. The sun was bright that afternoon, and her large office was almost as big as mine. She had a nice sitting area, an enormous desk, and a glorious view of the city.

She rose from her desk, looking at me with a hesitant smile. "Mr. Hunt, it's nice to meet you in person." She walked around the desk in purple stilettos with a teal dress. Tall, thin, and pretty, she looked like the perfect woman for my dad. She had obvious grace judging by the way she carried herself. I could tell she used to be a model because she was beautiful. It was hard to believe she was in her forties.

I shook her hand. "It's nice to meet you too. Thanks for meeting me on short notice."

"It's no problem." She gripped my hand firmly before she released it. "I was hoping I would meet you someday. I guess someday is today. Come, take a seat." She indicated the couches on the rug. It was cozy, like someone's living room.

I sat across from her, unbuttoning the front of my jacket.

She stared at my face hard, as if she was looking for something. "I'm sorry...you look so much like your father."

"I get that a lot."

"Your father looks unbelievable for his age. You two look like—"

"Brothers." I smiled. "It's true. Tatum told me she'd be happy if I age as well as he did."

"I'm sure you will. The apple doesn't fall far from the tree."

"Hopefully." I sat back and rested my ankle on the opposite knee.

"So, what can I do for you, Mr. Hunt?"

"Please call me Diesel."

"Alright, Diesel." She crossed her legs and brought her hands together. "I'm assuming this has something to do with your father. That's the only connection I can think of."

"It does. I told him to invite you to our wedding, but he said no."

"Oh…"

"I know it's not because of you, but because of my mom. He probably feels like—"

"I totally understand," she said gently. "Really, I get it. Your father has made it very clear where he stands in life. He's widower, and he'll always mourn your mother. That's fine with me. Always has been." She smiled at me. "When he talks about her, I feel like I almost know her. He told me about the moment when he first saw her. It's refreshing to hear a man wear his heart on his sleeve, to be unashamed to admit he was in love. Not all men are like that. Most don't even understand what love is or care to find out."

My father was lucky he had a woman who was so understanding. When it came to Tatum, I was selfish. I wanted to be the only man in her heart—and in between her legs. I was very possessive of her. "Thank you for being so patient with him. I hope you keep being patient with him. My dad needs to move on with his life. I think he won't allow himself to be happy because he feels too guilty."

"I've caught on to that," she said with a chuckle.

"He's never actually been serious with a woman before. It'll take him some time to get used to it."

"I've got all the time in the world, Diesel. Your father is an incredible man. I'm not going anywhere."

Maybe I didn't have anything to worry about, after all. "Thanks. Tatum and I were wondering if the four of us could have dinner tonight."

"I'd love to. But perhaps we should wait until your father is ready to initiate that. I don't think he is."

"I know he's not," I said with a laugh. "So I'm giving him a push out the door."

"You're sweet, but I think we should let him do this on his terms. Our relationship has moved at a snail's pace. He's very conflicted about it."

"Because he likes you so much."

Her eyes softened. "I know he does. It's sweet."

"So, let's do this."

"How about we wait until after the wedding?" she asked. "I know your dad is getting emotional right now.

The first of his sons is getting married, and his wife isn't there to see it. Give him some time."

I wanted my father to be happy so much that I was rushing the process. My mother had been gone for over ten years, so it seemed long enough. But my dad had shut off everything until that moment. To him, this was like being with the first woman after he lost his wife. Those models in between didn't really count. They didn't mean anything to him. But this woman certainly did. "Okay. That sounds fair."

"Alright. I'm looking forward to it. You know, he talks about you a lot. He's very sorry about everything that happened."

I bowed my head and broke eye contact. "I know he is."

"And he loves you so much."

"I know..."

"He's lucky you're so supportive of this. I have no idea how my daughter will feel about it. Anytime I've dated someone, she's ignored it. She's never wanted to meet anyone I've seen, and I've never pressured her to. But I know Vincent is different, so she'll have to face it."

"What's her issue?"

"She's very close to her father," she said with a sigh. "In her eyes, I'm the one who broke up the marriage. But she doesn't understand that her father was physically and emotionally abusive toward me. She was too young to understand, and he's very talented at pretending to be something he's not when he's around her. He's had other girlfriends, and I suspect he treats them the same way he treated me."

I wondered if my father knew this. I suspected he didn't.

"So when she meets Vincent, she'll reject him. But she'll have to get over it because I'm not going to stop seeing him no matter how upset she gets. She's a lovely girl. I'm making her sound like a nightmare." She chuckled. "She's my whole world, and I love her with all my heart. But this is the one thing she's weird about. She's always wanted her father and me to get back together."

"Why don't you tell her the truth?"

She sighed and looked away. "I love that she has a relationship with her father. I never had one with mine. I don't want to take that away from her... I don't want her to hate him. He's good to her, he loves her."

If I knew my father ever raised a hand to my mother, he'd be dead right now. "My dad doesn't know this, huh?" I suspected he would have mentioned it. And if he didn't, he would have shown some anger when he mentioned Scarlet was divorced.

She shook her head. "No."

"Why?"

"Your father is an old-fashioned gentleman. If he knew...I know he would do everything in his power to make my ex-husband suffer. He would march over there and strangle him with his tie. Then he would use his wealth to make his life absolutely unbearable. I know how much he cares about me, and he would do anything to protect me."

She was dead-on about all of that.

"But I don't need to be protected. I've been out of that relationship for over a decade now. If he ever tried to touch me again, I'd break every bone in his body until he died from the pain."

"What makes you think I won't do that myself?" If my father cared about this woman, then I cared about her. And if that asshole thought he would get away with this, he was wrong. Karma always came back for everyone.

She smiled. "Because you know I don't want you to."

"Then what makes you think I won't tell my father everything?"

"If it hurt you, imagine how much it'll hurt him," she whispered. "I'll tell him when I'm ready. But right now, he's got other things to be concerned about. I'm not dropping my baggage on him right this second, especially when it's not a current issue."

I nodded in understanding. "Fair enough."

"Well, it was nice to meet you." She rose to her feet and shook my hand. "Congratulations on your wedding."

"Thank you. I'm very excited."

She smiled. "You have a whole lifetime of excitement to look forward to. This is only the beginning, and it only gets better from here. I don't know from personal experience, obviously, but I know through others. And when you have your first child...that will be the greatest day of your life."

Tatum and I were going to start trying to have a family right away. I knew I wanted kids, but I couldn't imagine what it would be like to physically hold them in my hands. I'd be responsible for a whole new life. But the idea didn't scare me because I'd always guarded Tatum like she was a piece of my heart living outside my body. My children would be no different. "Yeah...I have a lot to look forward to."

———

I walked inside the penthouse and hung my jacket on the coatrack. "Baby, I'm home."

She stepped out of the bedroom, still wearing the same outfit she wore to the office. Her heels were gone, and now she was barefoot. She walked up to me, her hips shaking as she walked. When she reached me, she gave me a hot kiss and squeezed my biceps with her fingertips.

I was hard instantly.

I knew her IUD was gone and now she could get pregnant at any moment. The idea made my cock twitch, its biological purpose taking over. I wanted to stuff her with my seed as many times as it took before she was big and pregnant. My hands shook just thinking about it. "Missed you."

Her arms circled my neck. "I missed you..."

I sucked her bottom lip then backed her up to the couch. I wanted to fuck her at the deepest angle possible, to make sure I got every drop of come inside that tight cunt.

She broke the kiss and turned her mouth away. "I didn't mean for that to get carried away."

"We always get carried away." I cupped her cheek and kissed her again.

She moved her mouth with mine for a few seconds before she pulled away again. "I think we should wait to have sex again until after the wedding."

I stared at her blankly. "I have no idea what you just said right now."

She pulled her hand from my face. "It's only a few days away. It'll make it more special that way."

"Baby, you know I always make it special."

"You know what I mean. It'll make it more special, and we'll be trying to get pregnant, so it'll be even more special for that."

I actually growled in her face. "I think it's a stupid idea."

"Diesel," she said with a chuckle. "It'll make you want to rip off my dress all that much more."

"Trust me, I already will."

"Well, that's how it's going to be."

I gripped her hips hard, venomously angry. "Baby...you have no idea what you're doing to me."

"It's only for a few days. And I also think you should sleep at your penthouse until then."

"No."

"I—"

"No," I repeated. "You don't want to have sex, then fine. But I'm sleeping beside you every night for the rest of my life. End of discussion." I stepped around her, pissed off that she had the audacity to ask me that.

But then the elevator beeped because someone was about to step into the penthouse.

"Someone coming over?" I asked.

"I didn't invite anyone. Maybe Thorn is just stopping by."

Last thing I wanted to deal with was company.

The doors opened, and Thorn stepped inside. He was dressed casually in jeans and a long-sleeved shirt. But he wasn't alone. Brett, Jax, Pine, and Mike stepped into the penthouse.

What the hell was going on? "What are you doing here?"

"Nice to see you too, asshole," Thorn barked. "Hurry up and change. We're going out."

"Why?" I'd never seen this group of people together under one roof.

"Why?" Brett asked incredulously. "You're getting married in a few days. You think we'd let you turn into a boring old man without a proper send-off?"

"A bachelor party?" I asked. "Guys, I'm way too old for that shit."

Tatum grabbed me by the arm and gave me a gentle squeeze. "Get changed and go."

"First, we're going to that bar downtown with the

topless ladies, and then we're going to the strip club," Pine said. "And then we're—"

"No naked ladies," I snapped. "I'm serious."

Mike rolled his eyes. "It's a bachelor party. Just accept it."

"I said no naked ladies," I repeated.

Tatum smiled at me. "Diesel, it's fine. I understand—"

"That's not why," I snapped. "I don't want to do that shit anymore. I'm over it. If you wanna go to a bar or a club, that's fine. But I'm not going to some damn strip club to watch naked women dance around when there's only one woman I want to see work a pole." I stormed off into the hallway toward the living room.

Titan's voice was still audible. "He's in a bad mood today."

"Why?" Thorn asked.

"I told him we couldn't have sex again until after the wedding."

Thorn cringed audibly. "No wonder he's so pissed off."

———

We had a private booth in the corner. We were on a rise so we could watch everyone on the dance floor. People were broken off into pairs, and groups of women shook their asses while all the men stared.

I downed glass after glass, my mind in two different places at once.

"What are you going to miss the most about being a bachelor?" Pine asked.

I turned my gaze to him, my fingers still wrapped around my cold glass. The ice cubes were starting to melt, and a frost permeated through the glass and directly into my palm. When I reflected on my single life, I couldn't come up with too many fond memories. "I guess our adventures on the yacht."

"Those were good times," Mike said. "When you party out at sea, you never have to worry about pissing off a neighbor. And the girls were always topless."

"What else?" Pine asked.

I'd been with models and actresses, some of them kinkier than others. I'd shared my bed with more than one woman at once, and sometimes more than two. I'd had women give me blow jobs before business meetings just to take the edge off. I'd had women do almost anything just to have the privilege to tell their friends they'd fucked Diesel Hunt. Did I miss that life of crowded loneliness? Not even slightly. "Nothing."

"You won't miss anything else?" Brett asked in surprise. "What about having your own place? What about going out and meeting a new woman for the first time?"

"What about waking up to someone whose name you don't remember?" Jax asked.

"Or threesomes?" Pine asked. "Come on, those were your favorite."

"No, I won't miss any of that." I looked at the people

having a good time on the dance floor again. "It was fun at the time, but I'm much happier now than I've ever been. Tatum is a woman who requires my full focus. I couldn't even handle another woman at the same time."

"She might be into that," Pine said. "You never know."

"Let's stop talking about what my fiancée might be into," I said coldly. I didn't share that information with anyone else. What we had was private.

"Geez, you're upright," Pine said. "I didn't think you'd ever be so pussy-whipped."

"I'm not pussy-whipped," I said. "I just found the right one. You will too, someday. You'll see what I mean."

Mike nudged Pine in the side and nodded to a pair of girls together on the dance floor. Both in sparkly dresses that barely covered their asses, they looked like easy targets. Landing two handsome, rich men would probably bump up their night. "Dibs on the right."

Pine nodded. "I prefer blondes anyway." He downed his drink then slid out of the booth with Mike.

Brett and Jax started talking, the loud music overhead blocking out their conversation on the other side of the table. Brett usually had a woman under his arm by now, but it would definitely happen by the end of the night. With his good looks and fortune, women were always taking shots at him.

"No sex until the wedding?" Thorn stared into his glass and shook his head. "Bullshit. You should leave her."

I chuckled because I knew he was kidding. "I'm not happy about it, but at least it's only for a few days. She tried to kick me out of the penthouse too, but I put my foot down that time."

"Good. So, how are things?"

"What do mean?"

"With both of you. Tatum seems really happy. What about you?"

I shifted my gaze to his. "You can't tell that I'm happy?"

"No, I know you are. But you hide it pretty well. She told me that she's submitted to you...pretty big accomplishment. I didn't think it was possible."

I wouldn't freely talk about my sex life with Tatum with anyone, but since she'd mentioned it to him first, I thought it was okay. "She likes it. At least with me, she does. It used to be about control with her because she didn't trust anyone. But she trusts me more than anyone else on the planet. We both know I rightfully earned it."

"Absolutely." He shook his glass before he took another drink. "Must be nice."

"It is nice." It was the greatest feeling in the world, to see a woman like Tatum drop her weapons and armor and yield to me—her king. I didn't realize how much I liked being in control until I fell for her. Now I wanted to possess her harder and deeper. Just thinking about it made me want to run home and fuck her. "Is that how you and Autumn operate?"

"Not really," he said. "With her, it's pretty...vanilla."

"Are you okay with that?"

He took another drink before he answered. "Surprisingly, yes. I haven't really felt the need to be dominant with her. I mean, I am the dominant one. But I've never tied her up or anything like that. She makes missionary feel like the best sex I've ever had."

"I'm glad you took the next step."

"Yeah, me too," he said with a smile. "We'll see where it goes. I'm already pretty obsessed with her, so I imagine it can only progress in one direction. But we'll see what happens."

"I knew I didn't want to be with anyone else the second I had Tatum."

"Yeah, I picked up on that," he said with a chuckle.

"You just know. And you can lie to yourself all you want, but the truth will get to you eventually. You're like a sponge, and the truth is water...it seeps in."

He finished his drink and set the empty glass on the table. "So you were serious when you said no strippers?"

"Absolutely."

"I guess I respect that. I'd rather see Autumn on a pole than some random woman anyway."

I hid my smile, knowing Thorn was far deeper in the relationship than he realized. "The whole reason why I'm getting married is because I don't want anyone else. And if I don't want anyone else, why would I want to see some chicks get naked? The tradition doesn't make much sense to me. I've committed my whole life to this woman. That devotion started the moment I asked her to marry me. It doesn't start when I say I do. It started the second she put on that ring."

He nodded in agreement. "You're a good guy, Diesel. I'm glad she's marrying you. She's an amazing woman, so she deserves to be with an amazing man. I know you guys will make it."

"Thanks, man."

"And I'm glad I didn't marry Tatum, because if I did, I wouldn't have Autumn right now...and that would suck."

I'd predicted this a long time ago. I knew it would happen, but I didn't say I told you so. I'd save it for later. "She's an incredible woman too."

"I know." He ran his fingers through his hair. "She's out of my league. Thankfully, she doesn't notice."

"You could easily be in her league. Seems like you're getting there."

"You're right. I'm getting more pussy-whipped by the day."

"It's not so bad," I said. "Just remember, she's getting dick-whipped too."

He chuckled. "Dick-whipped...good one."

———

It was three in the morning when I walked into the penthouse I shared with Tatum.

I was dead tired.

We went from bar to bar, drinking and partying. Thorn and I ended up spending the most time together because we both had women waiting at home for us. The rest of the guys had a lot more fun than we did.

At least they didn't drag me into a strip club. I didn't want the cheap perfume on my clothes, mixed with the smoke from cigars. I didn't want to be caught dead in a place like that, not when I was getting married on Saturday.

That'd make me look like an asshole—whether it was my bachelor party or not.

I walked into the bedroom and spotted Tatum sitting up in bed. She was on her tablet, the dull light illuminating her face. Her hair was pulled up into a bun, and her face was free of makeup. She would normally be asleep by now, but she was wide awake. "Everything alright, baby?" I dropped my jacket on the armchair and yanked my shirt over my head. I was so tired I didn't care about brushing my teeth or washing my face.

"Couldn't sleep." She pulled her gaze away from the screen. "Have fun?"

"Yeah."

"See any strippers?" she teased.

I kicked off my shoes and dropped my jeans. "Nope. But I thought about you stripping for most of the night."

"I can arrange that in real life, you know."

"Yeah?" I changed my boxers then walked to the bed. "Tatum Titan strips?"

"No. But Tatum Hunt does."

Hearing her use my last name sent shivers down my spine. "She does, huh?"

"Yeah. Maybe she'll show you on the honeymoon."

I sat at the edge of the bed, controlling my thoughts

so my dick wouldn't get too hard. Once it turned into a rod, I'd have a difficult time controlling it. Then I'd be all over Tatum no matter how many times she told me no. "I hope she does."

She scooted to the edge where I sat and began to massage my back. She started at my shoulders then slowly migrated down.

I'd ordinarily push her hands away, but her touch felt so good. She knew how to apply the right pressure against my muscles, digging hard to flatten the knots in my back. She moved down and rubbed my lower back, making the tightness slacken.

"How does that feel?" she whispered.

"Really good."

She kissed my neck as she touched me, her tongue moving along my warm skin.

I closed my eyes and enjoyed her ministrations, my dick thickening on its own. Her hands were the sexiest part, the way she dug into me so aggressively. She touched a man exactly the way a man wanted to be touched. "Baby, I suggest you stop. Otherwise, you're gonna get fucked tonight."

Her hands stopped at my shoulders, her fingers still deep into my muscles. She sighed and pulled her touch away.

I opened my eyes and massaged my temple. "I know why you're still awake."

"Really?" She lay back in bed. "Why?"

"Because you need sex before bed." I set my alarm

clock then lay beside her. "You've been lying there hot and bothered all night." I rested my hand on my chest and stared at the ceiling.

"Or maybe I just wanted to make sure you got home safely." She scooted to my side of the bed and cuddled into me. Her face rested against my shoulder. "You worry about me all the time, but I worry about you just as much."

"I don't need you to worry about me."

"Yes, you do." She kissed my shoulder and closed her eyes. "I can't wait to be Mrs. Hunt..."

I closed my eyes when she said the name, feeling my muscles tense. "Me too."

"Only a few more days to go."

"And I can't wait to start a family with you."

I tensed again, feeling my heart race with excitement. There was nothing I wanted more than to make love to her all night and make a baby with her. I was honored that I was the only man that got to do that. But the thoughts made my dick harden in my shorts, and I knew it would distract me so I wouldn't be able to sleep.

Maybe I should have slept at my own place, after all.

CHAPTER NINE

THORN

I texted Titan. *You want to get dinner tonight?*

Just you and me?

Preferably. I wanted to talk to her about Diesel. We were leaving for Thailand in two days.

Sure. In an hour?

Yeah.

When I left the office, I met her at a sports bar that had awesome beer and great appetizers. Titan didn't eat much, so it never made sense to go to a restaurant. She just took a few pieces of the fries and focused on her salad. Now that she was getting married in a few days, she ate even less than usual.

"How are things?" I asked.

"Good." Her eyes moved to the TV in the corner, but she didn't follow sports very closely so she obviously didn't care what was on. "I'm regretting this no-sex pact I made with Diesel...and it's only been a few days."

"Well, it was a stupid idea. What the hell were you thinking?"

"That it would be uncomfortable but not unbearable..." She picked at another fry. "When he gets out of the shower, he purposely parades around the place with a towel around his waist. I feel like he's torturing me on purpose."

"I guarantee you that he is." If Autumn took sex off the table, I'd just seduce her too.

"How are things with your *girlfriend?*" She accompanied her tease with a smile.

"Great," I countered. "We're having lots of amazing *sex*."

Her eyes immediately narrowed at my jab.

"Unlike you."

"Don't remind me..."

"She's my date for the wedding."

"I told you monogamy isn't so difficult when you find the right person."

"It's been a week," I reminded her. "Let's not jump ahead."

"It's been more than a month," she countered.

"I just asked her to be serious with me last week. So, no, you're wrong."

"But you didn't sleep with anyone in that time period. Therefore, you were monogamous. Don't try to get out of this, Thorn. You're sprung over this woman, and let's not sugarcoat it."

I took a long drink of my beer because I didn't know how to deflect her statement.

Titan wore a smug grin.

I set my glass down and wiped my mouth with the back of my forearm. "Whatever...at least I'm getting laid tonight."

She grabbed a fry and threw it right at my face.

When it bounced on the table, I grabbed it and popped it into my mouth.

"You're a billionaire, Thorn. You don't need to eat food off the table."

"You think the kitchen is any cleaner back there?" I asked incredulously. "Unlikely."

"Diesel told me he had a good time at his bachelor party."

"He did? He was a bitch the whole time. Anytime a woman hit on him, he stormed off and made a scene about it."

She chuckled. "He's used to the media turning the story around on him, so that's probably why he's acting like that. He has to make a performance, that way no one can spin it against him."

"I guess that's true." A photographer once got a picture of Diesel kissing some woman in a club. He denied the allegation from the very beginning. I didn't believe him at the time, but now I did.

"What did you do when women hit on you?"

"No one did."

She cocked an eyebrow in disbelief.

"I got out of the way before they had a chance," I explained. "If I saw them making eyes at me, I ignored them. And if they came over to talk to me, I went to the bathroom. The guys think I have bladder issues now."

She smiled. "That's sweet."

"I think it's cowardly, but alright."

"I can't believe you were ever worried about being faithful. You're doing a great job."

"Again, it's been a week."

"A month," she corrected. "A month is a long time to sleep with the same person. I was in love with Diesel within two weeks."

"Let's not get ahead of ourselves here and toss the L word around."

"Whatever you say..." She drank her Old Fashioned and glanced at the TV again.

"Need any help for the big day?"

"Nope. Everything is taken care of."

"Kinda strange to think you aren't going to be Titan anymore. Our relationship will be different now. It used to be just you and me...now it's you and Diesel." I didn't consider myself to be an emotional guy, but losing Titan was difficult for me. She was my family. I cared about her like she was my own flesh and blood.

"That's not true," she said. "It'll be you, me, and Diesel—all three of us."

"You know what I mean, Titan." I looked down at my beer.

"Things will change, yes. But they already have. In the end, I know you and I will always be close. When you and Autumn get married—"

"Whoa, what the fuck?" I snapped. "I'm not getting married. I never even put that on the table."

"Whatever," she said. "When you get married some-day...you'll have someone, and I'll have Diesel. So we won't be as close anymore, but I know we'll still be family. I know we'll still have our own relationship...just like we do now."

"Yeah...you're probably right. How are you handling getting married?"

"I don't understand your question." She pulled the toothpick out of the glass and bit off the cherry.

"You're getting married. Your life is completely changing. It's not where you thought you would be a year ago. It's a drastic shift. Between you and me, how do you feel? It's normal to get cold feet. People don't feel doubtful about the person they want to marry. But they feel doubtful about how different their lives will be."

She stirred her glass as she considered the question. "I haven't thought about it in that way. Honestly, all I can think about is the man I get to keep for the rest of my life. There will be bumps in the road because we both like having things a particular way. But I know we'll work through them."

"Did you do the prenup?"

"No." She took another drink.

"No?" I was surprised Titan would even consider eliminating it.

"Diesel and I made our own legal document. We're committed to making the marriage work at any cost. I thought it was so romantic that I couldn't say no."

"What kind of legal document?"

"It's not really legal. It can't hold up in court. It's just our promises that we made to each other. If we ever feel the urge to be unfaithful, we'll talk about it and see what we can do to prevent it. If I can't be prevented, we'll seek counseling. If that doesn't work, we can discuss an open relationship. Whatever needs to happen, we'll make it happen. But divorce is a word we won't include in our vocabulary."

"That is pretty romantic."

"I know Diesel would never hurt me, and he loves me so much. I can't see that ever changing. And I would never hurt him. I don't think it will be an issue for us."

"Me neither."

"And he wants us to combine our strengths as well as our businesses. We have the capability to take over the world. Now he wants to execute it."

"Pretty awesome." They would be the biggest power couple in the world. "And you're going to start trying for a family right away?"

She nodded. "I'm getting old, Thorn…"

"You are not."

"I'm thirty. I'm running out of time."

I rolled my eyes.

"I want to have at least two kids, and I don't want to be pregnant the whole time. I want to have a break in between. So I have to do this now. Diesel wants a family too, so it's fine."

"He seems pretty eager to get started, actually."

She chuckled. "I know he is. He reminds me every day."

"Well, I'm here to talk if you need someone to listen. And I'll always be here to listen."

Her eyes softened, and she reached across the table to rest her hand on mine. She gave me a gentle squeeze before she pulled away. "My life is changing so much...but some things will always remain the same."

"Yeah. You're right."

The subject changed to work, and we talked about the things I'd be taking care of while she was gone for two weeks. It was a long honeymoon, but since Titan had worked aggressively for the last ten years, she deserved a long break. No better place to do that other than paradise.

Her phone started to ring, and Diesel's name appeared on the screen. "I've got to take this. He's probably pissed I didn't tell him I was meeting you..." She slipped out of the booth and stepped outside to take his call.

I enjoyed the rest of my beer then scrolled through my phone. I'd taken a few pictures of Autumn last night. She was asleep, but she looked so beautiful when she was cuddled into my side. We didn't even need a king-size bed because she pretty much slept on top of me. She was all over me—all the time.

I grinned as I scrolled through the pictures.

"Hey, I know you from somewhere."

I looked up from my phone, noticing the blonde bombshell looking down at me with a smile plastered on her face. Her hair was wavy like she was had just come from the beach. Her sweater fell over one shoulder, and she wore skinny jeans with brown booties. If this were any other time, I'd make a move. "You probably see me in the news a lot."

"Yeah, you're Thorn Cutler, right?"

"Yep." I didn't ask who she was. That sounded like an invitation for the conversation to continue.

"Was that Tatum Titan you were with a second ago?"

"Yeah. She had a phone call, so she stepped outside."

She tucked her hair behind her ear. "I think it's really cool that you guys are still friends. Not too many people could do that."

It would take years before people started to forget I was ever engaged to Titan. "Our friendship is pretty solid."

"Since you're sitting here alone, you want to get a beer? My treat."

A beautiful woman was offering to buy me a beer. Ordinarily, I wouldn't turn down an awesome offer like that. I'd wondered how I would behave in a situation like this. Would I be a sleazebag and immediately jump back to my old ways once the opportunity presented itself? I could get ass whenever I wanted, so I didn't need Autumn for that. But I wanted something else from Autumn—something that meant a lot more. "Thanks for the offer but...I have a girlfriend." I couldn't stop the smile from forming on my lips. I said the words out loud, and surprisingly, it felt good.

"Oh...I didn't realize." She smiled then turned away. "Nice meeting you."

"Nice meeting you too." When I looked up, Titan was standing at the next table, her arms crossed and a big grin on her face.

I rolled my eyes. "Shut up while you're ahead."

She moved back into the seat across from me, still showing the victory in her eyes. "Fine, I'll shut up. But that's only because you know exactly what I'm going to say."

———

I sat in the back seat as my driver took me to my penthouse. I called Autumn and placed the phone against my ear.

She answered almost immediately. "Hey, babe."

I grinned like a fool when I heard her say that. "Hey, baby. What are you doing?"

"Just got home, and now I have dinner on the stove."

"Dinner, huh?"

"Are you fishing for an invitation?"

"No. If I wanted to come over, I would just do it."

Her smile was audible over the phone. "You're coming over, huh?"

"How can I listen to that sexy voice and not?"

"It's easy. Just go to your penthouse."

That wasn't easy at all. I pictured her dark hair trailing down the center of her back as she stood in the kitchen. She was wearing one of my shirts, the length reaching her knees. "That's impossible when I picture how sexy you must look right now."

"Actually, I don't look very sexy. I just left the gym, and I'm in my workout clothes."

"With those tight leggings and sporty top?" I blurted.

"Yes."

"Fuck…"

She laughed into the phone. "Get real, Thorn."

"I am. I'll be there in five minutes. You can take off your pants now or wait until I get there."

"I know you like to do the honors."

My girlfriend was awesome. "I'll be there soon."

"Thorn?" Her voice suddenly turned serious, a direct contrast to our playfulness.

"Yes?"

"Titan told me about last night."

I was drawing a blank. "What happened last night?" I saw Titan for forty-five minutes over drinks. Nothing interesting happened.

"You told that sexy blonde you had a girlfriend…and you had a stupid grin on your face."

Oh, that. "Titan is a lying psychopath. Don't listen to her."

"That's too bad. I was going to give you the best sex of your life."

My cock immediately thickened in my slacks. I pictured Autumn bent over the kitchen counter, her leggings bunched at her knees. I pulled on her hair as I pounded into her from behind, crushing that pussy—the pussy I owned. "Okay...maybe she wasn't lying."

"That's what I thought."

———

Her hair stuck to her neck in the shower, and now that all her makeup had been washed away, her small freckles were more noticeable. She faced me under the water and ran her hands down my chest, feeling my hard body with the same enthusiasm she showed earlier when I fucked her in the kitchen.

The dinner she made never got eaten.

"So, what did you think?" She tilted her head back and rinsed her hair.

My eyes immediately went to her perky-as-fuck tits. "You rode me pretty damn good."

"Best you ever had?"

"No."

Her eyes moved back up to mine.

"You're always the best I've ever had." It sounded like a line, but I didn't mean for it to come out that way.

She smiled up at me, her plump lips looking irre-sistible. "Whether you mean that or not, I don't care. I just loved hearing you say it."

We got out of the shower and dried off before we returned to the kitchen. The vegan bowl she made was cold and the veggies were soft, but we served the plates and ate it anyway. I sat across from her at the table, sitting in my boxers because I didn't want to put my suit back on.

She was in a long t-shirt, her damp hair pulled over one shoulder.

"This is good."

"It tastes like shit, and we both know it," she said with a chuckle. "But it's edible."

I chuckled at her bluntness. "I'm sure it's great when it's fresh."

She took a few more bites before she drank from her water.

I stared at her as she stared down at her food. I loved watching her. It was like looking at the photos I had of her in my phone. "You want to have dinner then stay at my place tomorrow? We're carpooling in Titan's jet. Or, I mean, we're plane-pooling."

"I can't. I'm having dinner with my parents. But I'll meet you guys at her apartment."

"Why are you having dinner with your parents?"

She cocked an eyebrow. "What kind of question is that? Because they're my parents."

"That's not what I meant. I was wondering if it was a special occasion or something...like your mom's birthday."

She pushed her food around with her fork. "Well, it's actually *my* birthday."

Oh, shit. Did she tell me that, and I just forgot? I felt like the biggest asshole on the planet. I was certain she didn't mention it because I would have remembered. We'd only been seeing each other for a month, so it's like I was a complete asshole.

"My mom usually cooks dinner, and we have a small get-together. It's quiet, but I like it."

"That's nice," I said in a low voice. "I feel really stupid right now. I didn't know..."

"It's okay, Thorn. I never mentioned it, so how were you supposed to know?"

I still felt like a jerk.

"So I'll meet you guys in the morning."

"You can't come over after dinner with your parents?" I asked hopefully.

"I should go home and pack. But we'll be staying in the same room in Thailand, so we'll be together then."

She didn't invite me to her parents' place for dinner, and it made me wonder if they knew about me at all. Did she want me to come but thought it was too soon? Or did she not want me to come? How did I figure that out without asking? Maybe I shouldn't ask at all. "Baby?"

"Yeah?" She looked down at her food and took another bite.

"I'd like to come over for dinner with your parents...if you want me there."

She looked up again slowly, subtle surprise on her face. "You want to meet my parents?"

"Well, yeah. I want to celebrate your birthday with you." Whether she was with friends or family, I wanted to be there. I'd never met a woman's parents before, but Autumn had already met mine. I'd ask Titan for some advice before I went over there.

"I'd love that," she said. "I just didn't think you'd be ready for something like that."

"To celebrate your birthday?" I asked incredulously.

"You know what I mean, Thorn."

"I prefer it when you call me babe."

A smile melted across her lips. "You know what I mean, *babe*."

"I want to be there."

"You're sure?" she asked.

"Yes." I held her gaze with my own steady one. "You're going to have to coach me through it, though, because I've never met a girlfriend's parents."

"Because you've never had a girlfriend."

"Well...yeah."

"My parents are really nice. They'll love you."

"Did you tell them about me?"

She nodded. "I did."

I tried not to smile. "So...you said I was your boyfriend?"

"Well, I certainly didn't tell them you're some guy I'm fucking."

I chuckled. "Good call."

"At first, they were weird about the Titan thing. They didn't want me to be a rebound. But I explained to them what that situation really was. They didn't understand in the beginning, but I told them it wasn't really that strange. Royalty has marriages for convenience rather than love. Anyone who's someone seriously considers a business relationship for a marriage. When I put it into perspective, they understood."

"And they know that's not what we are, right?"

"Yes."

"Good." I wasn't with Autumn for any other reason than the fact that I adored her. "Should I bring anything?"

"No. My mom lives for this sort of thing."

"Reminds me of mine."

"I have a feeling they would get along well." She turned back to her food and kept eating.

The notion of our parents meeting would suggest we were getting married, but the idea didn't freak me out. It didn't make me feel anything. "So, is your dad the threatening type? Is he going to grill me?"

"I'm a twenty-seven-year-old woman," she said with a chuckle. "My dad doesn't need to grill the men I see."

"Did they meet your ex?"

"Max?" she asked. "Yeah, they liked him. They don't like him anymore, but they did at the time."

Maybe they wouldn't like me because they thought I

would do the same to her, which I wouldn't. Autumn could put on whatever spin she wanted, but I still thought the guy was an idiot. His wife couldn't hold a candle to Autumn—no way. "They're probably going to grill me pretty hard, then. But I'm prepared. I'll sweep them off their feet." I was good-looking, a billionaire, and I came from a great family. The thing they would care most about was the way I treated their daughter.

And I would treat her like a queen.

———

"Help me." I walked into Titan's office without knocking. She was holding up a pair of white heels so she didn't see me coming through the glass doors.

"What do you think of these?"

I shrugged. "They're nice. Why?"

"They're my wedding shoes. I just got them in." They were an off-white color, and real diamonds were constructed into the shoe. They were perfect for a woman as classy as Titan.

"To be honest, Diesel isn't going to give a damn about your shoes. Even when your legs are thrown over his shoulders and your shoes are right next to his face, he's still not going to give a damn. Just my thought..."

She smiled then set the shoes into the box. "You're right."

"He's gonna want some lingerie. Tell me you got some of that."

"Actually, I did." She nodded to the boxes stacked on the table against the wall.

"Then he'll be a very happy man. Good call."

She set the shoes on the table along with everything else. "What did you need help with? I need some help too."

"With what?" I asked. "Do you need something for the wedding?"

"No. I'm just having a hard time keeping my hands off Diesel. I'm not sure if I can make it another day."

I sat in the armchair facing her desk. "God gave you fingers for a reason, Titan."

"You know I can't do that. It's not the same anyway."

"Then I don't know what to tell you. This idiotic suggestion was your idea."

"True. I guess I'm the only one to blame." She sat down then closed her laptop. "So, what were you saying?"

"Today is Autumn's birthday."

"Oh, it is?" she asked. "I'll wish her a happy birthday."

"I'm going over to her parents' place for dinner tonight to celebrate."

She did a double take. "Thorn Cutler is meeting his girlfriend's parents? I can't believe it."

"Me neither." I knew how to dazzle anyone in a meeting, so I could do the same for these people. Gaining people's confidence was my specialty, and I'd use a lifetime of learning to do the same with Autumn's mom and dad.

"You want advice on how to make a good impression?"

"No. I know I can make a good impression. I'm a good-looking billionaire. I'm practically Prince Charming."

"Uh, Thorn." She shook her head slightly. "Autumn is worth over a hundred million."

"So?"

"You being a billionaire isn't going to mean anything to them. That's not what a parent cares about when it comes to their daughter."

"Then, what do they care about?"

"That you make her happy. That you treat her well. Prove that to them, and you're in."

I thought I made her happy. I did my best to treat her well. Would that be good enough? "I'm not sure how to do that, Titan."

"Well, you're going over there to celebrate her birthday with her parents. That's a pretty good sign. You could just skip it, but you aren't. That will mean something to them, especially if she tells them you asked to come."

"Looks like I'm off to a good start."

"I think you just need to be yourself." She propped her chin on her knuckles, her left hand resting on the desk. The diamond ring sat on her finger, the humble size perfectly matching her personality. "I know you really care about Autumn, more than you even realize. If I can see it, I'm sure they can too."

"I do care about her... I want them to like me."

"Then you're golden, Thorn. Just don't brag about

yourself. I'm sure they know exactly who you are, so you don't need to mention your money or accomplishments."

"Alright. Noted."

"Is that all you needed help with?"

"Actually, no." I'd given this a lot of thought and hadn't come up with a solution. "I don't know what to get her as a gift. There's a diamond bracelet at Tiffany's that's really nice, but I never see her wear jewelry. She either doesn't wear it because she doesn't like it, or maybe she can't afford something she really wants..."

Titan shook her head. "Don't get her diamonds. It's impersonal and empty."

"Uh, I don't think most women would say that."

"The only time you should buy diamonds for a woman is if it's an engagement ring. For this first birthday together, you should do something a lot more meaningful. I know you've only been seeing her for a month, but it needs to have some thought in it."

"Okay..." I tried to think of something, but I was drawing a blank.

"I can't help you with this, Thorn. This needs to come from you."

I rubbed my temple and sighed.

"You'll come up with something. You're one of the smartest men I know."

"Just last week you called me an idiot."

"And you are an idiot," she countered. "Sometimes."

————

Autumn didn't have a car, so I drove my Bugatti to the house in Connecticut. I wasn't trying to show off. The only cars I had were luxury vehicles that cost millions of dollars. If I had my driver take us, I thought that might look worse.

We pulled up to the house, a two-story white house with blue shutters. It had a nice yard with a large oak tree right out front. Trees were everywhere on the property, sprinkled with snow from the blizzard that came through last week.

I tucked her gift under my arm and then walked to the front door.

"Is that for me?" She was in black jeans and a beige sweater. An olive green scarf was wrapped around her throat, and she wore a thick black jacket on top. She'd had gloves on when she got into the car, but she'd stuffed them into her pockets.

"Yeah."

"You didn't have to get me anything."

"It's your birthday, baby. I wanted to get you something."

"Well, that was very sweet."

I took her hand and walked up to the front door. "They have a very nice place."

"Yeah, they love it. It's always quiet. Whether it's summer or winter, it's beautiful here. When my mom saw it, she said it was her dream house."

"It was really nice of you to buy it for them." She'd never said that, but I picked up on the subtle hints.

"They're my parents...they did a lot for me." She rang the doorbell.

I was close with my family, so I found it attractive that she was close with hers. Not everyone was generous when they had money. Oftentimes, people just became greedier. Autumn wasn't that way at all.

The door opened and revealed a woman in Autumn's likeness. With jet-black hair, green eyes, and a short stature, she looked like Autumn's sister. Her eyes fell on her daughter, and she beamed with obvious pride. "My baby is home." She pulled Autumn in for a tight hug. "Twenty-eight...I can't believe it." Her mother was thicker than her daughter, having a bigger waist and thighs, but she'd still aged very well.

"I know," Autumn said as she hugged her mother back. "Time goes by so fast."

Her mother turned to me next, and she gave me the same look of joy that she just showed to her own daughter. "You must be Thorn. We're so excited to have you over. Please come in."

"Thanks. Pleasure to meet you."

She shook my hand. "I've seen you on TV a lot. You look just as handsome in person."

"Oh...thank you." This was getting off to a good start.

Her father came into the entryway, a man with black hair that was quickly fading to gray. He wore a collared shirt and dark jeans. He was slender, like he spent most of his time on his feet. "Glad to have you join us." He shook my hand.

"I'm happy to be here, sir." I'd never called anyone sir before. People were always calling me that instead.

"I'm Walter," he said. "This is my wife, Emily."

I nodded. "Pleasure to meet you both."

"Let's sit down and eat," Emily said. "I made Autumn's favorite."

"Lasagna?" Autumn asked.

"Yes, sweet pea," her mother said.

Seeing their closeness touched my heart in a way I could never explain.

We sat at the dining table, and I left the present toward the opposite end. Her mother served the food. We started eating, and then Autumn exchanged a few words with her parents, asking about their lives while she hadn't seen them in weeks. She told them about the conference in Chicago and her working relationship with Titan.

I scarfed down the food because it was delicious. "This is amazing, Emily."

"I'm glad you like it, Thorn," Emily said. "Cooking has always been my favorite pastime. There's a cooking school just in town, so I'm there a lot with a few friends. Do you cook often, Thorn?"

"Not really," I said honestly. "I made Autumn dinner once, but I served the only dish I know how to make."

Autumn smiled at me.

Emily smiled wider. "That's sweet."

"You guys have a lovely home," I said. "Reminds me of *Home Alone*."

"Thank you," Walter said with a smile. "When Emily saw it, she knew she had to have it. And Autumn was generous enough to make that happen."

Autumn shifted her gaze to her food, her cheeks reddening.

"You guys have a wonderful daughter," I said. "The first time I met her was in her office. I was trying to make a deal with her, but she didn't bow down. She met my confidence with her elegance. I've never been so impressed in my life."

The pride shone in Emily's eyes. "I'm not sure how we got so lucky to have a daughter like her. When she was young, we knew she was special. Ahead of her peers and ambitious, she passed all of her courses with flying colors. And to top it off, she's extremely compassionate and generous."

"She must get it from you two." I wasn't trying to kiss their asses. It was just the most logical explanation. The apple didn't fall far from the tree. I inherited a lot of traits from both of my parents. I learned my professional tactics from my father and my affectionate manner from my mother.

"I'd like to think she does," Walter said.

The conversation shifted, and they asked me about my company and my involvement in Autumn's business relationship with Titan.

"Titan and I have been good friends for over ten years now. Once she was shot, I took over her holdings to help her out. Her fiancé has an empire even bigger than hers, and he had to manage that while taking care of her. My family company isn't as extensive as the other stuff Titan does. It's been in my family for over a hundred years now, so it's pretty self-sufficient."

Her parents asked me a few more questions about work before the conversation died away. They didn't interrogate me like I thought they would. They seemed accepting of me right from the beginning.

"Should we do gifts before cake?" Emily asked.

"Mom, you guys don't have to get me anything," Autumn said. "I'm almost thirty."

"No matter how old you are, you'll always be our little girl." Walter grabbed the gift and set it in front of her. It was a small gift, rectangular in shape.

Autumn ripped off the paper and then revealed a bracelet inside. It was silver with three different charms. Each one had a different letter. D, A, and M. It took me a second to figure out what it meant. The A in the middle was the initial for Autumn's name. And the two charms on the outside represented Mom and Dad.

Thank god, I didn't buy her diamonds. I would have looked like a total ass.

"Aww..." Autumn stared at it with a smile, the affection in her eyes. "That's so sweet." She clasped it around her wrist and examined it. "I love it."

"Now we'll always be with you wherever you go," Emily said as she patted her daughter on the arm.

The touching scene caused me to fall for Autumn even harder. Something about her relationship with her parents made me feel warm inside. Autumn was a strong woman who didn't back down in a fight. She could hold her own in any hostile situation. But when she was with her family, she was sweet and vulnerable like everyone else. She wore her heart on her sleeve and filled the room with affectionate warmth.

"Thanks, Mom and Dad." Autumn examined the bracelet again before she pulled her arm away.

"It's nice," I whispered. "Very thoughtful."

"Yeah..." Autumn cleared her throat and controlled her expression.

I grabbed my gift and handed it to her. "It can't be returned, so I hope you like it."

"I know I'll love it, Thorn." She ripped open the box then pulled out the scarf sitting inside. It was maroon in color with a small pattern woven into the fabric. Made of a luxurious cashmere, it was soft to the touch. She examined the pattern and finally deduced what it was.

I had it designed with formulas I noticed in her lab, equipment she used on a daily basis, and her name written in the stars. Science was her life and her passion, so I wanted to make something that was meaningful to her. She didn't care about money, only the legacy she would leave behind. She'd already contributed so much to the industry, and I wanted her to know she wouldn't be forgotten. Her name would always be written in the stars —and in my heart.

When I left Titan's office, I'd spent the next hour trying to think of something I could give Autumn. She wore scarves often, so I knew she loved them. But a simple scarf wouldn't have been enough. She may never wear this, but at least she would know I paid attention to every little thing she did.

"Thorn..." She ran her fingers over the material then looked at me. "This is so sweet..."

"Your legacy is in the making, baby."

She was touched by the gift her parents had given her, but she was even more touched by this. Her eyes softened, and if I looked closely enough, I could see the slight film of moisture coat the surface of her eyes. "I love it."

"Good," I said. "I'm glad."

Her parents examined the scarf next, both of them interested in the markings I'd had personally detailed into the fabric.

"I got such great gifts this year," Autumn whispered. "Thank you."

Titan gave me the best advice, and now I was so grateful I'd asked for it. Autumn didn't care about expensive things. She had money, but she obviously didn't care about buying an expensive car or jewelry. She was down-to-earth and humble.

Diamonds would have been idiotic.

I was so glad I thought of this. I could tell she really loved it.

And the smile she wore meant more to me than everything I owned.

———

Her father and I stayed in the dining room while the ladies went into the kitchen to clean up. We talked about sports, the coldness this winter season, and his reaction when Autumn told him she wanted to drop out of MIT.

I'd imagined meeting a woman's parents would be a lot more difficult than this, but it was the easiest thing in the world. Her father was nice, funny, and easy to talk to. Not once did I feel like he was watching my every move in the hopes I would mess up.

"Excuse me, I need to use the restroom." I left the dining room and went down one hallway, but it took me back toward the kitchen. I made a left to head toward the front of the house.

"So..." Emily's voice caught my attention. "Thorn seems pretty amazing."

"He is," Autumn said. "He's...perfect."

I halted in my tracks when I heard the smile in her voice.

"Sweet pea, your cheeks are red," Emily teased.

"I know," Autumn said quickly. "I hate that."

"And he's so smitten with you."

"You think?" Autumn asked hopefully.

"Yes, it's written all over his face," Emily said. "That man is in love."

"I don't know about that," Autumn said. "But he is a sweetheart."

Emily stacked some dishes in the dishwasher then closed it. "So, is this serious?"

I leaned against the wall in the hallway, feeling slightly

guilty for listening in on their conversation. But I couldn't help myself. I knew Autumn wouldn't lie to her mother. Whatever she said would be the truth.

"I...I don't know," Autumn said quietly.

"I can tell how you feel about him," Emily said. "It's written all over your face right now."

"Mom," Autumn warned.

"Come on, sweet pea," Emily said. "I know you. I haven't seen your eyes light up like that...ever. Not even with Max."

The mention of her ex immediately made me jealous, but when I heard the context, I realized there was nothing to be jealous about.

Autumn was quiet for a long time. "Momma...I'm in love with him."

My heart immediately expanded in my chest, a warm sensation circulating in my blood. My knees felt weak, and my chest ached because I stopped breathing. Her confession made me feel a million things at once. But one thing I noticed was I didn't feel repulsion. If another woman said that, I'd already be walking out the front door. But Autumn's confession didn't scare me at all. What scared me the most was that I wasn't scared.

I wasn't scared at all.

———

I took her home then walked her to the front door. Her gifts were tucked under her arm, and she'd been quiet since we left the house. I didn't give her any indication that I'd overheard her conversation with her mother, but she was extremely timid.

"Thank you for coming tonight," she whispered. "And for the gift. I love it."

"I had a good time. I liked your parents."

"They're great." She fished her keys out of her purse.

I didn't want to go home and sleep alone, even if our plane was leaving early. If I slept over, I'd have to get up even earlier just to pack my things. But right now, I didn't care about that. I could sleep on the plane. "I want to stay over tonight."

"You do?" she asked. "Even though you'll have to get up early?"

"Couldn't care less."

She got the door open and stepped inside. She set her things on the entryway table then shut the door behind me.

I wanted her in a way I never had before. My hands ached to touch her body, my mouth yearned for the kiss of her plump lips. We hadn't even turned on the lights to the townhouse, and my hand snaked into her hair. I kissed her in the entryway, my fingers grasping the soft strands like they were reins.

Her hand moved to my forearm, and she kissed me with the same heat. Her mouth was just as eager for mine. Her tongue entered my mouth, her warm breath filling my frozen lungs.

My arm hooked around her waist, and I brought her

closer into me, kissing her harder than I ever had before. I'd fucked her in the sexiest ways, had filled her with so much of my seed it dribbled onto the sheets, but now it was different. I didn't want to fuck her at all. My hands wanted to make love to her body. My kiss wanted to make her feel like a queen. My heart wanted to make hers feel safe.

We made our way down the hallway and into her bedroom. Clothes were falling off and scattering across the floor like breadcrumbs leading to the bed. When she wore nothing but her skin, I carried her to the bed then laid her down. I hooked her leg over my shoulder then widened her other thigh toward her waist.

I sucked her bottom lip then gave it a gentle tug before the crown of my cock pushed inside her.

She moaned into my mouth like she'd never taken my dick before.

I pushed through her wetness and slid completely inside, feeling her channel tight around me like fingers wrapped around a cock. My eyes were locked on her expression, watching her reaction to me. Now that I knew how she felt about me, I could see the clues everywhere. Her love was a bright beacon in her eyes.

How had I gotten this incredible woman to fall in love with me?

I was difficult, immature, stubborn, and idiotic.

And she was every man's fantasy.

I thrust into her gently, in the mood for slow sex instead of an aggressive fuck. I wanted to savor the way she stared at into my eyes, the way she ran her hands up my powerful chest. I wanted to feel the connection between our souls, feel the way her pussy tightened around me as she slowly approached an orgasm.

"Babe, I'm gonna come."

I loved it when she called me babe. It made me feel like her possession, like I belonged only to her. I'd never wanted to belong to someone before. My eyes were hypnotized by her beauty, by the way her eyes lit up in pleasure. Her beautiful hair was spread around her on the sheets, and her firm tits shook with my thrusts. "You're the most beautiful thing I've ever seen."

Her hands gripped my hips and pulled me harder into her as she tightened around me. She came with a satisfying moan, her mouth gaping open and her eyes locked on mine. "Yes..." Her hand wrapped around the back of my neck, and she dug her fingers into my hair.

Damn, she looked perfect right now.

Coming all over my dick.

Looking at me like I was the only man in the world.

So in love with me.

I liked that she was in love with me.

I deepened the angle and ground into her body, hitting her clit a little hard. My dick was balls deep, and I was surprised she could handle all of me. I was practically hitting her cervix. I wanted to come inside her not just because it felt incredible. I wanted to give her all of me, make her mine in the sexiest way possible.

I came with a moan, feeling the heat flush through my

body as it mixed with the adrenaline. I pumped my load deep inside her, feeling like a king filling my queen. There was no better feeling than coming deep inside this woman.

She grabbed my hip and pulled me deeper into her, wanting every single drop. "Thorn..."

I'd just finished an explosive orgasm, but now I wanted to fuck her all over again. Just a simple touch, a single word from her mouth could get me going again. I bent her knee to her chest and dug my hand into her hair before I kissed her again. My dick slowly softened inside her, but I knew it wouldn't be long until I was hard and ready again.

This woman always had me ready.

CHAPTER TEN

VINCENT

I stared at Scarlet across the restaurant table. We'd emptied a bottle of wine, and our plates were wiped clean of our meals. Now we were finishing our final glasses, the white wine perfectly complementing the meal we'd just devoured.

In a black dress with curled hair, she looked like a bombshell. Her hair was pinned to one side, exposing her petite shoulder in the one-strap dress. She always looked magnificent, but tonight, she looked absolutely stunning.

I couldn't stop picturing her on her knees.

She gave incredible head. The memory came to me in my dreams. It came to me when I was in the middle of a meeting with millions of dollars on the table. My mind became clouded by sex. I wanted to conquer her in my bed, press her so deeply into the mattress that she sank toward the floor. I wanted her to pull me deeper into her and whisper my name.

When my imagination ran wild and my hard dick pressed against my jeans, I forced the thoughts away. "I love what you did with your hair." It was the first thing that came to mind. It was pushed back and elegant. It wouldn't be easy to fist later, but I liked the way it looked.

"Thanks. So, your flight leaves tomorrow?"

"Yeah. I'm taking my own jet. Thorn and Autumn and a few other people are taking Titan's plane. But since they're staying for their honeymoon, everyone will come back on mine."

"Sounds like a good plan. When will you be back?"

"Four days."

She nodded. "You must be excited."

I was excited. My son had found the perfect woman to share his life with. I'd never have to worry about him. He had a good woman who would set him straight when he needed it, and she would be there for him when things got tough. I wouldn't be on this earth in fifty years, and I needed to know my sons would be okay. "Yes, I am."

"I'm happy for you. There's no greater feeling than seeing your child happy."

"You're right." One of the things I loved most about Scarlet was how much she understood what it was really like to be a parent. It was the hardest job in the world but the most rewarding. She loved her daughter more than anything in the world, and it was obvious in the way she talked about her. The other women I'd dated were too young to have children, so they never understood.

"I hope my daughter winds up with the perfect man. I'd die happy."

"I've got two more I have to worry about..." Brett was approaching forty, and Jax was still in his party phase. Diesel had been that way, too, until he encountered Titan. I didn't know if Jax would be so lucky to find someone the way Diesel did.

"They'll find someone. It'll happen when it's meant to happen."

We finished the rest of our wine, taking our time. Our comfortable silence was just as soothing as the alcohol. She was the perfect pairing to my drink, the strawberry to my dessert wine. "You'll be alright while I'm gone?"

She laughed into her glass.

I kept my straight face.

"Oh...you aren't joking." She took a sip before she set down her glass. "Vincent, you know I don't need you to look out for me. I've never needed a man for anything. That's why you're sitting across the table from me right this moment."

"Not true. I want to take care of you."

Her eyes softened.

She was an independent woman who didn't need me for anything, but that was why I wanted to give her the world. I wanted her to relax and be taken care of for once. I wanted to give her the world because it was so easy for me to do.

"I appreciate that, but I'll be fine. I'm having brunch with my sister on Saturday, taking my daughter out to dinner later that night, and my nephew is having a birthday party on Sunday. So my weekend is pretty saturated."

"That sounds nice." I wished I could attend those things with her. I wondered what her sister was like. I wondered if her daughter would like me.

"It'll be fine. I'm excited to introduce you to them when the time is right."

When the time is right. I wasn't sure when that would be, but judging by the way I wanted her so much, it would be soon.

I paid the tab, and then we left for my penthouse.

I never wanted to be presumptuous, but I hoped she was coming back to my place. "Are you coming over tonight?"

"Are you inviting me?" She placed her hand on my thigh.

"Yes."

"Then, yes, I'd love to."

We went to my penthouse and rode the elevator until we appeared in my living room. I pulled out my phone and picked a soothing classical song to play over the sound system. Whenever I was home alone, sitting on the couch doing paperwork, it was usually the music I listened to. Scarlet calmed me, so I thought the song paired with her perfectly.

I uncorked a bottle of wine and poured two glasses

before we sat together on the couch. Her legs were crossed, and she smeared lipstick on her glass as she drank. Her green eyes were on me, and she looked so beautiful I wanted to take her to bed right that second.

I restrained myself.

Alessia and the others were a lot more talkative. They told me about their day, the drama they had with friends and their parents. I listened attentively, but I didn't find their problems that interesting. Being with an older woman like Scarlet was much easier because she was vastly more mature. She didn't ramble on the way others did. Whenever she spoke, it was purposeful.

"I got tickets to this art showcase next weekend. Would you like to come with me?"

It was the first time she'd asked me to do something. It seemed like I was the one always controlling our relationship. "I'd love to." A part of me was hoping she'd ask me to meet her family, but since I hadn't asked her to meet my sons, that seemed hypocritical.

"What's on your mind, Vincent?" She set the glass on the coffee table and gave me her full focus.

I enjoyed the way she said my name. Her voice was deep, and it held power I immediately responded to. She was the most confident woman I'd ever been with, but that confidence never turned to arrogance.

"A lot of things." I sat back against the couch with my wineglass in my hand.

"Such as?"

"For one, I find myself hoping you'll ask me to meet

your daughter and your sister...even though that seems too soon. I haven't asked you to spend time with my kids, so that doesn't seem fair. A part of me wishes you were coming to the wedding with me. And I want to make love to you on my bed right now..."

She didn't blink once despite my blunt confession. Her expression didn't change, and she retained the same self-assured composure. Her gorgeous legs looked long underneath her dress, and the black nail polish on her toenails gave an extra sexy perk.

The chemistry rose between us, our mutual desire filling the room. I wanted to be between her legs, but I knew once I was, there was no going back. It would be the beginning of a long and happy relationship. It wouldn't be a meaningless fuck I could just brush off. My heart would be on the line, and I'd be stepping into something I'd been avoiding for over a decade.

Scarlet rose from the couch then faced me, her dark hair still pinned back and to the side. She wore a backless dress, so all she had to do was grab the strap and peel it down her beautiful shoulder. The fabric slowly dropped down her body until it fell to her waist.

Her tits were gorgeous.

Two pieces of tape were across her nipples, and she quickly removed both at the same time. Her nipples hardened immediately once they were free. Age had dragged down her tits slightly. They weren't perky like the racks I was used to seeing. But her flawless skin, her beautiful curves, and the pink color around her nipples made them stunning. My mouth ached to wrap around each one and suck.

She pushed the dress down to her feet, revealing her beautiful body in just a black thong. There was extra weight in her hips and stomach, but she still possessed a body that made me hard in my jeans. She was all woman, all feminine curves. A slight hint of stretch marks was noticeable below her belly button, but the scars were beautiful. They were battle marks from bringing her only child into the world. A young man wouldn't find that sexy, but I certainly did. Women would always be stronger than men because they were ones who created men to begin with.

No man could compete with that.

"Then take me, Vincent. You know how long I've wanted you."

My right hand formed a fist, and I clenched my jaw. Temptation was staring me right in the face, and I'd never been so tempted. I felt more aroused by her than I did with any of the others. She had a powerful inner beauty that outshone every model I'd been with. Gorgeous curves, beautiful eyes, and keen intelligence made her the most desirable woman in the world.

She stepped closer to me, her knee touching mine.

I wanted to yank that pin out of her hair and fist her hair. I wanted to smother her mouth with endless kisses. I wanted to feel those firm tits in my palms. I wanted to have a passionate night with someone I actually cared about. Good sex was easy to find, but fantastic sex was rare. There had to be more than just an attraction, a chemistry. There had to be raging hearts full of emotion.

My hands moved to her knees, and I felt her thighs with my fingertips. Her muscles were sculpted, and her skin was so soft. My heart accelerated at the touch, feeling my mind begin to fog with logical thought.

I sat upright and wrapped my hands around her legs. I kissed her skin, starting at her thighs and moving up to her stomach. My lips brushed over the lace of her panties before I placed gentle kisses along her stomach. I kissed her stretch marks then dragged my tongue across the delicious skin.

Her fingers dug into my hair, and she inhaled deeply, her body coming to life at my touch.

My hands glided over her hips and to her waistline, feeling her petiteness. I gripped her tightly, assuring myself she was truly real. I rose to my feet and lifted her at the same time, wrapping her legs around my waist as I carried her into my bedroom.

She cupped my face and kissed me, her fingers digging into my hair. She breathed hard into my mouth as her lips trembled against mine. Her tits dragged against my t-shirt as she moved, and her heavenly smell wrapped around me.

I laid her on my bed then pulled my shirt over my head.

She immediately pressed her bare feet against my chest, her toes digging into me. "You're so hard..."

I brought one ankle to my lips and kissed it. Then I kissed the other.

I dropped my jeans and boxers next then yanked her body to the edge of the bed. She sucked my dick so good last time, and I was eager to return the favor. I dropped to my knees and pressed my face between her legs.

"Oh god..." The second I touched her, her entire body tensed, and she locked her hands around my wrists. As if she hadn't been expecting me to kiss her in such a delicate place, her hips bucked uncontrollably. Her head rolled back, and she panted through my kisses, moaning louder than most women did during sex.

She was waxed and ready for me, so she obviously had been hoping things would heat up tonight.

That was a turn-on.

My mouth worked her nub, and I enjoyed her exquisite taste. She tasted exactly as a woman should taste —delicious. My arms hooked around her thighs, and I devoured her, enjoying her while taking my time. Listening to her writhe for me was satisfying. When she said she hadn't been on a date in a year, I could tell she hadn't been exaggerating.

My cock was hard and ready to go, but I stayed on my knees and pleasured her. I'd made her wait weeks before I would even kiss her. With Alessia and Meredith, I slept with them the same night I met them. My patience was a compliment since I only resisted because I actually cared about her.

I pushed her to the edge, making her teeter on the precipice of joy. She held her breath and dug her nails into my skin. "Vincent...Vincent." She repeated my name over and over again before she crashed into a world of pleasure. "God...yes." She bucked against my mouth and winced in pleasure, reduced to a woman riding a high.

My tongue kept working her body until her moment was completely over. "That was...wow."

I rose to my feet, my cock anxious to feel how wet she was. She didn't even need my saliva in order to take me. My cock was hard in a way it hadn't been in a long time. The beautiful women in my life fulfilled my sexual desires, but none of them got me so rock hard. If Scarlet enjoyed my mouth so much, I couldn't wait to see how much she enjoyed everything else I had to offer.

My knees sank into the mattress, and I maneuvered on top of her, my hard body rubbing against her soft skin. When her bare tits pressed against me, I felt my spine shiver. I leaned down and sucked both of her nipples, making her wince from the pressure. I guided my tongue into the valley between her awesome tits.

Fuck...the way she tasted.

My mouth moved up her neck until I found her lips. I kissed her hard on the mouth as my thighs separated her. My engine was revving at full capacity, and I couldn't slow down. Now that we were skin against skin, my breath came out shaky. My throbbing dick rubbed against her clit, and I imagined how she would feel once I was buried deep inside.

I forced my kisses to slow down.

I forced my body to stop.

I sucked her bottom lip before I moved my gaze to

hers. Her tubes were tied, so pregnancy wasn't an issue. I was clean, and judging by the fact that her sex life was unremarkable, she probably was too.

So I didn't ask. That was a conversation for horny young people.

I pointed my crown at her entrance and slowly sank.

Jesus...she felt incredible.

She dug her nails into my biceps and moaned in my face. "Vincent..."

She was tight, wet, and perfect. My cock could definitely make a home between her legs. I moved until most of my length was inside her. If I gave her any more, I'd just hurt her. I rubbed my nose against hers and felt her warm breath fall on my skin.

She locked her ankles together behind my back and ran her fingers through my hair. She looked at me with a gaze full of sex and something deeper. It was affection, it was trust, and it was something else too.

I kissed her slower this time, my lips moving with hers at a languid pace. She dug her fingers into my hair and kissed me with the same restrained passion. Our bodies moved together slowly, feeling each other rather than aggressively grinding.

I wanted this to last because it felt so good. I wanted to build her up to another orgasm before I filled her. She just came, so it might take a while. But it'd been so long since she got laid, it might take less than five minutes.

Sweat collected on our bodies, and the sound of our moving lips filled my bedroom. The headboard gently tapped against the wall from time to time. I hooked my arm under her thigh, and I pinned it back so I could move deeper inside her.

Her nails dug into me and her moans increased.

I was hitting her in the perfect spot. I could feel it. Sweat trickled down my chest and rubbed her against her tits. My balls tightened because I could feel how much she enjoyed me.

She dragged her nails down my back and moaned in my face. Her pussy tightened around me with impressive force, and she writhed underneath me as another explosive orgasm overtook her. "Vincent..." She pressed her mouth to mine but was unable to kiss me, her body electrified by the pleasure I was giving her.

I thrust into her harder, making the climax of the orgasm even stronger. My cock twitched inside her as I prepared to release. I couldn't stop myself from coming even if I wanted to. The all-or-nothing sequence had been initiated, and I couldn't hold back. Just as she finished her climax, mine began.

My hand latched on to her hair, and I shoved my entire length inside her so she would catch every drop of my come. I stuffed her deep, giving her everything I had. Even without seeing it with my own eyes, I knew my release was impressive.

She gripped my ass and pulled me hard into her. "So good..." She laid her head back and stared up at me with sweat gleaming on her forehead. Her tits rose and fell as she caught her breath. "Oh Jesus..."

My dick softened inside her, and I kissed her neck as I recovered from what I'd just experienced. Sex had never been that good with the flings I'd had. Fucking on my yacht in the Mediterranean had never been as explosive as what I'd just had with Scarlet. It was missionary and slow, but it was still fantastic.

She ran her hands through her hair and closed her eyes. "My god..."

I kissed the valley between her tits.

"Vincent, a man has never made me feel so good." She opened her eyes and looked up at me. "You're a god." Her arms circled my neck, and she kissed me hard on the mouth. "Not once in my forty-two years of life have I ever come twice..."

"Expect it to happen all the time now." My sweaty body was entwined with hers, and I wasn't thinking about how much our relationship had just changed. Now I was connected to her in a way I wasn't before. I adored this woman with all that I had. Now I saw her as mine.

I saw her as my everything.

CHAPTER ELEVEN

Diesel

I was so horny I couldn't sleep.

My dick was hard under the sheets, and it was throbbing just like a migraine did when it beat inside my skull. I glanced at the clock on my nightstand and realized my alarm would go off in thirty minutes.

I wasn't going to bother trying to go back to sleep.

Titan was fast asleep, tucked into my side like I was her favorite stuffed animal. Her hand was wrapped around my torso, and her breaths fell across my skin.

I maneuvered out of the bed and walked into the kitchen. I set my phone down along with my laptop then made a pot of coffee. We were leaving for Thailand in a few hours. I'd probably get some sleep on the long flight.

I sat down at the kitchen table in my sweatpants and opened my laptop.

My phone lit up with a text message from my father.

My father had never texted me in his life. *Give me a call when you get a chance.*

I hoped everything was alright. I immediately called him back.

"Hey, Diesel," Dad said in a deep voice. He seemed tired, like he hadn't slept all night.

"Everything alright, Dad?"

"Yeah, everything is okay." He continued to speak quietly, like someone might overhear him. "I'm sorry to drop this on you at the last minute. But...I was wondering if Scarlet could come along. It's okay if it's too late—"

"Yes." I couldn't wipe the smile off my face. "Bring her."

"Are you sure? Because—"

"Dad, shut up." I'd never said those words to him in my entire life.

He was dead silent.

"It's okay to move on. Mom would want you to. Shit, she would have wanted you to move on like five years ago. And Scarlet is super nice. She's pretty, smart, elegant... she's perfect for you."

Dad's silence suddenly filled with hostility. "How do you know that?"

Shit, I'd just incriminated myself.

"Diesel?"

Fuck. "I went by her office earlier this week."

His tone shifted. "Why?"

"I asked her to be patient with you... I don't want you to lose her."

"I've never interfered in your personal life—"

"Are you kidding me?" I snapped. "Fuck yes, you have. You tried to turn Tatum against me by making her that deal. You blackmailed both of us. Or did you forget all of that already?"

He turned quiet again. "You're right...but I meant that in a different context."

"Well, I wanted to meet her. And she seems pretty damn perfect. Don't push her away."

"I'm not."

"Then bring her. Let yourself be happy. And don't be afraid or ashamed to love this woman. Everyone knows how you felt about Mom. You don't need to continue carrying this vigil all the time. Love this woman like you loved Mom. It's okay. Mom would want you to." My mom had been compassionate and understanding. And she'd loved my dad as much as he loved her. It would pain her to know he was still suffering like this. "You know how much it would hurt Mom if she knew how sad you were. There's nothing she wants more than for you to be happy. Please be happy."

He sighed into the phone. "You're right. I don't think I can keep Scarlet at a distance anymore anyway..."

I didn't ask why. I knew it was none of my business.

"There's something about her... I knew it the first time I saw her. She's the first woman I've ever...felt this way about since your mother. I guess that made me feel guilty. But I know you're right. If I were dead and your mother were still here, I'd want her to fall in love again too."

"Absolutely."

"So...I think I'm ready."

"Good. We'd love to have her."

"You should check with Tatum. This is her big day."

"I don't need to check with her. She's gonna be thrilled when she wakes up."

"Are you sure?" he asked.

"Yes, Dad. How many times do I have to say it?"

He chuckled. "You're right. I'm a bit of an overthinker sometimes."

"Sometimes?" I countered.

"You're gonna turn into me someday, so watch it."

"God, I hope not. But Tatum did say she hopes I age as well as you do."

"Yes, I'm very handsome," Dad teased. "So, are you excited? Nervous?"

I shut my laptop and stared at the steam rising out of my coffee. "Very excited."

"And not nervous at all?"

"What's there to be nervous about?"

"Everything is going to change. You're solely responsible for another person now."

That didn't bother me. "I love her. I want to be responsible for her."

I could hear his smile over the phone. "Good answer."

"There's no one else I'd want to spend my life. I've had my share of women, and none of them interested me much. But Tatum...she's the one woman in the world who could bring me to my knees with just a few words. She earned my respect in a way no one else ever has. I'm a lucky asshole that I get to have a woman like that."

"Well said...minus the asshole part."

I chuckled. "Thanks."

"Well, let me know if you need anything. I'm very excited for this wedding. I couldn't be happier about the person you've chosen to spend your life with. I know she'll take care of you. And, of course, you'll take care of her."

"Thanks, Dad."

"I'll see you later."

"Alright."

"And thanks for letting me bring Scarlet along."

"She's great, Dad. I already love her."

"Thanks...I appreciate that."

———

Tatum came into the kitchen after she showered. She was just in her black bra and matching thong with a towel wrapped around her head. Her windows were tinted from the outside so she was never worried someone would see her in such revealing clothes.

I glared at her.

She poured herself a mug of coffee then approached me at the kitchen table. "Morning, Mr. Hunt."

"Morning...soon-to-be Mrs. Hunt."

She sipped her coffee then shut my laptop. "No working. Isn't that what we agreed on?"

My eyes moved down her body, looking at her perfect figure while trying not to drool. "We agreed on a lot of things..."

The corner of her mouth rose in a smile. "One more day."

"I can't sleep because my dick is hard all the time."

"Ooh...I wish I could make him soft."

I growled.

She sipped her coffee again. "I'll reward your patience."

"By getting knocked up."

"I hope so." She pulled out the chair and took a seat. "Is that why you were up early? Or is it because you're getting cold feet?"

I cocked an eyebrow. "Trust me, I'm not cold. I'm hot all the damn time."

"I hope so. Because Diesel Hunt, world's biggest playboy and most eligible bachelor, is finally settling down. It might be hitting him right about now..." She blew on her coffee before she took another drink.

"With every passing minute, I want to marry you more." My hand moved to hers on the table. My fingers grazed over her knuckles.

She gave me a faint smile.

"What about you? Afraid to let go of your name?" She knew she could tell me anything and I wouldn't get upset.

Whatever her feelings were, it didn't change the fact that she wanted me to be her husband.

"I guess it bums me out a little, but I'm looking forward to taking your last name. I'm excited to hear people call me Mrs. Hunt so I can see the devastation in the eyes of every woman around me..."

"That's possessive."

"Oh, and you aren't?" she countered.

I smiled. "Extremely." I brought her hand to my mouth and kissed it. "The first time we fuck, it's not gonna last long. I have to put that out in the open."

"Me neither."

I kissed her knuckles before I set her hand on the table. "My dad called."

"At six in the morning?" she asked in surprise.

"Wanted to know if he could bring Scarlet."

"Really? He changed his mind?"

"He did. He didn't say why, but I'm glad he's had a change of heart."

"Me too. He's a sweet man and deserves to be happy."

I didn't know if I would consider him to be sweet, but I was glad he had what he wanted. "I understand why it would be hard to move on from the love of your life. I couldn't imagine my life without you. But it's been ten years. It's time."

"It is."

"And she seemed perfect. I like her."

"I knew she was perfect when I read that article she

wrote. She's totally smitten with Vincent, and not because he's rich."

"No...it seems deeper than that. So, it's okay if she comes along?"

She rolled her eyes. "Of course. We made it clear she was welcome."

I drank my coffee and stared at my fiancée, excited we would be husband and wife when we returned to this penthouse. We hadn't decided on where we would live, and despite my lawyer's insistence, we didn't sign a prenup. We were in this together—until death parted us. "We never discussed where we would be living after we tied the knot."

"Do you have a preference?"

"What are the choices? My penthouse or yours?"

"There's unlimited options."

"I guess either place doesn't matter to me. But it doesn't make sense to keep both. One should go back on the market."

"I made the compromise to change my name for you, so I guess I should pick."

I didn't argue with that because it was fair. "Alright."

"I'd like to keep my place. It's the first piece of property I bought once I started making money. It has a lot of sentimental value."

"Fine with me. Then my place will go on the market."

"But...I'm considering getting a place in Connecticut."

I couldn't picture her living anywhere else other than Manhattan. "Really?"

"How do you feel about that?"

"Not sure, honestly. I've never pictured myself commuting. And I certainly can't picture you living outside the city."

"I admit being in Manhattan makes life easier. But I'm not sure how I feel about raising our kids in the city."

Our kids. I liked that.

"The city is just so constant, you know. I feel like they should have peace and quiet."

"Whatever you want, baby. But I don't think that's realistic."

"Really? Why not?"

"We're both devoted to our work. Making us both commute forty-five minutes each way every single day sounds like a waste of time. That's less time together. Less time with our family. Lots of people raise their kids in the city. It's not the perfect family setting, but it's a lot more manageable for us. I'm guessing you wanted to get a nanny?"

"Yes. But she won't stay home with them. She'll take care of them in my office as I work. I don't trust anyone to take care of my children without my supervision."

I didn't want someone else to do everything either. "Then it makes more sense to do it in the city."

"Is that what you prefer?" she asked.

I nodded. "We can always sell this place and get a nice townhouse a few blocks over. Maybe something in the Tribeca area. They have a lot of things to choose from, some of them with ten-thousand square feet. They have private yards, and they feel more like a house than a pent-house like this."

"Not a bad idea..."

"And you could sell this place."

"I don't know if I could ever do that. Maybe we could keep it...when we need some alone time."

I smiled at the thought. "I like that idea. I wish we could take advantage of it now..."

"Very soon, you'll be able to take advantage of it all you want. And you'll never have to sleep with a hard dick against your stomach again."

I could have taken the easy way out and beat off in the shower or something, but I wanted to fulfill her wishes. She wanted me to be burning hot for her, and that's exactly what she would get.

Even though I would have been burning hot for her, regardless.

CHAPTER TWELVE

TITAN

Diesel and I sat at the front of the plane, while Thorn and Autumn sat farther back in the comfortable leather armchairs that reclined all the way back into a full bed. Diesel's brothers were on the plane too, as well as a few friends of mine, including Isa and Pilar, whom I hadn't seen in forever.

We'd been in the air for a few hours, and Diesel busied himself on his laptop while I did the same.

I couldn't believe I was getting married.

I'd dreamed about this day my entire life. I only wished my father were alive to give me away.

I knew he would be proud of me.

Actually, I knew he was proud of me.

Diesel could attribute my vision to a hallucination under medication, but I didn't believe that. I never considered myself to be a particularly spiritual person, but that interaction was real.

Instead of being sad he wasn't here to share this day with me, I felt at peace. I felt like he was here even though I couldn't see him. He gave me his approval of Diesel since I couldn't receive it in real life.

It meant a lot to me.

Thorn approached our seats, dressed casually in sweatpants and a t-shirt. It was a long flight, so it didn't make sense for us to dress in our finest attire. "Titan, can we talk for a bit?"

Diesel didn't take his gaze off his computer. "You won't be able to call her that much longer."

Thorn took the seat across from me. He glanced at Autumn farther back in the plane before he looked at me again. "Autumn is asleep right now."

Now I knew who the subject of the conversation was. "What happened?"

Diesel kept reading on his laptop.

Thorn glanced at him before he turned back to me. "I guess you'll just tell him what I said anyway. I had dinner with Autumn's parents last night. Everything went fine. I liked them, and they seemed to like me."

Diesel looked up from his computer. "That sounds great, so I wonder why the tone is so solemn."

"She was helping her mom with the dishes in the kitchen," Thorn said. "I walked down the hall to find the bathroom, and I overheard them talking…"

"What did they say?" I asked.

"They talked back and forth a bit. Her mom asked how Autumn felt about me...other things were said. But at the end...Autumn told her mom she was in love with me." Thorn turned his gaze to the floor, his eyes fogged with memory.

"Aww..." Autumn was a master at hiding her emotions. She remained professional when we worked together, and whatever her opinion was, she could keep it from me if she wanted to. I knew she felt something significant for Thorn because of the way she looked at him. I hadn't necessarily thought she was in love with him, but I certainly wasn't surprised to hear she was. "You better not do something stupid like dump her at the wedding."

"I'm not gonna dump her," he said under his breath. "That's the last thing on my mind."

Now I suspected her feelings were mutual. "Then, what are you going to do?"

"There's nothing for me to do. She doesn't know I overheard her." The loud sound of the plane drowned out our conversation. She was sitting too far away to hear anything we were saying.

"So you're going to pretend you don't know anything?" Diesel asked.

"Yeah, I guess," Thorn answered.

"But you aren't freaked out by it?" I asked incredulously. "Freaking out sounds like the first thing you would do."

"Why would I freak out?" Thorn asked. "This is Autumn. It's flattering. Now I see it every time she looks at me. It's so obvious that I'm not sure how I didn't notice before."

"I know something else is obvious too…" Diesel turned back to his computer, like his sentence wasn't heavy with implication.

Thorn's eyes shifted to him. "What's that supposed to mean?"

Diesel ignored him.

Thorn turned back to me. "Titan?"

"I think Diesel is implying that her feelings are mutual," I said. "And honestly, I agree."

"What?" he asked with a laugh. "I'm not in love with her."

Diesel smiled slightly. "Whatever you say, man."

"I'm not," Thorn repeated. "If I did, I would just say it."

"Or you're too afraid to say it," I said. "And you shouldn't be. If Autumn is the one, you should be grateful you found her. Not everyone is so lucky. Sometimes people don't meet the right person until most of their life has passed…or they don't meet the right person at all. If that's how you feel, you shouldn't be afraid to say it."

"We're jumping ahead here," Thorn said. "It's been six weeks at the most."

"I knew I loved Diesel the first time he kissed me," I said quietly. "You just know, Thorn. I know you know…so just let it be."

He shook his head and looked out the window.

"I can prove it," Diesel said. "When a chick would tell

me she loved me, I'd dump her. And I wouldn't just end things, I'd destroy them. The second I knew a woman had those kinds of feelings for me, I ended it as soon as possible so I wouldn't hurt her more in the end. I wouldn't keep seeing someone if I knew I would never reciprocate those feelings. The fact that you're *flattered* by what she said tells us everything we need to know. So save yourself some time and stop lying to yourself. You love this woman...be a man and admit it." As if Diesel hadn't just put Thorn down, he turned back to his computer.

Thorn turned his gaze away, holding his silence from both of us.

"Is it really that terrible if you do?" I asked. "Falling in love is the best thing that ever happened to me. I was scared in the beginning, but now I have the greatest gift in the world. It's not like you're afraid of getting hurt. And obviously, you're capable of love."

"I guess..." Thorn clenched his jaw as he considered our words. "I just don't want to hurt her."

"Then don't," Diesel said. "Problem solved."

"You're oversimplifying the issue," Thorn said.

"No, I'm not," Diesel said. "From the moment I fell in love with Titan, I've never hurt her. It's not hard. Be faithful and be honest. Those are the only two things you need to do. The rest is easy."

Thorn watched him, his thoughts racing behind his eyes.

"I know you can be both of those things," I said. "You've always been that way. The fact that you don't want to hurt her suggests you never will. If that's how you feel, then tell her. Don't waste time by pretending she's not the love of your life. We're young and have so much time left on this earth...but it's going to pass quickly. Enjoy her as much as you can."

Thorn rubbed his palms together after considering everything we'd said. He stared at his hands, his chiseled face hard with deep thought. He took a deep breath then sighed quietly. "I shouldn't be bothering you with this... since you're getting married."

"You aren't bothering us." I placed my hand on his. "We're family."

"Then what does that make us?" Diesel asked as he indicated Thorn. "Family-in-law?"

"No," I said. "Just family." I turned back to Thorn. "You're overthinking all of this. If the time is right and you feel that sensation in your chest—" I pressed my hand over his heart "—just tell her. And smile when you listen to her say it back."

————

The weather was perfect when we arrived. It was sunny and beautiful, the temperature warm but the humidity not unbearable. Our bags were taken to our rooms, but when I stepped inside, I realized Diesel's suitcases weren't there.

"I hope they didn't lose your things." We had the presidential suite at the resort, with a private pool and our section of private beach to enjoy the crystal-clear water. A living room led to a patio that was big enough for twenty people. The place was stocked with a full bar along with many other amenities.

"They didn't." Diesel took a look around with his hands in his pockets. "I'm staying in my own room tonight."

That hadn't been discussed. "You are?"

"I can't go another night, baby." He faced me, his hands withdrawn like he didn't trust himself to touch me. His jaw was clenched, and irritation was in his eyes. "It's just too hard...I'm going to snap."

"I thought you wanted to sleep beside me every night for the rest of our lives..."

"I do. Very much."

I was used to having this strong man beside me every single night. I was used to his body heat, his powerful protection. I used to only sleep alone, but now the idea of being without him made me feel like I was stranded on a desert island. My life had been completely shared with him...and we weren't even married yet. My body ached for his, my nails wanted to dig into his flesh, and I was suffering as much as he was...but I still didn't want him to leave. But I refused to tell him that. I could go one night. "Alright."

"Don't be mad at me."

"I'm not," I whispered.

He moved his hands to my shoulders, and he pressed his forehead to mine. "One more night."

"One more night."

He kissed my forehead before he released me. "I'll see you later."

"Alright."

He walked out and shut the door.

The silence surrounded me, and it had never felt as suffocating as it did now. I used to live for quiet moments like this, to crave the silence of solitude. The only thing I'd wanted from a man was good sex. Then I wanted him out of my place as quickly as possible. No man had shared my bed in a decade.

But now my life was completely wrapped around Diesel. He was an extension of who I was. They say having children was like having your heart exist outside your body...and that was how I felt about Diesel. My heart was in his hand, and when he walked away, he took it with him...along with my soul.

———

I sat in the chair and patiently waited for the woman to finish my hair and makeup. My hair was in loose spirals, and my makeup was light. I preferred to look natural instead of overdone with foundation and mascara, and I knew that's how Diesel preferred me too.

I started to get nervous.

I wasn't nervous about the man I was marrying. I was just nervous in general. I'd made pitches to the biggest companies in the world without my heart rate increasing at all. I'd landed billion-dollar deals without losing sleep the night before. I was marrying the man I loved with the people closest to me present. There was no reason to be nervous.

But I was overwhelmed.

I put on my dress next, and it fit perfectly. Original and customized, the dress was the only one like it in the entire world. Made with real diamonds, premium lace, and a light fabric that reduced the heaviness of the dress, it was perfect.

I knew Diesel would love it.

Thorn walked inside in his gray suit with a pink boutonniere pinned to his jacket. He stopped when he spotted me in front of the mirror. Then he released a low whistle. "Wow...you look..." He approached me by the mirror and looked me up and down. "Let's just say it's a shame it didn't work out between us."

I chuckled, feeling the stress leave my chest now that someone had made me laugh.

"You look beautiful. I know I've seen you in this dress before, but it looks different now."

"Probably because I'm happy."

"Yeah." He gave me a deep look. "Yeah...that must be it."

"How is he?"

He grinned. "You don't want to know."

"What's that supposed to mean?"

"He's been pacing for the last hour and a half."

"Why? Is he nervous?"

"No. He says he just wants to get started already. He's anxious. Tired of waiting."

I pictured Diesel walking around his hotel room, his hands in his pockets with his head bowed down. The image touched my heart, knowing he was anxious to see me walk down the aisle toward him. "Aww..."

"I just checked on everything outside. It's set up and ready to go. Looks really nice."

"Great." I couldn't care less how it looked. I only cared about the man waiting for me.

"So..." He walked to the bar and made two Old Fashioneds. "This is the last time it'll be the two of us...Thorn and Titan."

He handed me the glass.

"I know...it's crazy."

"I'm happy for you. You deserve to be with the best... and Diesel is definitely the best."

"I'm very lucky."

He took a long drink.

I did the same.

"Anything you need?"

"No. I'm ready to go..."

"Nervous?"

"Anxious."

He spotted the flower crown sitting on the table, and he picked it up from the plastic case. "May I?"

"Yes."

He placed it on my head then adjusted my hair. His fingertips touched me lightly as he fixed everything, making me look perfect. "I've never seen you look so beautiful."

"Thank you, Thorn."

"Honestly, I'm pretty sad I have to give you away. You've always been my girl...in a different kind of way."

"I know. But we'll always be family."

"Yeah." He leaned in and kissed me on the cheek. "We should probably get going. Anything else you need before we get started? A few more minutes to collect yourself?"

I didn't need any more time. Diesel was pacing because he was too anxious to stand still. "No. I'm just as eager as he is."

Thorn stuck his hand in his pocket and pulled out a note. "He wanted me to give this to you before we left." He placed the paper in my hand.

I unfolded it and read the words.

Don't walk down the aisle.
Run.

-Boss Man-

I smiled as the tears formed in my eyes. "Diesel..."

Thorn tipped his head to the floor, giving me some privacy.

I folded the letter and handed it back to him. "Could you hold on to this for me?"

"Of course." He opened his wallet and placed it inside. Then he extended his arm. "Ready?"

I wrapped my hand around his arm. "Yes."

CHAPTER THIRTEEN

Diesel

There were only twenty guests at our wedding.

The perfect amount.

We were surrounded only by the people we were closest to. There were no paparazzi or prying eyes. We were tucked away on a private beach with just the sunset behind me. I could hear the small waves break against the shoreline.

It was a beautiful day in paradise.

But not as beautiful as the bride who was about to walk toward me.

My father sat beside Scarlet as he stared at me, the pride in his eyes. Everyone else looked at me too, but once Tatum made her entrance, no one would care about me anymore. Without knowing how she looked, I knew she would be the most beautiful thing on this island.

Finally, the harpist began to play, and the ceremony began.

My heart didn't race.

I didn't fidget.

I stood with my hands by my sides and waited in anticipation for the greatest moment of my life. Marriage wasn't something I'd fantasized about as I grew up. Even as an adult, I didn't care about it. There was no woman who could ever capture my attention for longer than five minutes.

Until I met my future wife.

Now I waited with steady hands, waiting for the greatest gift I would ever receive.

The unconditional love of the most wonderful woman in the world. She was strong as steel, unbreakable like metal, and soft like a rose petal. A woman too good for almost any man, she wouldn't just love anyone. I was the only one worthy of her affection. I was the only one strong enough to get her to surrender. Now she trusted me implicitly, knowing I would never betray her.

I earned that trust.

Thorn finally guided her away from the bushes that blocked my view of her. I couldn't describe the way Thorn looked or his expression because I didn't look at him once. I stared at the woman coming my way, the woman who was more beautiful than a cloudless, starry night. Her shiny hair was in spirals, and she wore a crown full of exotic flowers. Her white dress tight around her waist and full of diamonds. It was elegant and form-fitting, the most beautiful dress for the most beautiful woman.

I felt the emotion in my heart, but I didn't weep.

Just like my father and my mother, I had found that one special person who had my soul. I would love her every single day until one of us faded from this life. But until that moment arrived, I would cherish her every single day.

Because she was mine to adore.

With every step she took, I felt the connection between us grow. I wanted to yank her from Thorn's grasp and make her mine already. I wanted to feel the softness of this woman, to promise to love her with everything I had.

My eyes locked on her face, and I saw the moisture that had built up in her gaze. Emotion wasn't something she wore on her sleeve, but I knew my note would hit her right in the heart. Now she could barely keep it together as Thorn brought her closer to me.

Finally, she arrived.

My bride.

My wife.

The mother of my children.

The other half of my soul.

My everything.

Thorn placed her hand in mine and took a seat.

I felt her pulse in my fingertips, felt the emotion that seeped from her skin. I pulled her toward me and placed my forehead against hers. My arm moved around her waist, and I brought her into my chest, feeling the ache finally die away now that she was mine.

"Aww..." someone said in the crowd.

I finally released her and stood across from her, ready to vow to love her all my life.

She sniffed then wiped her tears away, unable to keep her emotion at bay. "My husband..."

My expression darkened as I stared at her face. "My wife."

———

I had my first dance with my wife.

In the center of the clearing while everyone enjoyed the cake at their tables, Tatum and I danced in a circle of torches with the stars up above. The quiet music played over the speakers, and our eyes were only on each other. Her hand was in mine, and I gripped the small of her back as I took the lead. I pressed my forehead to hers and closed my eyes, enjoying the second happiest moment of my life.

The first was when she said I do.

"I thought I would never find you..." she whispered to me, her gaze shifted down to the floor.

I opened my eyes and stared at the perfect woman in front of me. "I didn't think I would find you either."

"And now you're my husband... I'm in love with my husband."

"Not as much as I'm in love with my wife."

She smiled, her eyes bright with the film of moisture. "I don't have a mother or a father, but I feel like I have everything with you. You give me everything I'm missing. You've made me believe in love, hope, and trust..."

"You give me everything too, Mrs. Hunt."

She smiled wider. "That's what you're always going to call me, isn't it?"

My eyes locked on hers. "Always."

She moved her face into my chest and swayed with me. "This is the greatest day of my life."

"Mine too."

We finished the song together, lost in our joy while everyone watched from a distance. It didn't seem like they were there at all because it was just the two of us. We barely had a few bites of dinner or cake because we were too busy touching, kissing, or talking.

Thankfully, people left us alone.

When the song ended, I kissed her forehead. "Do you want to stay longer, Mrs. Hunt?" I'd spent the entire day talking to these people as I waited for my wedding. Now that I had my wife, I didn't give a damn about anyone else. I wanted to retreat to our hideaway, to make love endlessly. I didn't only want her because I'd been denied her for almost a week.

I just wanted my wife.

"No." Her fingers twirled the hair at the back of my neck. "I want my husband to make love to me."

My hand instinctively gripped her dress at the small of her back, hearing the sexiest confession I'd ever heard.

When she wore that gorgeous white dress and looked so beautiful, naturally, all I wanted to do was rip it off. "Then let's go, Mrs. Hunt." I took her hand and guided her to the tables where everyone was sitting. "Good night, everyone. My wife and I are going to bed."

"To bed, huh?" Thorn asked, his arm over the back of Autumn's chair.

I wrapped my arm around Tatum's waist and guided her away. "Good night."

People said their goodbyes as we walked off, and when we were finally in the hallway outside our room, the quiet surrounded us. I got the door open and stepped into the presidential suite she'd been enjoying on her own. It'd been cleaned, and now there were rose petals leading to the bed, along with champagne and chocolate-covered strawberries.

Neither one of us cared about any of that.

My hands remained steady as I unbuttoned the dozens of buttons that started at her neck and stopped at the top of her ass. I popped one after another, slowly revealing her beautiful flesh. When I reached the last button, I spotted the white thong underneath the dress.

I took a deep breath in anticipation.

I pushed the dress off her shoulders, watching it fall into a pile at her feet. My hands gripped her arms, and I kissed the back of her neck and the center of her spine. My hands curled around her body, and I cupped both of her tits, my thumbs flicking over the nipples. My breathing was unsteady, deep and hoarse. It was quiet in the room, so I could hear every sound she made, every soft moan that sounded deep in her throat.

My lips brushed against her ear. "Mrs. Hunt, turn around."

She slowly faced me, still standing in the center of her dress.

My hands explored her slender stomach and her perky ass like I'd never touched her before. She was gorgeous, prettier than I'd ever seen her. From the flowers in her hair to the bracelet on her wrist, she was more perfect than a doll.

I rubbed my nose against hers before I finally kissed her.

It was like the first time I ever had.

My hand cupped her cheek, and I breathed into her mouth, filling her lungs with heat and warmth. I sucked her bottom lip then felt her push my jacket over my shoulders. After one article of clothing fell, the others followed.

She stripped me until I stood in only my skin.

I pulled her thong off her ass and left her heels on her feet as I guided her to the bed.

I'd never been this hard in my life

I laid her on the bed then moved on top of her, her legs opening to me instantly. My hands burrowed into the sheets on either side of her, and I rubbed my dick against her clit. The slickness of her entrance smeared against the base of my cock.

She dug her fingers into the back of my hair and

pulled me more completely on top of her, her legs widening farther. She grabbed my base and pointed my cock at her entrance.

I slid inside slowly, greeted by nothing but wet warmness. "Mrs. Hunt..." She was so wet for me, just as aroused as I was. The last week had been torture, but the restraint had been worth it. She'd never felt so good.

"Husband."

I slid inside until I was balls deep. Our breaths were mutually strained and unsteady. I'd been with her hundreds of times, but this felt brand-new. Now that she was my wife and the only woman I would ever be with for the rest of my life, it felt different.

It felt better.

Being this committed to another person gave me the greatest high I'd ever known.

And the fact that we could start our family that very night made it even better.

My lips trembled against hers as I started to thrust.

"Diesel..." She dragged her nails down my back as she moved her hips with me. "I'm already going to come..."

I'd barely been inside her for a minute, but I could feel her walls tightening. I knew it was her abstinence as well as her emotional investment that made her this way. She was trembling in my arms, eager for more of me.

Thankfully, she was ready. Because I was about to blow.

"God...Diesel." She tightened around me instantly, her orgasm starting right from the beginning. She was desperate for me, needing my soul as well as my body. Her nails dug deeper, and her eyes gave me the most soulful look of love I'd ever seen. "I love you..." She buried her face in my neck as she rode out the rest of the climax.

I gave my final pumps then released inside her instantly, my moans louder than hers. I gripped her tightly, like she might slip away at any moment. I filled her with more come than I'd ever had, stuffing her with so much it immediately overflowed onto the sheets. Just a simple touch ignited us both, and we were already writhing for each other.

She held on to me like she hadn't just exploded around my length, and I clutched her just as tightly as I did before. That was a personal best for both of us.

I kissed her softly on the mouth. "I love you too, Mrs. Hunt."

CHAPTER FOURTEEN

THORN

My hand rested on Autumn's thigh as we watched Diesel and Tatum dance in the distance. Pressed tightly together and oblivious to everything going on around them, they swayed to the slow music. Titan's gown trailed across the floor as Diesel guided her. I'd never seen her so happy.

"They're so in love," Autumn whispered.

"Yeah..." I eyed her hand, seeing her fingers interlocked with mine. I wasn't holding Autumn close to me as we moved on the dance floor, but I was certainly happy. I could feel it all the way down to my bones. Having Autumn in my life vanquished all the terrible habits in my life. I didn't drink as much anymore, I didn't sit in dark clubs and watch women dance on poles, and I didn't care about work as much either. She filled a hole I hadn't realized needed to be filled.

Vincent sat beside his girlfriend, Scarlet, and watched his son dance with his new bride. They didn't share affection, but it was obvious they were linked together. Vincent hardly blinked as he watched the two of them move across the dance floor.

Scarlet placed her hand on his. "They're perfect together."

"They are," Vincent whispered. "I wish Isabella were here to see it...she'd be so happy."

"She is here," Scarlet said gently. "And she's very happy."

Vincent turned his gaze to her, his eyes softening slightly.

I didn't know Vincent very well because he was quiet all the time, but now I saw a different version of him. I saw him as a father, not just a crazy business tycoon. He wore his heart on his sleeve, and it was obvious he loved Tatum as much as his own son.

My parents were there too, sitting at a different table and staring at the newlyweds on the dance floor.

"You think we'll spend time with them this evening?" Autumn asked.

I scoffed. "No. The second the song is over, Diesel is gonna take his new bride away. That's what I would do. They'll see us in the morning."

Autumn squeezed my hand. "That's romantic."

"I'm telling you..."

The song ended, and they shared a soft kiss before they walked back toward us.

Diesel pulled her close to him and guided her around the tables. "We're going to bed."

I gave Autumn a meaningful look. "Told you."

She smiled back.

"To bed, huh?" I teased.

Diesel hooked his arm around her waist and guided her away. Her white dress glowed under the torches until it was gone from sight.

"Doesn't mean we can't enjoy all this free booze and food." I held my glass and clinked it against hers.

Vincent turned to Scarlet. "Thanks for joining me. Jax and Brett seem to like you."

"They're gentlemen," she said. "You've raised fine men."

Vincent's eyes softened again. "That wasn't all me, but thank you."

"Boys will look to the man in their life for example," she said. "All three of them looked up to you, and now they're strong, intelligent, and gentle. Look at the way Diesel is with Tatum. He's a whole different person."

Vincent nodded slightly, the fatherly pride in his eyes. "Thank you for saying that."

She patted his hand, a smile on her face. She looked like she was at least fifteen years younger than him, and even though she was a lot older than me, she was definitely pretty. She wasn't like the models I'd seen him with in the past, but she was definitely more compatible.

"Do you have kids, Scarlet?" I asked.

"One daughter." Her eyes immediately lit up at the mention of her. "She's twenty-two. A nursing student."

"That's nice," I said. "Does she look like you?"

"Exactly," she said. "People think we're sisters all the time."

"Because you look like you're in your twenties too," I blurted.

Her smile widened. "Thank you, Thorn..."

Vincent moved his hand to her thigh.

"I've always wanted to have a son," she continued. "But it didn't work out at the time. And my daughter was already a handful. As an only child, she was a bit spoiled. She needed a lot of attention."

"I have a brother, but I still needed a lot of attention," I said with a chuckle. "I'm a bit of a mama's boy."

"He is," Autumn said. "But in a cute way."

I squeezed her hand. "I'm glad you don't think I'm a sissy."

"It's not like you call her every day or something." Autumn sipped her champagne.

A guilty look came over my face.

She caught the expression. "Or you do..."

"She usually calls me right before lunch." I shrugged. "We talk for like fifteen minutes. She asks about the business, but we talk about other things."

She finished her glass before she patted my thigh. "It's okay, Thorn. I still like you anyway."

You still love me anyway. A part of me expected her to

say that, and a part of me hoped she would say that. "The music is still playing. Wanna dance?"

"We'll be the only ones out there."

"So?" I asked.

"And you don't strike me as the kind of guy who dances," she whispered.

"I'm not the kind of guy who has a girlfriend either, but I do." I rose to my feet and helped her out of the chair. I guided her to the dance floor and then pulled her into my chest. Just as Diesel and Tatum had been dancing before, I held Autumn against me and looked into her eyes. In a light pink dress that contrasted against her black hair, she looked like an angel without wings. Tatum had looked beautiful in her wedding dress, but Autumn reached a whole new level of perfection.

"I'm happy for that." Her face was nearly touching mine. "They found a perfect getaway where they don't have to be gawked at by reporters. On Monday, it's bound to be all over the news. But at least they got to have some privacy in the moment."

"There will be lots of speculation when they realize I gave her away."

"I'm sure there will be."

The fire from the torches reflected in Autumn's eyes, her gaze dancing like the flames. Her black hair was pulled over one shoulder, and just like Diesel, all I wanted to do was take her back to our room. "I never want to go back."

"Never?" she asked playfully.

"I'd rather stay here with you...have a honeymoon of our own."

"To have a honeymoon would require us to be married first."

I could freak out at the mere suggestion, but I didn't. After what Tatum and Diesel said on the plane, the words had slowly sunk deeper into my skin with every passing hour. I lay beside Autumn in bed unable to sleep because it was all I could think about. It made me happy to know she loved me, and that could only mean one thing.

I was a goner.

The rest of my life was staring back at me. It was too soon to make a claim like that, but now I knew. All my late nights with random women were over. Weekends in the club were long gone. My single life passed before my eyes, and now I was in a completely different place. Just as Diesel changed the instant he met the right woman, the same had happened to me.

I'd tried to fight it as long as I could, but it was pointless.

It was my fate.

I should accept it like a man.

"What?" Autumn must have noticed the intense way I was staring at her. I couldn't remember the last time I blinked because my gaze had been locked on her for an eternity. Everyone enjoyed their wine and dinner by the tables, oblivious to our quiet moment.

"I like to look at you."

"I know," she whispered. "But I've never seen you look at me quite like that."

Without being able to see my own face, I knew exactly what my expression meant. I knew what kind of feelings were pounding in my chest. The tightness in my throat could only mean one thing. The overwhelming feeling wasn't as frightening as it used to be because I'd finally laid down my weapons and dropped the fight.

I surrendered. "It's the same way you're looking at me."

CHAPTER FIFTEEN

VINCENT

Hand in hand, Scarlet and I walked down the beach in the darkness. The torches along the path around the resort gave us enough light to see where we were going. My slacks were rolled up, and my shoes were left behind.

The waves rolled up the beach, soaking our feet in the warm water.

"That feels nice." Scarlet stayed close beside me, her dress short enough that the water didn't damage the elegant fabric. "I can't remember the last time I went on vacation. Anytime I travel, it's usually for work."

"Me too." I was glad I'd brought Scarlet along. Otherwise, I'd be walking along the shore on my own, thinking about my wedding day. It was the greatest day of my life, and because of that, it hurt. But Scarlet lifted my spirits and made me appreciate what I did have. I was a healthy man with a growing family. Now I had a daughter.

"What changed your mind about bringing me along?"

When I'd asked her to come along, there wasn't time to talk about it. "Diesel."

"Yeah? What did he say?"

"I called early that morning and asked if you could come along. After we were...together...I knew it was the beginning of something. Not the beginning of a meaningless relationship, but the beginning of something deep. I don't want to look back on this day and wish you'd been there to celebrate my son's wedding. He told me he was thrilled I'd changed my mind. He also told me he'd stopped by your office."

She looked down at the water, her expression exactly the same even though she'd been caught in a secret. "Diesel is wonderful. When he came by my office on your behalf, I thought that was the sweetest thing in the world. He wants you to be happy more than anything else in the world."

I'd been touched by the gesture once the surprise wore off. "He's been much better to me than I was to him..."

"He doesn't see it that way, Vincent. Your son loves you."

"I know he does..." Isabella was gone, but she left three pieces of herself for me to enjoy.

"I'm glad you changed your mind. I'm having a great time."

"So am I." I dropped her hand and moved my arm around her waist.

She suddenly stopped walking and turned to me, our feet digging into the sand. Her eyes reflected the moonlight, and the light from the torches highlighted the small smile on her face. She rose on her tiptoes and kissed me on the mouth.

My hand immediately dug into her hair, and I felt my possessiveness come forward. This woman felt like my treasure, something only I got to enjoy. The second I'd made love to her, everything changed. My heart opened and pulled her inside. Now she had infected me everywhere, becoming a part of who I was. She made my life worth living, made happiness easy. "Thank you for being patient with me."

"Of course." Her lips brushed against my mouth as she spoke. "I'd do anything for the man I love."

I didn't react because her words didn't surprise me in the least. I knew she loved me even though she'd never told me. She proved it in every other way, by being patient with me, by writing that article about my character. As much as she wanted me, she went at my pace because that was what I needed. Most women wouldn't settle for half of my heart, but she loved me so much that she didn't care. "And I'd do anything for the woman I love."

CHAPTER SIXTEEN

Titan

The sunlight stilled peeked from behind the blackout shutters and made its way into the room. I felt the heat on my forehead before my eyes opened. I squinted as I looked at the brightness burning inside the bedroom.

Diesel's arm was around my waist as he slept peacefully beside me. His chest rose and fell as the sheets were tucked around him. Six foot three of all muscle, his tight body looked gorgeous in the sunlight.

I wanted to go back to sleep, but the sun was too bright. My eyes turned to the alarm clock on the nightstand, and I saw that it was almost eleven.

Damn, what time did we go to sleep last night?

I sat up in bed and pulled the sheets over my chest. My hair was a mess, so I tamed it the best I could with my fingertips.

Diesel must have realized I'd moved because his hand

reached toward me. "Mrs. Hunt?" He spoke with his baritone voice, his words raspy.

"Does that mean you'll never call me baby again?"

He cleared his throat. "Probably not." He grabbed my elbow and pulled me back to the bed. "Why would I when I have a much sexier name to call you?" He pressed my back to the sheets then moved on top of me, his morning wood anxious to be inside me.

My fingers immediately dug into the hair at the back of his neck, and I opened my legs to him, eager for my husband's thick cock. "True."

He rested his body on his elbows, positioning himself between my legs in the laziest way possible. It was too early for anything complicated. He still had sleep in his eyes, and my body wasn't fully awake yet.

But I was definitely wet.

He guided his dick inside me, and he slid in easily. "Always ready for me..."

"That's just your come from last night."

He moaned in my face. "You've got to be pregnant by now."

"Maybe..."

He thrust gently inside me, his ass tightening as he moved. "That would be a great wedding gift."

Neither one of us had brushed our teeth, but that didn't stop me from pulling his mouth to mine and kissing him. Our lips moved together in mutual passion, and once our tongues danced together, I felt my spine shiver. He'd made me climax many times throughout the night, so I knew my mojo had been ground down.

But I could already feel another.

"Husband...harder."

His hand fisted my hair, and he secured his grip before he thrust into me at a more rigorous pace. The headboard tapped against the wall, and his cock thickened inside me. My slickness completely enveloped him, mixed with all the come he gave me the night before.

Now he was hitting me in the perfect spot. "Right there..."

"So tight, Mrs. Hunt."

I loved hearing him call me that. Titan was long gone, and now I was a Hunt. I'd be a Hunt for the rest of my life. My nails cut into his skin and slid all the way down his back. Marks were scattered all over his body from the savage way I'd dug into him all night. "Yes..." My head rolled back, and my pussy exploded around his big dick.

Diesel fucked me hard into the mattress, bringing me to an even deeper climax just as he released inside me at the same time. His seed was so heavy I could feel it fill my channel. After all the orgasms he had yesterday, I didn't think he'd have anything left to give.

But he certainly did.

He groaned in my face as he finished, his cock twitching as it began to soften. "Jesus..." He rubbed his nose against mine before he kissed me. "I know what we're doing for the rest of the day."

My hands ran up his hard chest. "I'd love to...but I'm pretty hungry."

"Tatum is hungry?" he asked incredulously. "I've never heard that before."

"Well, I don't have to worry about fitting into my wedding dress anymore. And I'm gonna gain a bunch of weight when I'm pregnant anyway, so whatever."

He grinned. "Good point. I'll order room service."

"No, let's go out."

He stared at me like I'd said the wrong thing. "Why would we leave the room?"

"I want to see everyone before they leave. We took off yesterday."

"It's our wedding. We can do whatever we want."

"Yes...but we also have the rest of the day...and two weeks of just the two of us. Come on, Diesel."

Like a bear, he growled at me.

I kissed his chest then his neck. "Do it for your wife..."

"You can't pull that trick on me."

"Yes, I can. It's one of the perks of being Mrs. Hunt."

After a sigh, he rolled off me. "Dammit."

―――――

I wore a short white dress with a new flower crown in my hair. Everyone was seated at a table on the deck of one of the restaurants. Diesel and I had rented out the entire resort, so there wasn't anyone else there to bother us.

"Wow, I didn't think we'd see you two again." Thorn walked up to us and shook Diesel's hand. "And I've never seen you in shorts. It's a good look for you."

Diesel had toned legs, so he looked amazing in anything. "Did you guys enjoy your evening?"

"We had a great time." He gave me a one-arm hug. "But not as great of a time as you did."

"Probably not." Diesel left my side and hugged his father.

"So, how's the baby-making going?" Thorn asked.

I rolled my eyes. "Hope that question was rhetorical."

"You never know," he said. "Maybe you're already knocked up."

"I don't think his swimmers are that fast."

"I don't know... You made him wait a week. Droughts do crazy things to men."

Autumn came to his side and gave me a hug. "You look just as beautiful as you did yesterday. I love your dress."

"Thank you," I said.

"Congratulations," she said. "I've been to a lot of weddings, and I can tell you two are genuinely happy together. It's nice to see."

"Thank you." I knew Diesel and I had something special, and I wouldn't trade it for anything in the world.

"So, I'm not sure what I'm supposed to call you now," Thorn said. "It's been Titan since the day we met. And I'm not going to say Mrs. Hunt every time I want your attention."

"She has a first name." Autumn hooked her arm through his.

Thorn shook his head. "Tatum doesn't sound right...at least from me."

"Hunt?" I asked. "It's only one syllable. Titan was two."

Thorn said the name to himself. "Hunt...Hunt." He nodded. "That works. Hunt, it is."

I moved around the table and greeted everyone else. I hadn't said more than a few words to Thorn's parents yesterday, so I chatted with them now. Then I moved to Isa and Pilar and whispered some of the details of what happened last night. Jax gave me a big hug, and Brett kissed me on the cheek. I went from being an only child to having two brothers. I moved around the table farther until I came back to Diesel.

Diesel was still talking to his father and Scarlet.

"You looked so beautiful yesterday," Scarlet said. "And the way Diesel looked at you...I'll never forget it."

"Thank you," I said. "I'm really glad you could be here."

"Me too," Scarlet said. "I've had a great time. Vincent has been so happy since we got here. He's so relieved his son found the right person. He adores you...he's told me many times."

"He's definitely a great father-in-law. I got lucky."

"He and Diesel are a lot alike... I don't think they even realize it."

Vincent finished speaking to Diesel before he

embraced me. He kissed me on the cheek then hugged me to his chest. "Mrs. Hunt, you look beautiful today." A softness entered his eyes as he looked at me, glancing at the ring on my finger. His wife had worn the same name for so long, and now I was the second one to have it. I knew that was what he was thinking. It was written in his eyes.

"Thank you."

Diesel circled his arm around me again. "She wanted to have breakfast with all of you. I wanted to stay in the room."

"Breakfast?" Thorn asked. "It's eleven thirty."

Diesel ignored him. "So, we're gonna eat then head back to the room."

"Wow," Thorn said. "Diesel really wants a baby."

Vincent turned his gaze back on me. "Are you trying to start a family?"

I'd told Thorn because he was my best friend, but I wasn't sure if Diesel wanted anyone else to know. "Yeah...we are."

Vincent turned his gaze on Diesel, seeking confirmation.

"It's true." Diesel looked down at me affectionately. "We're working on it."

Vincent slid his hands into his pockets, clearly speechless. "I...I'm happy to hear that. Wow, I'm going to be a grandfather."

Scarlet rubbed his back. "This has been a really exciting weekend for you, Vincent."

"Yeah...it really has." The affection burned in his eyes again. "I'm excited. I hope everything works out for you."

"I'm sure it will," Diesel said. "And if it takes a while... that's fine with me too." He grinned then rubbed his nose against mine, not caring about the PDA he was showing in front of his father.

But I did care. "Let's sit down and eat, husband." I took his hand and pulled him to the table.

He pulled out the chair for me then leaned over to kiss me on the forehead. "Best nickname ever."

CHAPTER SEVENTEEN

VINCENT

Once the weekend was over, everyone prepared to leave on my private jet while Diesel and Tatum stayed behind to enjoy the rest of their honeymoon. Scarlet had to get back to work, and the office never stopped for me.

We said our goodbyes at the front of the resort. Tatum and Diesel shared words with everyone else, then came to us last.

"Thank you for coming," Tatum said. "It's been such an amazing weekend. I'm sad it's over."

"We had a great time." I stared at my son with more pride than I'd ever felt. Anyone could get married, but to marry someone as phenomenal as Tatum was rare. Diesel didn't settle for anything less than the best, and I respected him for it. I would never have to worry about him, not when he had such an amazing partner. "I'll never forget it as long as I live." I embraced Tatum first, holding her close the way a father would hug his daughter. She was a Hunt now, but I'd already loved her like my own. I knew her father wasn't there to share this magical day, but I could be what she needed. "I love you, sweetheart."

She gave me the softest expression I'd ever seen. "I love you too, Vincent."

"You're welcome to call me Dad...if you want." I patted her back before I stepped away.

"Alright...I will."

I hugged Diesel next. "I love you, son."

"Love you too, Dad." He patted my back.

"Make me a grandchild." I kissed his forehead before I stepped away.

"I'm working on it," he said with a chuckle. "And I won't let you down."

Scarlet and Tatum exchanged a few words and a long hug.

Diesel noticed them absorbed in their conversation, so he nodded to the left. "Let's talk over here..."

I followed him to the side, my hands resting in my pockets. "Need some honeymoon advice?" I teased.

"No, it's actually about Scarlet."

"Oh?"

"She and I talked in the office for a while, and since you guys are serious now...I feel obligated to tell you something."

"I'm listening."

He glanced at the women to make sure they weren't listening before he looked at me again. "We talked in her office about her ex-husband. I can't say what we talked about, but you should ask her about it the next time the moment is right."

My heart immediately began to pound. "Son, you're scaring me."

"Nothing to be scared of, necessarily. But there's something I think you should know. So ask her about it. I know I'd want to know."

I sighed, feeling my jaw clench. I knew her ex was a bad person. She'd made that clear. I just hoped that *bad* meant he was a cheater or a liar...and not something more sinister. Now that I loved this woman, I'd kill anyone who even looked at her wrong. "Thank you for telling me, Diesel."

"I got your back, Dad. But be casual about it. Don't tell her I said anything to you."

I nodded. "Alright."

He hugged me again. "Call me if you need anything."

"I thought I was supposed to say that to you?"

He shrugged. "It's funny how things change."

———

Scarlet didn't sleep over when we returned to New York. We both had work in the morning, and we were exhausted after all the flying after the short weekend. I went to work and listened to people congratulate me on my son's wedding. Now it was all the media could talk about, the union between two of the richest people in the world.

Now my son bumped me on the Forbes list.

He and Tatum were officially the richest people in the world.

I smiled when I thought about it. Every parent wanted to see their child do better than them. Diesel had achieved the impossible and bypassed me in wealth. I couldn't be prouder.

I skipped lunch and focused on work because I had too much to do. The hours flew by, and before I knew it, it was past five. I was too tired to work out, so I just went home and hopped in the shower.

Now that my mind wasn't occupied by numbers and reports, I thought about what Diesel had said to me. Scarlet was hiding something from me, and now that we were serious, she needed to tell me.

I could wait for her to come to me, or I could just ask her about it.

The gentlemanly thing to do would be to wait.

But I didn't want to wait.

I sat on the couch with a glass of scotch right as she called me.

I answered. "Hello, sweetheart." Using her first name seemed strange now. I'd made love to this woman in my bed, had come inside her many times. Addressing her in the way everyone else did didn't seem fitting.

"Hey." She wasn't her cheerful self. The single greeting highlighted all of her sadness. "I'm sorry to be so presumptuous, but could I come over? I'm standing in your lobby, and the security guard is staring me down."

I walked to the elevator and hit the button. "Of course. You're always welcome." We hung up, and then she rose in the elevator to my floor. She stepped out in jeans and a black blouse, looking as beautiful as always but with sadness painted across her expression.

She moved into me, rose on her tiptoes, and kissed me.

My arms circled her waist, and I kissed her back, loving the curves of her body. She was a petite woman, perfect to fit inside my powerful arms. I squeezed the fabric of her blouse tightly with my large hands, scrunching it as I enjoyed her soft mouth.

I could kiss her forever.

She pulled away first, her eyes heavier than usual.

"Tell me." My hand cupped her cheek, and my fingertips rested on her neck.

"The owner of the magazine saw that I was at Diesel's wedding. She knows we're serious, and she's asked me to do some immoral reporting. She wants me to write an explicit narrative about what it's like being in a relationship with you. And she wants me to dig into Diesel's relationship with Tatum, especially since Thorn gave her away at the wedding. I told her it was a conflict of interest...she didn't care. So she gave me an ultimatum. I write the articles or I lose my job. So, I quit."

I slowly lowered my hand to her shoulder, hit with the weight of her sorrow. Scarlet had run that magazine for quite some time, and she did an outstanding job. To be harassed into doing something she didn't want to do was completely unprofessional. She loved being the editor of *Platform,* but she walked away from it...for me.

She was loyal to me.

"Sweetheart, I'm so sorry..."

She bowed her head. "I really loved working there. I dedicated so much of my life to that magazine. I worked late nights without being paid for it, and I went above and beyond. To be reduced to someone that is so easily replaceable...is insulting. I feel like I have more value than being able to report about the Hunts. It's just work, and I shouldn't take it so personally...but I do." She stepped into my chest and rested her face against my body.

I enveloped her in my arms, protecting her against the pain the only way I knew how. "It'll be alright."

"I have money in my savings and a few investments, so I'll be fine until I can find something else. But, honestly, I don't want to go somewhere else. I believed in that magazine. She made a mistake letting me go."

"Yes, she did."

She sighed against my chest and stayed there for a long time. She closed her eyes and used me as a crutch to lean on. "I'm so glad I have you. I was so upset, and now... I feel a lot better." She breathed into my chest before she pulled away and looked up at me.

My hand moved into her hair, and I pressed my forehead against hers. "You never have to worry about anything as long as you have me." I could make all her problems go away with the snap of my fingers. I knew exactly what I was going to do to fix this, and I would tell her once it was done.

She smiled. "You're so sweet to me, Vincent."

I kissed her softly on the forehead. "How about some dinner?"

Her hands slid up to my biceps. "Honestly, I just want to go to bed..."

It was seven o'clock, so I knew she wasn't interested in sleeping. She was only interested in me. "Sounds good to me."

———

I lay behind her and kissed her exposed shoulder. I trailed my lips across her body then to the shell of her ear. "I'd like to meet your daughter."

"You would?" She looked at me over her shoulder, looking beautiful with smeared makeup and swollen lips.

"Yes."

"I have to be honest and tell you she'll probably be difficult."

"I deal with difficult people every day."

She chuckled. "I just mean, she's not sweet like your sons. I don't want you to be disappointed if she doesn't approve of you."

"I'm sure she'll come around, eventually."

"She is close with her father, unfortunately..."

Now was my opening. I should probably wait until a

better time, but my curiosity was too strong. "Will I be seeing him often?"

"No. I never see him. We spend every event separately, which I don't mind. For her college graduation, I'll have to be in the same room with him. But even then, I'll be in the opposite corner."

"May I ask why there's such hostility?" Now the ball was in her court. She could either tell me now or postpone it.

But she'd better tell me now.

A long sigh escaped her lips. "I'm only telling you this because you have a right to know. He used to be jealous and possessive of me. At first, I thought it was romantic. But then he turned violent and angry. The relationship became an abusive one. I tried to leave for a long time until I finally had the courage to run. The first two years were difficult because he kept trying to pin me under his thumb. One night, he broke in to my apartment to get to me. I was ready for him, and I beat him with a baseball bat until half of his ribs were broken. After that...he finally left me alone. We say very little to each other now."

A flush of pride washed over me when I heard that story. She took matters into her own hands and did what every woman should do. But that pride didn't last long because depression quickly replaced it. The fact that this man had ever laid a hand on her sent me into a kind of rage I'd never known. The last time I was this angry was when that careless piece of shit hit my wife with his car.

Scarlet didn't look at me. "I can feel how angry you are..."

I kissed the back of her neck to offset my hostility. "It's hard not to be."

"It was a long time ago. I'm fine now. He doesn't bother me anymore."

"Doesn't change the fact that it never should have happened." I pulled her closer into my chest and kissed the back of her head. "Nothing will ever hurt you again, sweetheart. I can promise you that." I couldn't protect my wife after she got into that car, but I would never make the same mistake again.

"You don't need to protect me, Vincent. That's not why I need you."

"Then why do you need me?"

She turned to look at me over her shoulder again. "Because you make me happy."

———

Three days later, it was done.

The money had been wired into the account, and one of my corporations was on the deed of ownership.

I was the new owner of *Platform* magazine.

It wasn't cheap, but I knew it was the best investment I'd ever made.

I couldn't wait to tell Scarlet when I saw her later. She'd be shocked, of course. She'd probably refuse in the beginning, but I would wear her down.

I wasn't going to let some corporate asshole make my woman feel like shit.

No one fucked with Vincent Hunt.

My PI walked in the door a few hours later. "I got the information you asked for." He tossed the folder onto the desk.

I opened it and took a look inside. I had the asshole's full name, address, bank statements, photo ID, and his personal routine. He owned a bar in Brooklyn and spent his afternoons behind the counter. "This is perfect. Thank you."

"Anything else, Mr. Hunt? You want me to send someone down there to intimidate him?"

Who could be more intimidating than me? "No. I got it."

He walked out of my office.

I stared at his name, searing it into my memory.

Colin David.

———

In the middle of the afternoon, the bar was depressing. Mostly old men hung out in the low-lit room. Guys played pool in the back corner, and the sports channel was on every TV.

I spotted him the second I walked inside, immediately regretting wearing my five-thousand-dollar tailored suit into a run-down piss-hole like this. He was in black t-shirt and jeans, sporting dark hair and a somewhat sculpted body. He was good-looking, but his habits hadn't preserved his age the way Scarlet had. He looked my age even though he had to be a decade years younger.

I approached the bar but didn't rest my hand on the wood, too dirty for the fabric of my suit. Everything about this shitty joint was disgusting.

Colin walked toward me. "What can I get for you, man?"

"You think I'd drink anything in this dump?"

He obviously hadn't been expecting me to say that because it took him at least two seconds to even process my words. His eyes narrowed, and his jaw clenched automatically. He probably saw hotheads on a daily basis, but he still couldn't control his anger. "What did you say, asshole?"

"I said this shithole is a dump," I said calmly. "And you fit in perfectly."

He paused as he stared me down, but he didn't immediately throw a punch or grab a bat under the counter. He must have recognized my face, knowing I was too rich and well-connected for him to throw a punch. He had some form of a brain, apparently. "Get the fuck out of my bar."

"Not until I introduce myself."

"I know who you are," he snapped. "No matter how rich you are, I'll never want your money. So fuck off."

"You recognize me, but you have no idea who I am." I leaned toward him over the bar. "I'm Vincent Hunt, the tenth richest man on this planet. I have the power to throw your tortured body into the river and make sure the police never find it. And even if they did, I have the cash to make them look the other way. I have the power to burn this shithole to the ground and make sure you never see a penny from the insurance company. I have the ability to make your life absolutely insufferable. I can take away all your rights and all your freedoms." I snapped my fingers. "Just like that."

He was absolutely still, alternating between anger and fear.

"I'm also the man Scarlet loves."

He couldn't stop his face from reacting.

"She's my woman. And she told me exactly what you did to her. She may have broken your ribs with a bat to scare you off, but I'll do something a million times worse. If you ever cross her, ever look at her, ever stand within five hundred feet of that woman, I'll break every individual bone in your body, all the toes, all the fingers, and even your skull. Do you understand me, asshole?"

His hands clutched the counter, and his knuckles turned white because he gripped it so hard. Paralyzed, he knew there was nothing he could do. He knew he was a small fish in a big pond, and I was the biggest shark in the goddamn ocean. He was nothing compared to me. He was just a pathetic excuse for a man who had preyed on someone weaker than him. And we both knew the tables had turned. Now he was the weak one...and I was his worst nightmare.

I held my hand, my thumb and forefinger pressed

together. "You don't want to know what happens when I snap my fingers." I wouldn't hold back in my vengeance. If he was anything less than cooperative, I would enjoy his slow torture. "Do you understand me?"

This time, he answered immediately. "Yes."

"Good." I finally turned away from the bar, making sure I didn't touch anything. "Have a good day, Colin. I hope you enjoy being under my thumb for the rest of your life." I turned my back to him as I walked out the door, unafraid of his retaliation.

Because we both knew he was a little bitch.

———

When I got home, I called Scarlet. "How was your day?"

"I did two cycling classes because I didn't know what to do with myself. But my thighs are going to look really great in a few weeks."

They already looked fabulous. "Would you like to come over for dinner?" I used to take her out all the time, but now it seemed like we both preferred the privacy of our homes. Now that everyone was talking about the wedding, I was avoiding cameras even more.

"Always. Just assume that's my answer."

I smiled. "Then get over here."

"Should I pick up anything?"

"No." Just her bare skin was more than enough.

She arrived fifteen minutes later, taking the elevator with the code I gave her. Now she could come up whenever she wanted. It was practically the same thing as giving her a key to my place. But if she ever needed somewhere to retreat, my penthouse was always open to her.

I greeted her with a kiss by the door and squeezed her petite waist. "I missed you today."

"I missed you too."

I would love to come home and see her every day. It was too soon to ask her to move in, but the idea of sharing my space with her didn't scare me at all. It would be nice to have someone there all the time. It was one of the things I missed most about Isabella. There was always a hot dinner on the table and a warm smile on her lips when I walked in the door. When we were young, our kids would run around creating havoc all over the place, but I loved it.

"What's for dinner?" she asked.

"My maid cooked up chicken and veggies."

She grinned. "I'm gonna lose so much weight with you."

"Not my intention. You're perfect the way you are."

"For such an aggressive man, you're unnaturally sweet."

"I'm just sweet to you. Trust me, you wouldn't want to work with me."

"Yeah, you're probably right."

Little did she know, I was about to be her new boss.

We sat down to dinner at the table and talked over our meal. I told her I hadn't spoken to Diesel that week. He was hidden away from the world on his honeymoon. Brett and I had lunch yesterday, and I saw Jax on a daily basis. She told me about the guy her daughter was still seeing. Their relationship seemed to be getting serious.

"I'm going to start applying to new places this week." She swirled her wine before she drank it. "One week away from work and I'm already bored out of my mind." She chuckled then swirled her wine again.

I'd been waiting to tell her the news at a different time, but it looked like this was happening now. "Actually, I have a job offer for you."

She shook her head and chuckled. "I appreciate that, Vincent. But I really don't want to work for you. The idea of sleeping with my boss sounds like a bad idea."

Hopefully, that wasn't the case in this situation. "I wouldn't be your boss. You would be the head of the company. I'd just be a private investor."

She smiled like she thought this was all a joke. "If you're going to pay to tie me to your headboard, you know I'll do that for free."

The idea was immediately arousing. "I bought *Platform* earlier this week. I made an offer that couldn't be refused, and now it's mine. I don't intend to change anything about the way it's run. And I want you to resume your position as the editor in chief. Run it the way you always have."

She dropped her wineglass on the table, and the red contents spilled everywhere.

I threw my napkin on the table and captured the pool

before it could spill onto the hardwood floor. I quickly contained it then turned my gaze back to her.

Scarlet was still stunned. "I...I'm sorry."

"It's alright. No harm done."

She slowly found her voice again. "You really did that?"

I nodded.

"You bought my magazine?"

I nodded again. "It's always good to diversify. I don't have any assets in fashion publishing."

"But Vincent... This is... There are no words."

"You'll take the job, right?"

She never answered the question. "I can always work somewhere else. There will always be a job out there."

"*Platform* isn't just a job to you. It's so much more."

"But that's not your problem, Vincent. You didn't need to do that. I'm not dating you so you can throw money at all my problems and make them go away."

I didn't throw money at Colin. "You're the woman I love, Scarlet. I'm sorry, but I'm going to make every little pothole in the road disappear. I'm going to pave the way with a red carpet. Whatever you want, I'm going to make it happen. You will always be surrounded by my power and privilege everywhere you go, even if I'm nowhere in sight. You are now royalty in New York City. I hope you don't turn down my offer just to make a point. I know you love me for me, not for the things I can do for you. But if you really want me, you're going to have to learn to accept my generosity."

She grabbed my glass of wine from across the table and took a long drink. Her eyes slowly faded from shock to conflicted calm. She took another drink, savoring the taste on her tongue.

I continued to stare at her.

"I really love *Platform*... I don't want to say no."

"Then don't. It's yours."

"Vincent..." She pushed the glass back. "I don't know what to say."

"You don't need to say anything. I love you, and I will give you the world every chance I get."

"I know...but I can't believe how lucky I am. You could have any woman in the world, but you chose me. I've never been really loved by a man. I've never been treated with such respect and adoration. It's unfortunate that I finally found the right man so late in life, but I'm thankful that I found you at all."

I found her hand and squeezed it. "I'm lucky too. You've been so patient with me."

"Because you were worth waiting for," she whispered.

I'd been with a lot of women who didn't mean anything to me. I never wanted to actually care about someone else. I wanted to wait until I was well enough to truly adore someone the way I adored my wife. And now she was here. "You were worth the wait too."

Her eyes softened. "Of course, I want that job."

"Then it's yours. I just want to make some changes."

"Such as?"

"I want you to model a line of clothes for women your

age. And have models your age as well, women who are beautiful without all the plastic surgery. We should make a fashion line that embraces an aging woman with elegance and beauty."

She smiled. "I think that's a great idea."

"Then let's do it."

"I'm going to enjoy working with you. You didn't get to the top without being the smartest man in the world."

"Actually, I'm not at the top anymore. Diesel is." I smiled with pride.

"And I know where he learned it from..." She grabbed the cloth napkin on the table and finished cleaning up. "Sorry about this. I'm not a clumsy person. I was just—"

"It's fine. Really." I grabbed the napkin and set it to the side. "We'll clean it up later."

"You really do let me get away with anything."

"Pretty much."

She refilled her wineglass and focused on eating again.

Now that I finished telling her one surprise, I had to move on to the next. She would probably be annoyed by what I did, but I didn't feel bad about it. Colin needed to know he'd made enemies with the most powerful man in the world. He thought he could take advantage of Scarlet because she was a small woman, but he didn't anticipate that she would one day stand behind the strongest man in the city. Should have been more careful. "There's something else I need to tell you. But you aren't going to be happy about it."

"That sounds ominous...what is it?"

"I had a little talk with Colin."

She did a double take, clearly surprised that I even knew his first name. She never told me any of that information.

I set my fork down and waited for her anger to rise.

"You...what?"

"I went by his bar in Brooklyn."

"And how did you know any of that? I never mentioned it..."

"The second you told me what he did, I had a guy dig into him. Got all the information I needed then confronted him."

"Oh no..." She dropped her fork. "Vincent...what were you thinking?"

"I just gave him a warning."

"He hasn't bothered me in eight years. He's not an issue anymore."

"I don't care if he's an issue or not." I couldn't keep my suave coolness anymore. My anger was frothing like hot milk in an espresso machine. "He tortured you because he thought he could get away with it. Now he's paying the price. Now he's made enemies with a bully a hundred times stronger...and I'm gonna make him walk on eggshells for the rest of his life. I threatened to kill him if he ever came near you again."

She covered her face with her hands. "Vincent...he's the father of my child."

"He won't mention it to her."

"What if he does?"

No man would admit he was a pussy to his daughter. "Trust me, he won't."

"And he hasn't bothered me in—"

"I don't give a shit. That fucker will pay for what he did to you. Giving him chronic anxiety is how I attempt to do that—in a nonviolent matter. I would have just paid men to jump him, but out of respect for your daughter, I didn't."

"Vincent, if you want my daughter to like you, this isn't the way to accomplish that."

I wanted her respect, but I had to put Scarlet first. "You need to tell her what really happened. She has the right to know."

She quickly looked away. "I can't do that, Vincent."

"Yes, you can. You're letting her believe a lie."

"I don't want her to hate her father."

"She should hate her father and forgive him in her own time. He has to face the consequences of his actions. This isn't about getting her to like me. This is the right thing to do. Have you ever been worried what he might do to her?"

She shook her head. "He would never hurt her. He's only like that with women he 'loves.'"

"She needs to know, Scarlet. You can tell her, or he can tell her."

"Colin will be the last person to mention it."

I narrowed my eyes. "He's a puppet on the string, and I'm the master. If you want him to tell her, I can make it happen. That little bitch is under my thumb now."

"I don't know…"

"It would be better coming from him," I said. "She'll know it's the truth, and she might be more likely to forgive him since he brought it up to her on his own terms. He waited ten years to do it…but at least he's doing it."

She dragged her hands down her face. "Maybe I shouldn't have told you…"

I could admit I'd done something irrational, but when it came to Scarlet, I was fiercely protective and aggressive. She'd become one of the most important people in my life, and I had to make sure she was safe. "You did the right thing, Scarlet. If we don't address this now, there's no reason why he won't bother you again."

"If he did, I'd break his ribs again with a bat," she threatened.

"And I'd rather you not deal with that all. Your daughter is living a lie, and it's very important to me that she likes me…or at least accepts me. If she's still upset because she thinks you gave up on your marriage too easily, I'll never stand a chance. I know my sons like you, and I want her to like me."

She stared at me solemnly. "I want her to like you too."

"And you know that's very unlikely."

She gave a nod.

"So how do you want to do this? Do you want him to tell her? Or do you want to do it?"

She considered it for a long time. "I think we should do it together—as a family."

My eyes narrowed. "I don't want him anywhere near you."

"I understand that. But this is a family matter. She's our daughter, and I want to work through it. She'll be upset with him, but I want her to know that I want her to forgive him."

I was stunned by her response. No other woman would feel that way about her ex-husband. The fact that she wanted to preserve their relationship was a testament to her commitment to motherhood. She didn't care about herself, only her daughter.

It reminded me of Isabella.

"Have you forgiven him?" I asked.

"He's never apologized."

"But you want her to forgive him."

"I don't have any connection to him. He's her father... it's completely different."

I might not agree with all of that, but I had to respect it. If I'd ever raised a hand to Isabella, I'd have expected all of my sons to defend her and turn their backs on me. I'd have expected them to make me pay for what I did. But we had different philosophies. "How do you want to do this, then?"

"I'll call him."

"No, I want to be there. If I'm present, it'll make this process a lot smoother."

Scarlet must have known that was the best compromise she would find, because she agreed. "Alright."

———

We walked into the bar and headed to the counter. Scarlet walked with her hand held in mind, not the least bit afraid coming face-to-face with her former attacker. She knew I was there to protect her, but she also knew she could break his ribs again if she needed to.

Colin spotted me immediately and tensed behind the counter with obvious fear.

That's right, bitch.

I got to the counter and stared him down.

He didn't even notice his ex-wife until then. He took his time wiping down the mug he was holding before he finally walked over to us. Both hands rested against the counter, and he stared at us timidly.

I never took my eyes off him.

"Colin." Scarlet walked up to him, a woman far too classy to be inside this dirty bar.

He stayed silent.

"I think it's time we told Lizzie what really happened between us."

He heaved a deep sigh, full of anger and aggression that he couldn't act on. "And I have to cooperate, otherwise, I'll get stuffed in a dumpster?"

"Not quite," she said. "I can tell her on my own, or we can tell her together. You have a choice."

He bowed his head, his left hand still gripping the rag. "Scar, I—"

"Her name is Scarlet." He lost any privilege to call her by a nickname.

He didn't look at me. "We haven't spoken in...eight years. That's a long time."

"Yes," she said. "And it's been nice."

The corner of my mouth rose in a smile.

"I have a girlfriend now," he said. "We share an apartment together here in Brooklyn. I really like her and want to ask her to marry me."

"I don't see what that has to do with this," she said gently.

"I mention it because...I've thought a lot over the past eight years." His eyes moved to the surface of the bar. "The way I acted...the way I treated you...it was wrong. I hate myself for what I did. I'm a lot different than I used to be. With Mary, I'm different. I wish I could have been that way to you, and I'm sorry I wasn't. I didn't know how to control my anger, and...there's no excuse. I shouldn't even bother trying to justify my behavior."

Scarlet was clearly speechless.

"I was in the hospital for a few days because of my broken ribs." He spoke quietly so the other patrons in the bar couldn't hear him. "That gave me a lot of time to think. I couldn't believe I broke in to your apartment and I was waiting for you. I wasn't even sure what I was trying to do. It was a reality check for me. It made me realize I didn't want to be that guy... I never want to be that guy again."

"I appreciate your saying that," Scarlet whispered.

"Lizzie is my whole world," he continued. "I don't want her to hate me for what I did, especially since I'm not that guy anymore. If we tell her...she'll never forgive me."

"That's too damn bad," I snapped.

Scarlet turned to me and placed her hand on my forearm. "Vincent, please."

I sighed and shut my mouth.

She turned back to Colin. "She'll forgive you. She'll need a few months to let it go, but I know she will. That's why we should tell her together. I want her to forgive you, and I'll tell her that myself. I love the relationship you two have. I don't want you to lose it either."

He bowed his head and sighed, gripping the counter at the same time. "God, I'm dreading this..."

"I am too," Scarlet said. "But she thinks I'm the reason we aren't together. I want her to meet Vincent and give him a chance. Anytime I introduced her to a man I was seeing, she wouldn't give him the time of day. And I know it's because of you."

He nodded.

"And I'm going to spend the rest of my life with Vincent. I need her to like him."

All the anger I felt immediately disappeared from my body. I turned to her, feeling my heart swell to twice its size. My fingertips felt warm, and my entire body flushed with the comfortable heat. I stared at the side of her face, touched by her words.

"You're engaged?" Colin whispered.

"No," Scarlet said. "I don't know if we'll ever get married, but he's the man I love. I want our daughter to love him too. He's not going anywhere, and I'm certainly not going anywhere either."

My hand moved to the small of her back, and I rested it there, reacting to her statement in silence.

"So, how do you want to do this?" Scarlet asked. "You want me to tell her?"

"No," Colin said quietly. "Let's do it together...and hope for the best."

CHAPTER EIGHTEEN

THORN

A week went by, and all Autumn and I did was work and fuck.

But not at the same time.

My mind was cluttered with endless thoughts and feelings. During the wedding, I felt my feelings only deepen for Autumn. I pictured my own wedding, something I'd never done before. I imagined where we would live together. I imagined what our children would look like. I'd always wanted my own family, and now I pictured what that would be like with Autumn.

Maybe Diesel and Tatum were both right.

A part of me argued I was just being logical about the relationship. I needed to marry someone, and Autumn fit all of my requirements. I was just excited about starting a family, and I needed a uterus to do that.

But I also knew that was bullshit.

If Autumn ended up with someone else, I wouldn't be so logical about it.

I would be devastated.

Toward the end of the afternoon, Autumn arrived in my office. Sexy in tall heels and a tight skirt, she rocked the room like a model on the runway. She made being a geek the next biggest trend. She smiled when she walked inside, her bag over her shoulder. "Hey."

My response was nothing but a stare.

She sauntered to the desk and stopped in front of me. "I have some stuff we need to go over. We're behind on preorders, and if I don't order new equipment and hire more employees, I'm not going to fulfill them. I don't know if we need to get approval from Tatum or if we can just move forward."

I interlocked my fingers behind my head.

She cocked her head to the side. "Are you going to say anything?"

I nodded to the double doors. "If those weren't made of glass, you'd be bent over this desk right now."

She kept a straight face but couldn't hide the blush that entered her cheeks. "You just fucked me good this morning."

"And I want to fuck you again." I wanted to do exactly what Tatum and Diesel were doing. I wanted to fuck her a million times until she was finally pregnant and round. "It's been almost eight hours."

"Maybe we can revisit this conversation once we're done with work for the day..."

"Whatever you say, baby." I finally rose from my desk, my hard-on obvious in my slacks.

Her eyes glanced down, seeing the obvious bulge.

"Show-off..."

"You're the only one I'm showing off for."

———

We left the building together, hand in hand. "You want to get some dinner?"

"I think we should keep a low profile. I've been bombarded by reporters left and right."

"I don't give a damn. There's a deli right on the corner. Want to go there?"

She moved closer into my side and walked with me. "You don't care about all the people taking pictures of us?"

"Why would I? I'm being photographed with the sexiest woman on the planet. It's not like it makes me look bad."

We arrived at the deli and ordered our food at the counter. We took a seat in the booth and ate our sandwiches and shared a bag of chips. There was hardly anyone in there despite the hour. We ate in comfortable silence, and I stared at her as I considered how I would fuck her when we got back to my place.

She seemed to be thinking the same thing because a slight smile was on her lips.

A few minutes later, the bell rang overhead as

someone stepped inside. The sound of a little girl laughing filled the restaurant. My back was to them, so I couldn't see who they were.

But Autumn obviously recognized them. She stopped eating and stared at them, her face immediately turning as white as snow.

I turned around to glance at them, and all I saw was a handsome man, a pretty wife, and a cute kid. I turned back to her.

Her head was down, and all of her playfulness had evaporated.

"What's wrong?"

"Nothing." She rolled up her sandwich even though she hadn't eaten much. She ignored the bag of chips too. "I had a big lunch. Want to get out of here?"

She never appeared frantic. She was always confident even in the most hostile situations. "What is it?"

She glanced at the people again, who were still standing at the counter. "That's Max." She kept her voice low so they wouldn't overhear us. "Pretty awkward that we're the only two people in here..."

"Oh..." Now I'd lost my appetite too, thinking about the man who broke Autumn's heart.

She slid out of the booth first, ready to leave before they turned around. She didn't even take her sandwich.

I stood up to follow her. I was about to walk with her to the door, but I turned to look at him instead. A handsome guy with short brown hair, he was my height with a nice smile. His arm was around his wife while she held their daughter.

They seemed happy.

Autumn stopped at the door and looked at me, her eyes narrowed.

I didn't know what I was doing. I wasn't thinking at all. I walked up to Max and tapped him on the shoulder.

"Thorn," Autumn hissed under her breath.

Max turned around, immediately defensive because he had no idea who I was.

I extended my hand. "I'm Thorn Cutler. You're Max, right?"

He hesitated before he shook my hand. "Yeah...do we know each other?"

"No." I nodded to Autumn by the door, who looked thoroughly embarrassed. "But you remember Autumn."

Max glanced at her, and when he turned back to me, he was even more confused.

"I just wanted to thank you for leaving her for someone else. If you hadn't done that...I wouldn't have found the love of my life. She's the most amazing woman in the world, and I can't believe she's mine. I love her more than you ever did... and I would never trade her in for someone else." I gave him a cold look before I turned away, leaving my words behind so they could sink into his flesh. Autumn deserved to walk away from that relationship with dignity. I wanted him to know that he'd made a mistake, that Autumn was loved by someone else more than he could ever love his wife.

I walked out, Autumn trailing behind me. "I'm sorry... I know you must be pissed at me." I paused before I turned around and faced her wrath.

She wasn't mad at all. In fact, her eyes were wet with tears. "I can't believe you said that."

"I wasn't thinking... It just makes me mad that guy hurt you so much."

"So...did you mean any of that?"

"Of course, I did." I'd walked up to him, and words just started pouring out of my mouth. I switched into instinct mode, talking without forethought. I wanted that guy to feel guilty for what he did, but I also didn't want him to pity Autumn anymore. She was over him, and she had a much better man now.

"Then you love me?"

I didn't even realize I'd said it until that moment. I was running my mouth and talking with my heart instead of my brain. But if I said it without thinking, then it really must be true. That wasn't how I wanted to tell my woman I loved her—not for the first time. But the damage had been done. "Yeah...I do."

"Thorn..." She moved into my chest and wrapped her arms around my neck. "I love you too."

Seeing her heartfelt reaction chased away any doubt I had. I'd never wanted my life to change, but then I met a woman I wanted to change everything for. She didn't love me for my wealth or my power, not when she had her own. She loved me for me...and you couldn't put a price on that. "I know you do."

"You know?" she whispered, her eyes still wet.

"I heard you tell your mother last week."

She tensed in my arms, her eyes turning rigid. "You heard that...?"

"I was trying to find the bathroom, and I overheard."

"Oh..."

"But it didn't scare me. Made me really happy, actually. That's when I started to realize how I felt about you."

"Yeah?"

"And Diesel and Tatum said a few things to me too. I guess I was scared to tell you... And then it came tumbling out when I told Max off. Sorry...that isn't how I wanted to tell you."

"Don't apologize...I loved it." She cupped my face and rose on her tiptoes to kiss me. She moved closer into my body, her tits pressed right against my chest. Her lips trembled against mine, but her passion was unmistakable.

I squeezed the steep curve of her back, positioning her as tightly as possible against my body. My mouth moved against hers, and the sensation felt right. I never wanted to kiss anyone else. I only wanted this woman— this perfect woman. People stopped to take pictures of us, but I didn't care what anyone thought.

Because I was happy.

CHAPTER NINETEEN

Tatum

The last six months of my life had been pretty crazy.

I lost the love of my life.

Got him back.

I was shot.

And I got married.

A lot of stuff to happen in such a short amount of time.

But all my struggles had been completely worth it in the end. There were times when I wanted to give up, to retire and live out my life away from the public eye. There were times when I wanted to give up on love and settle for convenience. There were times when I wanted to give up on humanity altogether.

But I was glad I didn't.

Now I had everything I could ever want.

I sat on the floor and leaned against the wall in the

bathroom with the pregnancy test stick in my grasp. The previous two weeks had been spent locked away in a tropical paradise as we enjoyed the beautiful beaches by day and each other at night. We rarely slept, but all the good sex made it worth it.

Now we were back in New York, and I was sitting in my bathroom.

Staring at the test that would change my life forever.

It was positive.

I was pregnant.

I held the plastic stick in my hand and stared at the plus sign inside the indicator. Bright and blue, it was the most beautiful thing I'd ever seen. I didn't think it would be possible in such a short period of time. My IUD hadn't been removed much before we started to try for a baby.

But now I had a bun in the oven.

Diesel would be happy.

I finally left the bathroom and walked into the living room. Diesel was sitting on the couch with his laptop in front of him. He'd worked all day, but he was still catching up on everything he missed. He didn't have someone to cover his stuff the way Thorn did for me. He was shirtless and barefoot, looking like the sexiest man in the world right in my living room. A cold beer sat on the table, and the game was on the TV.

After spending two weeks together, it made sense that we would be sick of each other by now, but we certainly weren't.

I slowly walked behind the couch, unsure how I wanted to tell him the good news.

He turned to me when he realized I was there. He must have noticed the expression on my face because he asked. "What is it, baby?"

I sauntered toward him then moved into his lap. "I have good news."

"What?"

I pulled the stick from behind my back and held it up for him to see.

It took him a second to understand what he was looking at. He stared at the plus sign blankly before his hand reached out to grab it. He stared at it harder, and then suddenly, every hard line of his expression faded away into softness. He sat forward farther, gripping it with his other hand like it might tumble out of his fingertips. Then the biggest smile spread across his face, lighting up his eyes like the New York skyline. I'd never seen him so happy, not even the day he married me. "I can't believe it..."

"It didn't take long, did it?"

He chuckled. "No, it didn't."

I rested my head on his shoulder and hooked my arm through his. "Little Hunt..."

"Our little Hunt."

"I wonder if they're going to be a boy or a girl."

"I don't care."

I smiled.

"My baby is on the way..." He took a deep breath then

released. "I know it's happening, but I still can't believe it. With our love, we made something. It's incredible."

"I'm going to get cranky and chunky, so it's not going to be a fairy tale all the time."

"I'm looking forward to that. I want to take care of you."

"I know you will, Diesel."

He set down the stick and kissed me on the forehead. "I'm so happy, baby."

"Me too."

"Let's keep this to ourselves for a little bit...enjoy it."

"Okay," I whispered. "But not too long. I won't be able to explain why I'm smiling all the time."

———

Thorn caught me up on what I'd missed. It took us two days to cover everything.

"That's it," Thorn said. "Are you sure you don't want me to stick around for a little longer?"

"No. You have your own things to do, Thorn."

"Because I don't mind."

I rolled my eyes. "You just want to see your girlfriend all the time."

"Pssh," he said. "I see her every night in my bed."

Now it was my turn to roll my eyes. "Too much info."

"What about you? Is Diesel still hammering you every night?"

"Yes..."

Thorn caught the smile on my face. His eyes narrowed like a cat that just saw a bird out of the corner of his eye. "What's that look for?"

"What? I'm a newlywed."

"No, that's a different smile. This smile means you're hiding something."

Now I had two people who knew me better than I knew myself. It was frustrating sometimes.

"What is it?" he pressed.

"Nothing."

"You're pregnant, aren't you?"

"What?" I asked incredulously. "What would make you think that?"

"Because you aren't going to smile just because you're getting good sex. You're going to smile for a different reason...and that's the only one I can think of."

I couldn't look him in the eye. It was too damn hard.

"Holy shit, you are pregnant."

"Diesel and I wanted to keep it as a surprise a little longer...but that's obviously not going to happen."

"Yes!" Thorn threw his fist in the air. "That's so awesome. Congratulations." He came around the desk and hugged me.

I didn't want to lie about it anymore, so I just embraced it. "Thank you."

"I can't believe this, Hunt."

It was still taking time for me to get used to my new name. "I know...Diesel was really happy."

He pulled away and pressed his hand against my stomach. "Can you believe there's a little person growing inside you?"

I swatted his hand away. "There's nothing to feel yet. But no, I can't believe it either."

Thorn slid his hands into his pockets. "I'm really happy for you. Everything came together for you in the end, and you got everything you wanted. Imagine if you did marry me... You wouldn't have any of this."

"I know..."

"And I wouldn't have Autumn...a very scary thought."

I smiled. "You've got it bad, Thorn."

He rubbed the back of his neck as he grinned. "I told her I loved her the other day."

"What?" I asked in shock. "Thorn Cutler told a woman he loved her?"

"It just slipped out...but I'm glad I said it."

"Wow. We both have something to be happy about."

"Yeah, we do."

"I'm happy for you, Thorn. Now I'm really happy we never got married. Autumn is wonderful...perfect for you."

"Yeah, she is," he said in agreement. "I'll never let her go."

"Family for you anytime soon?"

"I don't know about that...I've gotta marry her first."

"And when is that happening?"

"I don't know. I'm not sure."

"You know, you don't have to wait a year before you do it. If you know, you know."

"True..." He stepped away and dismissed the conversation. "Looks like everything worked out for both of us in the end."

"Of course it did. We both deserve it."

He smiled at me before he grabbed his satchel from the chair. "I guess I'll head out, then."

"Thank you for everything, Thorn. I really appreciate it."

"You don't need to thank me, Hunt. When I go on my honeymoon, I know you'll cover for me."

"You're right. I will."

Jessica spoke through the intercom. "Mrs. Hunt, there's a Bridget Creed here to see you. She's stopped by the office a few times while you've been away."

I raised an eyebrow, having no idea who that was. "Bridget Creed?"

Thorn's eyes nearly popped out of his head.

It took me a second to realize where I'd heard that name before. Thorn had mentioned it over a month ago.

The woman who could possibly be my mother.

Thorn looked terrified.

"Hold on, Jessica." I turned to him. "What aren't you telling me?"

Thorn didn't hold his secret for long. He was backed up against a wall. "She's stopped by a few other times to talk to you."

"And?"

"That's about it. She wants to see you."

"Because?"

He sighed before he spoke. "Diesel did some digging... and confirmed she's your mother."

I didn't react because not a single emotion came to mind. I suspected this woman could be my mother, but whether she was or wasn't, it didn't make a difference to me. She'd walked out of my life. That door was shut, and she couldn't walk back through it. "Of course, Diesel stuck his nose where it doesn't belong."

"Good thing you married him," he said sarcastically.

I crossed my arms over my chest. "Does she want money?"

"She claims she doesn't. I told her she should just leave you alone. You're a grown woman, and you don't need her. But she wanted the chance to talk to you in person before she gave up."

"So maybe I should just have this conversation so I can get rid of her?"

He shrugged. "I'll stay if you want."

"No, I'll be fine."

"Are you sure? If I thought she was dangerous, I would stick around."

"I can handle it, Thorn. I'm annoyed I have to spend time dealing with this, but ignoring her won't do anything."

"Maybe you should tell Diesel."

I glared at him.

"Look, you're married and pregnant now. I'll call him on my way out."

"Fine." He probably would be ticked if I didn't inform him what was going on.

"Alright. Give me a five-minute head start." He walked out and disappeared.

I sat behind my desk and considered what I would say to this woman. If she really wanted a relationship with me, she wouldn't have waited until I was turned thirty to start one. It didn't make any sense. She didn't care about me for the past twenty-five years, so why start now? She had her own kids, so it wasn't like being a mother wasn't in her plans. She had them later, but she still didn't reach out to me when it mattered. Maybe when I was a teenager, it would have been different. But she'd waited too long.

I told Jessica to usher her inside. She walked through the doors a moment later.

I almost couldn't believe what I was looking at.

It was me in eighteen years.

I remained behind my desk and didn't stand up to greet her. I carefully hid my reaction behind a stoic mask and didn't give her any insight into what I was thinking. Dressed in a black skirt with a white blouse, she even had similar taste in clothing.

She didn't try to shake my hand. Instead, she lowered herself into the chair, her purse over her shoulder. She didn't possess the same confidence I had. She was timid, hardly making eye contact. She took a deep breath and then finally looked at me, really looked at me. She took in my features with a shifting gaze, looking at my eyes as well as my cheeks. She breathed deeply, her eyes watering slightly.

I still didn't show an ounce of emotion. "I know who you are."

"Yes..." Her voice broke, so she cleared it. "I assumed."

"I'm not trying to be cold or cruel, but whatever your intentions are, I'm not interested."

She lowered her gaze, taking my insult with obvious hurt.

"I don't judge you for leaving my father and me. Being a mother may have been too difficult for you. I understand you were young and afraid. You did what you had to do for yourself. You made the right decision for both of us. Staying would have just hurt all of us in the end. So, you don't need my forgiveness because you don't owe me an apology. However...you forfeited your right to contact me for any reason. For that, I don't forgive you. I'm a very busy woman, and I don't have time to sit here and listen to whatever you have to say." My own words made me sound like a bitch, and I knew it. But I couldn't change the way I felt. I couldn't force myself to care when I didn't. She abandoned me with a man who could barely keep a roof over our heads.

"Tatum, I agree with everything you just said. However, I do owe you an apology. I never should have left you. I have two sons, and they've been the best things that ever happened to me. I shouldn't have left you. I should have stayed."

I didn't know what to say, so I continued to hold her gaze.

"I wish I knew you, Tatum. You've grown into such an incredible woman, and I couldn't be prouder of everything you've accomplished. I still can't believe you're my daughter... The way you've conquered the world and everyone that stood in your way. You're an inspiration to women everywhere. I know I have no right to be proud of you because I have no connection to you...but I'm very proud."

I ended eye contact once the guilt washed over me. "Why now, Bridget? Why did you wait so long?"

"It's a very sad story. I'll give you the short version of the long version. I was diagnosed with breast cancer eighteen months ago. Through treatment, I was able to defeat it. My doctors say the cancer is gone, and it's unlikely to return. But having that experience...thinking about my death...made me realize all the things I didn't do. I've been so afraid to contact you because I knew this would be your attitude, but I had to do it. I had to try. I had to at least apologize to you because you deserve to hear it. If you ever change your mind, ever want to know me or your half brothers, we would love to have the honor."

My heart slammed in my chest, and I felt the emotion creep into my veins. I shouldn't care about any of that, and I was embarrassed I did.

"I know you don't have children yet. But when you do...you'll understand. You'll understand they become your entire life. You'll love someone so much forever. I walked away from you when I shouldn't have, but that didn't mean I stopped loving you. I've always considered myself to be your mother even though I never earned the title."

The door opened, and Diesel stepped inside, a line of perspiration on his forehead because he must have run here. He adjusted his jacket and straightened his tie as he stepped into the room, casting a shadow over both of us. He unbuttoned his jacket and took a seat on the couch against the other wall.

I only glanced at him.

Bridget turned and looked at him. "Congratulations on your wedding. I saw pictures...you looked beautiful."

"Thank you," I whispered. I was still thinking about her last comment, about having children. I had a baby growing inside me right then, and even though I'd only been pregnant for a few days, my life was totally different. I wasn't the same person anymore. I was a mother even though my child wasn't completely formed. It made me feel a new level of empathy, a new level of compassion. My child would be born and not have a grandmother. Diesel's mother was gone, and my father was dead. All we had was Vincent. It seemed unfair to deny my baby the right to know where it came from.

Bridget turned back to me, watching me with sad eyes. She'd aged well, and she looked wealthy, like she didn't need money or help. Her pearls were real, her wedding ring was large, and her clothes looked like they were designer quality.

Maybe she didn't want me for money. "I'll never give you a penny of my fortune. If that's what this is about, you're wasting your time. You can spend years trying to butter me up, but I'll never change my mind."

Her eyes shut momentarily. "I'm not interested in that, Tatum. My husband is a wealthy man, and I have everything I need. I mean, he's not wealthy like you and your husband...but we do just fine."

I loved hearing Diesel being referred to as my husband.

"Your father was a good man. When I saw you on TV one day and realized it was you...I wasn't the least bit surprised. Your father was always optimistic even in the worst circumstances. That kind of attitude must have carried on to you. You never give up, no matter what the odds are. That's something you inherited from him."

"Along with a lot of other great things..."

"Of course," she whispered. She looked down at her fingers, her eyes cloudy with old thoughts. "I should let you get back to work. I'm sorry I've taken up so much of your time already. What I said still stands. If you ever change your mind...you'll find me." She rose to her feet and gripped her bag tightly. "I'm grateful you've given me the chance to apologize. That's what I wanted more than anything else." She turned to the door and slowly walked out.

Diesel shifted his gaze to me, his arms crossed over his chest.

Even on the other side of the room, I could tell what he was thinking.

Bridget walked out and shut the door behind her.

Diesel didn't lower his gaze. "She seems sincere."

I turned away.

"I forgave my father when I didn't want to...and I'm glad I did."

"Diesel, let it go..."

"Our baby could know their grandmother."

I sighed, my eyes on the desk.

"I won't say her behavior was justified. She made a huge mistake, and it shouldn't be swept under the rug. But now you have an opportunity to connect with the only family you have left."

"You're my family," I whispered. "Thorn is my family."

"You know what I mean. There's no harm in giving it a chance. You might like where it goes."

"Why are you saying this?" I turned back to him. "You're the most protective and paranoid person I know."

"Because I know this is what you need," he said firmly. "I read people very well, and Bridget seems sincere. Her husband is a millionaire, so she obviously doesn't need money from you. And you have two half brothers."

I looked away.

"What is the harm in trying?"

"I don't know this woman. She's a total stranger."

"I saw the look in your eyes, baby. You can pretend they didn't soften, but we both know they did. What if she dies tomorrow? Would you regret rejecting her?"

I sat in silence.

"You would, baby. Now give it a try. I know you're afraid to get hurt, but at the end of the day, you always have me. You always have Little Hunt."

I stared at my hands.

"Your father would want this."

I felt my body tense as I stared at my wedding ring. I felt the truth crash through me like a powerful wave. The vibration shifted up and down before it made its way directly to my heart. My father would have told me to leave the past where it belongs and embrace the present. He would tell me to extend forgiveness to everyone who asked for it. He would want me to have someone now that he was gone.

Diesel walked around the desk to me and placed his hands on my shoulders. His fingers slid down to my elbows, and he gripped me gently. "Baby."

I rested my head back against his waist and looked up at him. "Yes...my father would have wanted that."

He leaned down and moved his large hands over my flat stomach. He pressed a kiss to my lips then looked down at me. "He's the wisest man you've ever known. Listen to him."

CHAPTER TWENTY

Vincent

I couldn't think straight.

I kept pacing in my penthouse, downing nearly a full bottle of wine over the course of an hour. My eyes kept shifting back to my phone, waiting for a call or message from Scarlet. She was with Colin right now, talking to Lizzie about the real reason they divorced ten years ago.

Colin had seemed sincere in his apology, but that didn't make me stop hating him.

I would always hate him.

No amount of time would ever make his actions acceptable. There was no forgiveness for something that appalling. The idea of letting Scarlet be in an enclosed space with him set my teeth on edge.

It reminded me of Isabella. I wasn't there to protect her. Now it was happening again... I wasn't there for Scarlet.

After what seemed like an eternity, the phone finally rang.

"About fucking time." I answered and placed the phone against my ear. "Sweetheart, how did it go?"

"It played out exactly as I suspected," she said with a sigh. "Lizzie stormed out once she realized what her father did. Said she never wanted to speak to him again... and she apologized to me."

"Is he gone?"

"Yes, he already left. He's pretty down."

Like I gave a damn. "You want me to come over?"

A smile formed in her voice. "Why do you think I'm calling?"

Despite the stressful day, I smiled too. "I'll be there as soon as I can."

My driver dropped me off at her building, and I took the stairs to her floor. Before I could knock, she opened the door and greeted me with a hug.

I held her in my large arms and squeezed her against me. My hand touched her soft hair, and I smelled her perfume. My face moved into her neck, and I felt her pulse right against my lips.

She squeezed me back, her fingertips dragging down the back of my jacket.

I held her that way for a while, finally feeling sane now that I could embrace her in my arms. That asshole was gone, and she was in the same perfect condition as I'd left her. "I'm sorry things didn't go so well."

"It has to be this way." She pulled away so she could

look up into my face. "But Lizzie will get through it. I'll talk to her again and guide her back to her father. I don't blame her for storming out because it's a lot to take in. She thought she knew her father...and then realized she didn't know him at all."

"Yeah, I'd be devastated too."

"It's a new beginning...baby steps."

"I'm glad she apologized to you."

"Me too. And I told her about you...she wants to meet you."

"Really?" I asked.

She nodded. "And I know you aren't going to like this, but...I would really like it if we could all have dinner together."

"Of course, we can. I've been looking forward to it."

"No...I mean with Colin."

I didn't like that one bit. "He's not in your life anymore, so I don't see why he needs to be included."

"Because we're starting over. Colin wants to marry this woman, and I want to be with you. It would be nice if Lizzie could have both of her parents in the same room at the same time. He seemed really sincere in his apology. He started crying in front of his own daughter..."

"If you expect me to ever pity that man, you're wasting your time."

"Vincent, please."

I didn't want to cooperate. I wanted to know Lizzie but not to spend time with that shithead. But I also wanted to make Scarlet happy. She'd been patient with me from the beginning, and she was great with my sons. She understood my pain over Isabella and never cared about sharing me. I should do the same for her and understand they were still a family, even if they were divorced. "Okay...but only because I love you so damn much."

Her eyes lit up like the Fourth of July. "Thank you. I appreciate it." She moved to her tiptoes and kissed me, her mouth pressing against mine.

I squeezed her into me, taking everything I could get.

"I'd offer you dinner, but I don't want dinner."

"I don't want dinner either," I said against her mouth. "Unless you're the main course."

———

A week later, Scarlet finally convinced Lizzie to have dinner with both of her parents—and me.

I was nervous as hell.

I'd never done this before, met a girlfriend's child. There was so much pressure on the situation. I needed Lizzie to like me because I adored her mother. It would hurt me if my sons didn't accept the woman I loved.

I had to make this work.

We arrived at the restaurant hand in hand. Lizzie was already there sitting at the table alone with a basket of tortilla chips and a cup of salsa. Her arms were crossed, and she didn't look comfortable at all. But she looked just like her mother, exceptionally beautiful.

"Hey, honey." Scarlet reached the table first and smiled down at her daughter.

"Hey, Mom." She stood up and hugged her mom, giving her a long embrace that probably wasn't normal. When she finally pulled away, she looked right at me.

I lost my footing for a second, but I recovered my confidence instantly. "Lizzie, it's nice to finally meet you." I extended my hand.

She took it without smiling. "You too."

"Your mother has told me a lot about you... She's told me everything, actually. She's very proud of you."

"Thanks. She's told me a lot about you too." She was taller than her mother and exceptionally thin. If she didn't want to be a nurse, she could be a model instead. She was lucky she'd inherited her mother's beauty. "But I already know who you are. I see you on TV a lot...you're kinda famous."

"Unfortunately," I said with a smile.

"My mom told me you bought *Platform* since her boss was a jerk to her."

I hadn't anticipated her knowing that. My smile faltered. "I enjoy making your mother happy. It's a hobby of mine."

"Well, thank you. My mom is an incredible woman, and she works really hard. It's nice to know someone can take of her for a change."

This was going a lot better than I expected. "I want to take care of her for a long time."

Lizzie finally smiled before she turned back to the table. "So you have three sons, huh?"

"Yes." I sat across from her while Scarlet sat beside her daughter. That meant I'd have to sit directly next to Colin, but I'd rather be the one than Scarlet. And Lizzie wouldn't want to sit beside him either. "They're all grown men. My middle one just got married and is starting a family."

"That's exciting," she said. "My mom has pestered me about grandkids a few times..."

Scarlet shrugged. "I'm not getting any younger."

"Your mother tells me you're a nursing student," I said. "That's a very noble profession."

"Thanks," she said. "I really enjoy it. You're there with the patient through every step of their recovery. I enjoy having that intimate kind of relationship. Doctors are in and out...but you're always there."

"That's great," I said. "Your mother is very proud."

"Well, she would be proud of me no matter what I did," Lizzie said with a laugh.

Scarlet smiled and wrapped her arm around her daughter's shoulders. She kissed her on the forehead then squeezed her into a hug.

Lizzie let the touch linger even though she was uncomfortable.

I liked watching the happiness in Scarlet's eyes, seeing the way she loved her daughter the way I loved my kids. That was one thing we had in common. Our hearts lived outside our bodies when it came to them.

Scarlet pulled away and rubbed Lizzie's back. "I love you, baby."

"I love you too, Mom."

My eyes softened at their interaction, seeing so much of Scarlet in Lizzie it was like they were sisters. She was much younger than any of my kids, so I saw her as more of a child than an adult, even though it was a ridiculous thing to think.

"Thank you for agreeing to meet your father," Scarlet said. "He's excited to see you."

Lizzie immediately tensed at the mention of her father. "I don't know, Mom. I can't believe he did that to you."

"It was ten years ago," Scarlet said gently.

I didn't give a shit how long ago it was.

"It doesn't matter, Mom," Lizzie whispered. "It was wrong."

"Yes," Scarlet said. "But I want you to forgive him. He's your father, and I would never want you to hate him."

"How can you be so calm about it?" Lizzie asked.

"Because I know he's sorry," Scarlet said. "I know he's not the same man. You shouldn't punish someone for who they used to be. It's irrelevant at this point. I would much rather we be a family than be separated."

She was far too kind.

Lizzie sighed. "It'll take me some time to feel that way..."

"That's okay," Scarlet said. "Baby steps."

Colin arrived a moment later, doing the walk of shame as he entered the restaurant. He didn't greet Scarlet or try to hug Lizzie. He just sat down, bringing the awkward tension with him.

I would never shake his hand or make him feel welcome around me. He would always be on eggshells in my presence, a shadow of a threat constantly on his mind. I wouldn't raise a hand or cause problems on Scarlet's behalf.

"Hey, sweetheart," Colin finally said to Lizzie. "I'm glad you met Vincent. He's a nice guy."

I wore the same expression, but I felt the surprise in my chest.

"Yeah," Lizzie said. "I like him a lot."

Now my heart thudded again, this time with excitement. My eyes immediately went to Lizzie's face, seeing the sincerity in her eyes. Then my gaze shifted to Scarlet.

She was grinning at me—the happiest woman in the world.

———

"She adores you." Scarlet sat beside me in the back seat of the car as my driver took us back to my place.

"That's a little strong..."

"She does." Instead of sitting against the other window, she sat beside me in the middle of the seat. Her hand was on my thigh, her nails painted vibrant red. "Colin mentioned your conversation in the bar to Lizzie.

That's how it got started. I told her I'd been seeing you for a while, and I told her what you did with *Platform*... She was impressed. She knows you care about me to do all those things."

Now I got even more satisfaction from yelling at Colin. "That's good to know."

"I'm so relieved...you don't even know."

"You really thought she wouldn't like me?"

"She never gave any of my old lovers a chance."

I tried not to get jealous when she mentioned the other men she'd been with. It was ridiculous to feel that when I'd been married to the love of my life. Completely hypocritical. I swallowed the emotion and pretended it never happened. "I'm different. I wasn't going to give up until I had her seal of approval."

"You're right...I should have assumed." She linked her arm through mine and rested her head on my shoulder. "I'm excited that we can both spend time with her. I want you to be part of her life."

Scarlet seemed certain she was spending her life with me. But honestly, I felt the exact same way. The only reason why I didn't ask her to marry me was because it seemed too soon. Maybe in a few months, I would reconsider the idea. But for now, what we had was perfect. The fact that it was enough for her meant a lot to me. She never applied the pressure, but she always showed her commitment. "I just got my first daughter... I wouldn't mind having a second."

My phone started to vibrate in my pocket, so I

glanced at the name on my watch. It was Diesel. If it were someone else, I would have just ignored it because it was past seven. I answered. "Hey, Diesel."

"Hey, Dad. What are you doing?"

"I'm heading home with Scarlet. What are you doing?"

"I wanted to see if you could stop by. Jax and Brett are here too. We have some news."

I grinned because I already knew what the news was. I could barely contain my excitement. "We'll be right there."

CHAPTER TWENTY-ONE

Diesel

Jax and I hadn't had much time to reconnect, but we still felt like family. We still felt like brothers. He was just as excited as Brett was. "I'm gonna be Uncle Jax. It has a nice ring to it."

"I'm so happy for you guys." Brett hugged Tatum tightly. "I know we've got almost nine months to go, but they'll be here in no time."

We weren't planning on telling them right when they walked in the door, but they put the pieces together almost instantly. Thorn already knew about it because Tatum couldn't hide anything from him. He and Autumn unfortunately couldn't join us tonight.

And I was certain my dad figured it out on his own too.

"What are you hoping for?" Brett asked as he held his beer in the living room. "Boy or girl?"

"Either," Tatum said. She looked exactly the same as she did last week, but to me, she was glowing. She was glowing like the brightest star in the sky. Her stomach was just as flat and fit as always, but I imagined the baby growing inside her—the baby I put there. "Diesel and I will be happy as long as it's healthy."

"If she's a girl, she'll be a princess," Brett said. "Diesel will let her get away with anything, and once she blossoms into a woman, he'll lock her up in some tower somewhere..."

"Uh, no," Tatum said quickly. "She won't be a princess. She'll be treated exactly the same as if she were a son. That means pushing her just as hard and setting the expectations just as high."

"Aww," he said. "She'll be a little version of you."

"I hope so." Tatum was never a pampered girl, so of course, she'd expect the same from her daughter.

I didn't picture my little girl playing with dolls and makeup. I wanted her to be interested in more than being pretty and popular. In the real world, those two attributes only got you so far. You needed more than that to succeed.

"I'm going to be real with you," Brett said. "Diesel is gonna spoil her like crazy when you are looking the other way."

"Spoiling here and there is different," I said. "And I want to spoil all my kids...once in a while."

"Diesel and I have similar views on parenting," Tatum said. "So I think this will work out well."

I wrapped my arm around her waist, and I pressed a kiss to her lips. "And if we fuck this up, we'll just keep making more."

She chuckled against my mouth. "I guess that's one way to look at it."

The elevator doors opened, and my father walked inside with Scarlet. He was already smiling, and he never smiled. He knew the news before I formally announced it.

"Glad you could make it." I hugged my father before I kissed Scarlet on the cheek. "I know it was short notice."

"I just introduced Vincent to my daughter." Scarlet's arm hooked through his. "They really hit it off."

"That's great," I said. "But I'm not surprised. My dad is a pretty great guy."

His eyes softened. "That's nice of you to say, son."

I patted his shoulder. "So, how do you feel about being a grandfather?"

His smile widened, and a whole new expression appeared on his face. He wasn't on the verge of tears the way I'd been when Tatum told me the news, but he was definitely happy. Just like he was at the wedding, he was overjoyed. "I'm very excited."

Scarlet beamed as well. "Congratulations. There's nothing better than being a parent."

"I'm very happy," I said. "I think we'll make great parents. And even if I'm a terrible dad, I know Tatum will pick up the pieces."

"Diesel, you'll be wonderful," my father said immediately. "Don't worry about that." They moved to Tatum next, and my father hugged her for a long time, embracing her just like she really was his daughter.

I watched them from the entryway, seeing almost all the people I cared about most gathered around. My life changed the moment I felt for Tatum, and now it was changing in a whole new way. I was responsible for my wife and would lay down my life to protect hers. But now I would be responsible for a whole new person, a person I created with the love of my life.

How did I get so lucky?

Just a year ago, I was bored and empty. Nothing gave me meaning. And now I waswatching my father hug my wife as if he loved her just as much as he loved me. I wished my mother were here to share the moment, but I knew her spirit was in the room.

Tatum and I had an unconventional relationship. It started off as something physical and meaningless but developed into a bond so profound I could feel it in my bones. I didn't believe in destiny or fate, but something had told me she was meant for me.

That she was made just for me.

I was the only man who could handle such a powerful woman. She never would have met another man who was so secure with his own success that he never resented her for hers. I was the only man who could erase the memory of every single guy before me. I was the only one who deserved her.

I earned her.

And now she was mine for the rest of my life.

I watched her stare up at my father, a beautiful smile on her face. I'd watch her smile at me every single day for the rest of my life. I'd watch her smile at our children in the same way. Time would tear down our bodies, but we would still be beautiful together. Our children would grow into powerful people, and our love would continue on. One day, we would be buried together on a plot of land. For eternity, we would remain side by side. We would forever be the Hunts.

And she would forever be mine.

The elevator doors opened, and Bridget stepped out with her husband by her side. Her eyes immediately went to Tatum, the only person she really cared about. She turned her gaze back to me. "Hello, Diesel. Thank you for inviting me."

"Of course." I didn't shake her hand or hug her. It felt too strange.

When Tatum finished speaking to my father, she noticed me standing next to her mother in the entryway. Her eyes narrowed, and she immediately turned pale. She handed her glass of water to Brett and slowly joined me.

"I asked her to come," I explained.

Tatum masked her look of anger once the surprise dissolved in her veins. She'd done the same thing to me when she tried to repair my relationship with my father. She never gave up on us—and I was grateful she didn't.

Bridget stared at her, treasuring Tatum's expression. "I didn't mean to intrude. When Diesel invited us, I couldn't say no... I always love to see you."

My arm circled Tatum's waist, and I spoke on her behalf. "I think we're going to have to take this slow...but we're open to a new beginning." I turned to Tatum, silently asking her to agree with me.

Tatum nodded. "Yes...my father would have wanted that."

Moisture immediately sprung to Bridget's eyes, and her hands went to her chest. "That's... Thank you so much."

"Would you like to tell her?" I looked at my wife.

Bridget kept her eyes on Tatum.

Tatum paused for so long it didn't seem like she would say anything. Everyone else in the room picked up on the tension, so they watched us. Her hand immediately moved over her stomach. "Diesel and I are having a baby..."

"Oh..." Bridget gripped her chest harder. "That's... that's so wonderful. Congratulations. I'm so grateful you shared that with me." Her hands moved toward Tatum in an attempt to hug her, but she quickly withdrew her embrace, obviously thinking it would be inappropriate.

I dropped my hand from Tatum's waist in case she wanted to move into the embrace. The choice was up to her.

Tatum nodded. "Thank you...we're very excited." She didn't cross the space in between them and kept her distance. Physical affection was obviously too soon for her. "Please, let me get you something to drink. Be comfortable in our home."

The offer wasn't much to a regular person, but coming from Tatum, that was a big deal. She was officially opening the door and letting Bridget walk inside. Her guard was up, but her walls weren't nearly as high as they used to be.

She was taking a risk.

She took a risk on me.

I took a risk on my father.

Thorn took a risk on Autumn.

My father took a risk on Scarlet.

We all had to take risks sometimes. If we didn't, we wouldn't find the things that brought us the most joy. Opening the door allowed bad things to get inside, but a lot of good things too.

Opening the door to Tatum was the greatest decision I ever made. I knew she felt the same way.

And I knew this was another door that needed to be open.

EPILOGUE

TITAN

"Isabella, stop running." I placed my hands on my hips and stared down at my five-year-old daughter. She'd been running around the house with crayons in her hand because she refused to put on her shoes so we could leave.

Isabella stopped in her tracks, timid with fear. She dropped the crayons on the hardwood floor.

"Put on your shoes."

"Can you help me?" She hopped onto the chair and looked at her pink sneakers.

"You know how to tie them."

"It's hard..."

"You can do it, sweetheart." I showed my little girl how to do everything, but I didn't baby her. She needed to learn because I wouldn't always be around to help her. She needed to stand on her own two feet as quickly as possible.

Isabella sighed before she began the long process of getting each shoe on and taking forever to tie each one correctly.

I didn't rush her.

Diesel called me for the third time.

"I'm leaving right now. Isabella is putting on her shoes." I shut my laptop on the desk and grabbed my purse from the table. I'd worked all day at the office with Isabella strapped to my side. Our nanny was sick, so I had to run business with my daughter in tow.

"We've been here for fifteen minutes. You want me to come help you?"

"No. Just be patient."

Nathan yelled over the line. "Dad!"

"Shh," Diesel said in the background. "Mommy is coming."

"Mommy!" Nathan yelled.

Whenever our nanny called in sick, I took Isabella and he took Nathan. We couldn't handle more than one kid at a time while we were focused on our projects. Nathan behaved better with Diesel, and Isabella was a lot quieter with me.

"I'll be there soon." I hung up.

Isabella was done with her shoes, so we both left the office. I didn't pick her up and carry her to the elevator. We walked whenever possible. If I were willing to pick her up all the time, she would be the happiest little girl on the planet. But I wasn't doing that.

My driver took us to the restaurant, and we finally

made our way inside. Since there were too many people around, I scooped her up in one of my arms and carried her to the table where everyone was waiting.

"There's my girl." Diesel stood up with Nathan in one arm. He leaned in and kissed Isabella on the forehead.

"I thought you were talking about me," I teased.

"Then let me do that again," Diesel said with a chuckle. "There's my girls." He kissed me on the forehead next.

We traded kids because we hadn't seen either one all day. I held Nathan against my chest and smiled down at my three-year-old son. He looked so much like Diesel that my heart melted every time I looked at him.

"There's my granddaughter." Vincent came to Diesel's side and took Isabella away. "Beautiful, as always."

"Hello, Grandpa." She covered his nose with her hand.

"Hello, sweetheart."

Scarlet stood beside him and grabbed her small hand. "I like your dress. You look very nice today."

"Thanks, Grandma."

Scarlet took her next, her wedding ring shining in the restaurant.

Vincent eyed both of them with a smile on his face.

"Sorry we're late." Thorn came in next, his twin boys sitting in each arm. "We had a toy emergency. Don't ask." He rolled his eyes then greeted me with an awkward hug since he didn't have any arms to embrace me.

Autumn came in behind him with their daughter. "Brittany couldn't find her stuffed bear, and you know she can't go anywhere without it." The dark-haired girl in her arms had it held tightly to her chest.

"It shouldn't be an emergency," Thorn said. "But it was absolute chaos."

Autumn hugged me next. "Hello, Nathan."

He waved.

I took Brittany from her arms, and she took Nathan. "Hey, Brittany. How are you?"

She just held the bear to her chest and stared at me. She was very shy, which was unusual since both of her parents certainly weren't. But she was adorable, looking like a perfect blend of Autumn and Thorn.

"Let's eat." Thorn sat down. "I'm starving." He looked around the table and saw that Vincent was the only one without a baby. "Vincent, take one." He handed Connor across the table into Vincent's arms.

Vincent didn't seem to mind at all.

Now we all had a baby except Diesel. His eyes were on me, and he watched me hold our son against my chest. His eyes were soft, just as they always were when he saw me hold our children.

"What?" I asked, feeling his gaze intensify.

"You want to have another one?" he asked right in front of everyone. "Make it three?"

"Don't. Do. It." Thorn pointed at me. "Don't even think about it. Two is plenty. Don't go for three. Two parents and three kids doesn't add up."

Autumn rolled her eyes. "He's exaggerating."

"Hell no," Thorn snapped. "I had to take all of them

to work with me one day... Let's just say it was one of the worst days of my life."

"Shh," Diesel said to him. "I'm trying to convince my wife to let me knock her up again."

"Keep your legs closed, Hunt," Thorn barked. "You'll regret it if you don't."

There was no way I could keep my legs closed around my husband. Even if I wanted to, he would force them apart. "A third baby doesn't sound so bad..."

Thorn shook his head then grabbed the menu. "I need a big-ass beer."

Scarlet held Isabella until she started to cry in her arms. She handed her back to Diesel.

"See?" Thorn said. "It never stops."

"You'll regret the day it does stop," Vincent said quietly. "So enjoy it every moment you can."

Thorn turned his gaze on Autumn and shared a look with her. His features noticeably softened, and he brought his son closer to his chest. "Yeah...you're right. Vincent is always right."

Diesel hummed under his breath until Isabella stopped crying. Within a minute, she was back to being her calm self. She grabbed Diesel's nose and chin.

He was used to their hands constantly touching every-thing, so he was immune to it. He read his menu without being fazed by the constant touching. When Isabella slipped her fingers into his mouth, he playfully nibbled on them.

When I saw the way he was with our kids, there was nothing I wanted more than to have a third one.

Diesel caught me staring at him, so he stared back. "You thinking what I'm thinking?"

"Probably."

He chuckled then adjusted Isabella to a different leg so he could grab his water glass. "Dad, what are you and Scarlet doing tonight?"

"You want us to babysit?" Vincent held Connor in one hand while the other rested on Scarlet's thigh. "So you can make me another grandchild?"

"Pretty much," Diesel said. "Our nanny has the flu."

"And you have to do this tonight?" Vincent asked incredulously.

"Hey, you want another grandkid or not?" Diesel asked. "Jax isn't even close, and Brett and Natalie just got serious. I'm all you've got right now."

"Now he's threatening us with grandchildren," Scarlet said. "Well played, Diesel."

"I'm just yanking your chain," Vincent said. "We'd love to babysit, and not so we can have another grandchild. We love watching them."

"Yeah?" Thorn asked. "You want to watch ours too?"

"Thorn," Autumn said with a laugh. "Stop it."

"Hey, it was worth a shot," Thorn said. "When Autumn's parents watch the kids, it's impossible to get them back. They hog them too much."

"Aww, that's sweet." I thought of my father and how much he would love to meet his grandkids. But at least my mom was around. She came over once a week to spend time with the kids. Our relationship had progressed, but it was nowhere near perfect. It seemed like we were friends rather than mother and daughter, but it was better than nothing.

"Or do you want to watch them now so Tatum and I can sneak off?" Diesel asked.

I grabbed a piece of bread and threw it at Diesel's face.

Isabella laughed.

"Sometimes I feel like I already have three kids," I snapped.

Diesel grinned back, loving the way Isabella laughed. "That's pretty accurate, actually."

The waiter finally arrived with children's menus and took our orders. When everyone was distracted, I stared at my husband and reminded myself not to take anything for granted. I had the perfect life, luxuries that couldn't be bought. I had a wonderful husband and two beautiful children. My life was perfect.

I treasured it every single day.

I treasured it even more because it could have been so different. I took a chance on love, and I was rewarded with happiness I never thought I would experience. I got something people dreamed about but never actually experienced.

Letting go of Titan was the hardest thing I'd ever had to do, but combining my life with someone else's brought me more joy than I ever could have imagined. Diesel and

I were one person, and we had two wonderful kids to show for it.

I couldn't be happier.

Diesel must have known what I was thinking because he gave me a soft expression.

I gave him the same look in return.

And we both just knew.

AFTERWORD

Thank you so much for following me and Diesel and Titan on this journey. I've loved writing their stories, and I'm so grateful that you've enjoyed reading them. If you haven't left a review yet, please consider writing a few words. I'd truly appreciate it.

Stay tuned for my next story...

xoxo,

Vic

MUSE IN LINGERIE

by Penelope Sky

Chapter One

Sapphire

I sat alone at the bar with a scotch sitting in front of me. The amber liquid was strong down my throat, but not strong enough to fill me with the warmth I needed to survive this nightmare.

My mother's house had been repossessed by the bank. The single asset I inherited had been taken away from me with the snap of a finger. Now I didn't have a place to live, and what was worse, I still had to pay off the loan.

All because of my brother, Nathan.

His girlfriend left him, he got mixed up in the underworld, and he made a gamble he couldn't afford to lose. The guys killed him once his pockets were empty, and since Nathan had so much debt racked up, the government took the house to pay off everything he owed.

I couldn't believe this bullshit.

The house had been left to both of us, so we were both on the deed. Since I had better credit, and I was the more responsible one, the loan had been made out in my name. Now I had to pay for his stupidity by losing everything.

And I mean everything.

The house was gone. I still owed five hundred thousand dollars to the bank. My financial aid for college had been canceled because my credit was shit. Now I owed money for an education I couldn't afford to finish.

But that wasn't the worst part.

The crew that Nathan got mixed up in hadn't been compensated for the money they were due. They couldn't take the house because the government beat them to the punch. Knuckles, the leader of their organization, was one of the biggest crime lords in the world. Everyone spoke of him like a myth because they hadn't seen him in person.

Lucky bastards.

He was untouchable by the police because he had more power than any man should.

They called him Knuckles because that was his weapon of choice—his bare hands.

And I was his next victim.

I stared at the piece of paper sitting in front of me. Scribbled in black ink were simple words.

Three days, sweetheart.

Knuckles liked to play with his food before he went in for the final cut. He was torturing me, watching me struggle without a penny to my name. In random places, I would find these notes, usually slipped into my backpack when I rode the subway. Since I was homeless, I was crashing on people's couches.

And lying about my circumstances. They thought my place was being fumigated.

It was such a stupid lie I couldn't believe people actually believed it.

I only had three days of freedom left before Knuckles closed in on me.

And turned me into his personal sex slave. He promised there would be whips and chains. He promised there would be pain and pleasure. He promised he would get every cent he was due between my legs.

It was the final punishment for Nathan—even though he was long gone.

Knuckles warned me not to leave, that there would be dire consequences if I did. He had the resources to find me, and once he did, there would be a lot more pain than pleasure. There would be brutal torture along with his cock ramming me in every hole I possessed.

Fuck, I couldn't believe this was happening.

I wasn't sure who I was more pissed at. Nathan, Knuckles, or myself.

Myself because I should have known what Nathan was up to. I shouldn't have been so absorbed in my studies and work. I should have had a clue to what was going on around me. Nathan lived with me... How did I not see it?

I finished my scotch and ached for another, but I simply couldn't afford it. One was enough for the day.

The TV in the corner switched to Entertainment Tonight, and Lacy Lockwood appeared on the screen. One of the most beautiful models in the world, she was blonde with blue eyes and a body that would make every man fall to his knees. She modeled the most luxurious lingerie created. It was the kind of stuff that every woman wanted a man to buy her. It was beautiful, simple, and elegant. "Conway Barsetti is a genius. Everyone compliments my appearance, but he's the man who deserves your praise. He's the most meticulous and brilliant man I've ever known. Even on my worst days, he makes me feel beautiful."

With a size zero and a smile like that, how bad could her worst day really be?

The image changed to Conway Barsetti, standing for pictures outside one of his fashion shows. In a gray suit that fit him like a second skin, he stood in front of the cameras with pure indifference. It was like dozens of people weren't taking his picture at all, the bright flash hitting his eyeballs over and over. His hands rested in his pockets, and his broad shoulders contrasted against his narrow hips. For a man who designed clothes, his tastes were very simplistic. He turned his head slightly to give another angle for the photographers, his intense expression hardening like he was annoyed.

Not once did he smile.

And he obviously wasn't going to.

He had deep brown hair that looked black without the sun hitting it directly. Green eyes smoldered in vibrant intensity. His jawline was chiseled like the bone had been molded from a sculpture. His face had been cleanly shaven, but it was obvious he could grow facial hair overnight. A large Adam's apple protruded from his throat. Instead of looking like the designer who belonged behind the camera, he looked like he should be the focal point of everyone's attention.

He was damn gorgeous.

There were a few other interviews with the models, all gushing about the designer they worshipped like a god. Maybe they were being genuine, or maybe they were just kissing his ass to get a better spotlight. The show was taking place in Milan. Then then camera turned back to Lacey Lockwood.

"Conway Barsetti is always looking for the perfect woman to show off his art. I was sitting in a coffee shop when I was approached. My life changed forever in that moment, and I couldn't thank him enough for giving me this opportunity." The camera turned back to Conway, showing him shaking hands with a few other men in suits.

As I sat there pissing away whatever money I had left on a good drink, I watched this beautiful man living the dream. Rich, admired, and a level of beautiful that could only be described as stupid, he had everything. Women were plentiful, and money wasn't an issue. He could order as many drinks in that bar as he wanted.

I'd never been jealous like this before.

I was never rich, but I'd always had everything I needed. I had a roof over my head, food on the table, family, and an education. If you ask me, that was living the American dream. With the snap of my fingers, it was all taken away.

And there was nothing I could do about it.

I stared at the screen a while longer, watching the images change as they showed more aspects of Conway Barsetti's life. It showed his Italian villa in Verona, surrounded by vineyards and gorgeous land. It showed him posing outside a building in Milan, a bicycle leaned up directly beside him. Every image was more beautiful than the last, and not just because he was in it.

It was a beautiful place.

I'd never been to Italy. I'd never been outside the U.S. I'd been too busy being broke and going to school to afford such a lavish trip.

But now I had nothing. Just enough money to buy a plane ticket.

Knuckles threatened to hurt me even more if I ran. In three days, I would officially be his possession. Calling the cops wasn't an option because he'd kill every friend I had. But the idea of letting this man have me made me sick to my stomach. I wasn't going to wait around until he caught me off guard and wrapped his hand around my neck. I wasn't going to let someone turn me into a slave. I wasn't going to pay for a crime I didn't commit.

"Conway Barsetti's team just announced they'll have a special one-time opportunity for women to audition for a

spot on the runway. The auditions will be held in Milan..."
The reporter's voice trailed away once I tuned her out.

I left some cash on the table and grabbed my bag from the floor. Knuckles might be watching me that very moment, but I wasn't going to sit around until he appeared out of the darkness. I was going to run like hell until he caught me.

And I'd never stop.

Chapter Two
Sapphire
Even with only a few bucks in my pocket, Italy was a beautiful place.

The most gorgeous place I'd ever seen.

The small towns were surrounded by vineyards, flowers, and marketplaces full of fresh produce along with homemade cheeses. Wine was more plentiful than water, and strangers had no problem sharing with someone they didn't even know. Not having money to pay for food wasn't an issue because everyone was so generous.

If I were in America, I'd look like a beggar on the street.

I took the bus to the neighboring towns around Milan and explored them. It was easy to be a tourist when the most beautiful sights were all free. I slept under the stars because it was warm, and I showered in public restrooms. It wasn't my finest hour, but it certainly wasn't the worst either.

It was still better than being a slave.

At first, I looked over my shoulder every other minute, expecting to see that horrific man watching me. But three days had come and gone, and he obviously knew I was no longer in New York City. After a quick search, he would find the manifesto of the plane I was on. There was no doubt in my mind he'd tracked me to Italy. But since I was only using cash and not checking in to hotels, there was no way to trace me.

It was like I didn't exist.

Being homeless was a freeing experience.

The feds would keep searching for me since I owed so much on my mortgage, and they wouldn't stop until they put me in prison or took all of my wages from whatever job I managed to pick up. I would work forty hours a week just to be piss poor for the rest of my life. I couldn't even afford to resume my education.

Starting over in a foreign country sounded like my only option.

I just hoped no one caught me.

I didn't have a false sense of my appearance. I understood I was pretty, but I certainly wasn't model material. But if I could ask for a job doing something else, like sewing or being an assistant, I could make some money to get by. And I would also work for a very powerful man. It might make it difficult for Knuckles to touch me. That was also the last thing anyone would expect me to do, get a job working for a famous man. People would assume Conway Barsetti would turn me in, but judging by the empty expression in his eyes, he wouldn't give a damn who I was running from. He had more important things to do—like count his money and his women.

I returned to Milan later that night with a bag full of bread, cheese, grapes, and crackers. The villagers I met had pushed more food into my arms than I could carry. I ate most of it when it was fresh and saved the rest for dinner. I slept in a hostel that night and had a bed and a real shower after a few days without that kind of luxury.

Tomorrow, I would head to the audition and hope for the best. I didn't have nice clothes, but my clothes shouldn't matter because I wasn't looking to be a model.

I'd even be a janitor—if it paid enough.

***

I had to check in like everyone else and was given a number to stick against my clothes. All the women there were already in heels and lingerie, dressed up for the part. Beautiful, skinny, and with enormous hair, they were all qualified to be the next model for Conway Barsetti.

I was the only one fully dressed—and that made me feel naked.

Most of the women raised their eyebrows when they looked at me then whispered something to their friends in Italian. Some even laughed at me, like I was an idiot for showing up dressed in jeans and a t-shirt. My makeup and hair were done, and I dressed nice for a walk through the park, but in that context, I looked like the biggest freak on the planet.

Numbers were called, and women worked the stage like it was the real deal. They strutted, pivoted, flipped their hair, and threw smoldering gazes at the men sitting behind the table.

Conway Barsetti wasn't there.

He must have more important things to do than pick out his next model. Or maybe he was watching—but he couldn't be seen. I was a bit crestfallen when he was nowhere in sight. A beautiful man like that was fun to stare at.

They finally called my number, 228.

I walked up the stairs and passed the woman who just hit the runway. She didn't contain her laugh as she passed me, wearing a silver bra and panties and heels that were so tall she was practically walking on her toes.

I ignored her and walked up to the table where the three men sat. All dressed in suits, their eyes moved over my body, taking in every feature with experienced gazes. It wasn't the look I received from men when I went downtown in a short dress. It was pragmatic, completely observational.

The one in the middle spun his finger. "Turn and walk."

"I'm not here to audition to be a model." I kept my hands by my sides and didn't bother with a fake smile. I wasn't there to impress them with my appearance, but my mannerisms. "I have a lot of other skills I think will be useful to the Barsetti lingerie line. I can sew, clean, cook, organize...anything. I'm looking for work, and I'm willing to fill any position you may have."

The man in the middle had dark hair and eyes. A pen

was held in his fingertips and he absentmindedly rotated it within his fingers. His eyes were dark like coffee, with just a splash of cream. "Modeling is the position we're trying to fill. You want it or not?"

I immediately wanted to challenge him until he caved and directed me to someone who could hire me in a different field, but judging by the hostility in his eyes, he was already fed up with me. It was unlikely anyone spoke to these men that way, not when they could make dreams come true. "Do I look like the modeling type to you?" I showed up in jeans and a t-shirt with flat sandals on my feet. I wasn't photogenic like the rest of them. I didn't smile with perkiness or smolder with my sensuality. I was plain and boring. I knew it—and they knew it.

"I don't know," he said. "You haven't walked the runway yet."

"I don't think my ability to walk is the deciding factor here." I crossed my arms over my chest. "Look, I'm desperate for work. I just moved here, and I've got twenty euros in my pocket. I can do anything."

"Then walk the runway." He flicked his wrist and indicated to the stage with his pen. "Or leave." He challenged me with his dark look, telling me his patience had been officially drained. The other two men watched me in silence, hardly blinking.

I swallowed my pride and did as they asked. I'd seen two hundred and twenty-seven women walk that runway all afternoon, so I knew exactly what to do. I knew how to hold my shoulders, how to shake my hips, and how to pivot. I felt like an idiot for doing it dressed that way, but I was desperate.

And desperate people did desperate things.

I walked to one point of the stage and then turned back, walking with a straight back and tense posture. I didn't smile or wear a smoldering expression. That was where I drew the line.

The man in the middle set his pen on his clipboard. "Scars?"

"Excuse me?"

"Do you have scars?"

"No."

"Lift up your shirt."

My eyes narrowed. "Excuse me?"

"I need to see your skin," he said. "Blemishes, acne, etc."

"Just take my word for it."

He made notes on a piece of paper then snapped his fingers at me.

I placed my hands on my hips, regarding him with an ice-cold expression. Something told me that snap was specifically for me—and I didn't care for it. "Do I look like a dog to you?"

"Woof." An asshole smile spread on his lips. "Get your ass over here and take this. It has your instructions."

"My instructions?" I slowly inched forward, my eyes on the small piece of paper he held in his hand. "What does that mean?"

"It means you're going to the next stage." He placed

the paper in my hand. "Show this to the men at the door otherwise you won't get in."

"Whoa, hold on." My eyes scanned the information written down. It had an address as well as a time. "You're seriously considering me?"

"Yes, sweetheart." He still wore that asshole smile.

"Don't call me that." Anytime I heard that name, I felt the terror constrict my throat. Knuckles was the only man to ever call me that, so I'd developed a deep aversion to the horrific nickname. No man would ever call me that for the rest of my life. "And are you insane? Do you see all the gorgeous women out there?"

"You don't think you're gorgeous?" He cocked an eyebrow. "It doesn't matter what you wear. Real beauty can't be hidden. Now get off the stage. We have a lot of women to see."

I stared at the paper again, unable to believe what just happened. I didn't know how much models got paid, but it was definitely enough to get an apartment and have a hot shower every day. It could be enough for me to start over. "When I said I wanted a different position, I wasn't lying. Is there really nothing else?"

He crossed his arms over his chest. "You're the dumbest woman who's ever graced this stage. You just won the lottery, but you're too stupid to realize it. You'd rather sew in a factory than be a Barsetti model? No, you're the one who's insane." He leaned forward and stared up at me, his eyes burning like a raging forest fire. "Are you gonna take it or not? We're supposed to hand out ten invitations. If you don't want it, I'll give it someone who actually gives a damn." He reached his hand out to snatch it from my grip.

My hand immediately formed a fist around the paper, concealing it within my palm.

He leaned back and smiled. "Good...maybe you aren't that stupid."

"You're only choosing ten women?"

"Yes."

"And I'm one of the ten?" There were thousands of women lined up in the street, all dressed in their best. They were exotic, beautiful, and eager. I showed up hoping for a job mopping the floor or sewing buttons and lace, but I was given something they'd all kill for.

"Yes." He nodded to the stairs. "Now go before I change my mind."

I kept the invitation tucked into my palm, feeling my pulse pound around my grip. It was a sunny day in Milan, and the sun was beating on the back of my neck. I felt the sweat collect underneath my breasts in my top. But those physical nuisances paled in comparison to the choice I had before me.

The last thing I ever wanted to be was a model. I didn't judge women who took off their clothes to make a living, but I'd never been interested in the lifestyle. I didn't have the right attitude, and I was far too stubborn to follow directions. Knuckles threatened to torture me worse if I ran, but I did it anyway. Anyone would have told me it was the dumbest mistake of my life, but I didn't care.

I'd rather run than surrender.

Modeling for Conway Barsetti wasn't ideal, but it would give me something I couldn't find anywhere else.

Protection.

I'd be surrounded by people all the time, living in the shadow of one of the greatest designers of our generation. A man worth billions had serious power. He wouldn't care about protecting me, but he would certainly care about his brand.

Maybe this was a blessing in disguise. "I'll be there."

Chapter Three

Sapphire

10.

They stuck the number against my tiny black bustier. It was so tight I could only take a half breath. Even though models didn't wear thongs on the runway, I was required to wear one—that way every detail of my body could be seen.

The black thong matched the lace of my top, and there was a tiny pink flower right below my cleavage line for color. I'd never worn lingerie in my life, so it was my first time being put on display like this.

And I had to wear it in a room full of strangers.

A woman did my hair and makeup, transforming me into a woman I hardly recognized. Body makeup was rubbed into my skin, hiding even the slightest blemish from being visible. My hair was three times bigger than usual, and there was so much mascara on my lashes that my eyelids actually felt heavy.

I couldn't believe I was doing this.

But what other option did I have? Anyone could judge me for making money with my body, but when I was on the run from a psychopath, I didn't have many options. I didn't speak Italian, so finding work was difficult. I needed something that required very little talking.

And modeling required no talking.

The other nine girls were perfect for the part. Tall, beautiful, so thin I wondered if they ever ate, and perfect. Some of the girls made friends with each other, and none of them could contain their excitement for being selected in the top ten. I wasn't sure how many models they were looking for, but I would assume only half of us were likely to be picked.

I doubted I would make it to the next stage.

But then again, I didn't know how I got here to begin with.

"Line up." A middle-aged woman in glasses clapped her hands and pointed across the stage. We were inside one of the Barsetti studios, an entire auditorium full of rows of seats. The balconies were decorated with elegant Italian designs and an enormous fresco was painted across the ceiling.

The girls filed in a straight line, starting at number one.

From left to right, we formed a line. I was the last one

in line, and I wondered if my placement had anything to do with my odds. Maybe the best candidates started at the front.

The man who had selected me stood in one of the aisles, the other two men sitting with their clipboards. He held his phone to his ear, listened to something, and then shoved it into his pocket. "Conway Barsetti is arriving." He sat down with the other two men, leaving the aisle seat open.

It turned dead silent in the auditorium. People weren't even breathing. The girls sucked in their invisible stomachs and pinned their shoulders back, ready to impress a man who was impossible to impress.

I straightened my posture and mimicked them as much as possible, but it didn't stop me from feeling stupid. I didn't know how to be sexy. These women were masters at it, knew exactly what a man like Conway Barsetti wanted to see. I was totally clueless when it came to stuff like this.

But if he didn't pick me, I would ask for other work. I wasn't leaving this place until I had an income. Italy was expensive, and I couldn't rely on good people giving me free food all the time. I had to carry my own weight. I would clean toilets if that's what it came down to.

The silence continued to stretch endlessly, everyone afraid to breathe too loudly like it would disrupt the anticipation. I hadn't seen a room become this tense for anyone in my life. Even when the President of the United

States appeared on TV, people weren't this rigid. It seemed like I was waiting for a king.

A ruler.

At the exact same time, both doors swung inward and opened the entryway. Sunlight entered the room, and the silhouette of a man was seen. In a black suit and royal blue tie, a man carrying broad shoulders and endless power entered the auditorium. His presence infected every inch of the room, filling the air with his potent authority. I felt it with every breath I took.

A young woman followed behind him, a clipboard in hand with her pen held in her fingertips. She constantly stayed a few feet behind him, her body just as poised as the models on the stage.

Once he was away from the sunlight, his visage was finally visible. His chin was marked with a noticeable line of scruff, but it was expertly manicured. His hands rested in his pockets, and a shiny watch reflected the stage lights. He held himself with better grace than all of us on stage.

All eyes were on him.

He knew it, but didn't seem to be affected by it.

He took a seat in the chair reserved along the aisle for him. The woman who followed him around took a seat directly behind him. The men who had escorted him there shut the doors then lingered in the back, turning into motionless statues now that they weren't needed.

Quite a performance.

The woman on stage with us addressed us again. "Now

that Conway Barsetti is here, let's get started. When I call off your number, you'll walk to the edge of the runway, pose, and then return to your position. Cue the music."

Instantly, music erupted over the speakers. The lights were cranked higher.

My eyes looked at the spot where Conway was sitting, but I couldn't make out much of his features. His green eyes slightly reflected the lights coming from the stage, and it seemed like he was staring at me.

But that must just be in my head.

Number one went and strutted to the edge of the stage. Her heels clanked against the floor, but she didn't falter in her steps. She posed at the end, flipping her hair profoundly before she turned and walked back. She was in a thong just the way I was, but she obviously didn't feel even remotely uncomfortable showing her entire ass to the men in the audience.

I kept my posture, but the sky-high heels were already killing my feet. After five minutes of wearing the damn things, I was in pain. How did models bear the pain and still strut like they owned the stage? It was a mystery to me.

Number two went next.

My eyes moved back to Conway Barsetti's figure in the audience. His elbows rested on the armrests, and his hands came together in the center of his chest. His watch was more noticeable, and he wore a black ring on his forefinger. His face was still mostly hidden in the shadows, but now there was no mistaking what he was looking at.

Me.

Number two did her best work and returned to the line, but Conway Barsetti missed her entire performance.

He couldn't actually be staring at me, not when there were nine better candidates performing for him right at that moment.

Number three took off.

His green eyes were locked on me, not even blinking. He stared at me with an intense gaze that was almost hostile. It wasn't clear whether he hated me or wanted me. Maybe he was ticked his assistants had placed me in the top ten. Perhaps it irritated him that such an unworthy woman wore one of his greatest designs.

Number four went next.

His eyes were still on me.

I turned my eyes away, his heated gaze becoming too much. I suddenly felt vulnerable, like an antelope standing in the tall grass of the Serengeti. There was a lion watching me. I couldn't see him—but I could certainly feel him.

I'd been threatened by worse men, Knuckles being the top pick. But I always hit back with the same force they struck me with. If a man tried to disrespect me, I did the same to him. Allowing myself to be intimidated simply wasn't an option. To live your life in fear was to not live at all. Despite learning all those lessons, I felt trepidation when he stared at me.

I felt like he could see right through me, see all my fears and doubts. He could read my mind like words on a page. He could feel every emotion like it was wafting from my skin. He could sense my vulnerability, knowing I was slowly coming undone.

His image on TV was nothing compared to the real thing.

He may be beautiful, but damn, he was terrifying.

He was thirty feet away from me, but his presence projected so far it seemed like he was standing right in front of me.

The lights put me on display, and all I could do was stand there and take his stare. I was already nervous to walk in my heels, but now that his harsh eyes were watching me like a pair of binoculars, I didn't feel as strong as I did before.

I felt like a mess.

Now we were on number six.

She didn't make it to the edge of the stage.

As if Conway Barsetti was speaking through a microphone, his voice projected throughout the entire auditorium, but he accomplished it without raising his voice. "Numbers one through nine, you're dismissed."

Number six froze at the edge of the stage, in midpose. She looked over her shoulder at the older woman in charge of the audition, shocked and looking for direction. The other girls looked at each other too, devastated by the announcement.

Then they all looked at me—furious.

The woman in charge faltered before she found her voice. "Uh, head backstage, please..." Judging the fear in her voice, this had never happened before. Conway Barsetti hadn't even seen all the models before he dismissed them.

He hadn't even seen me move yet.

He was about to be disappointed.

Heels tapped against the stage as all the girls walked off, their silent fury audible in my ears. They moved behind the curtain, and within a few seconds, the sound of their heels ended. Then all I could hear was my own breathing.

And it was loud.

Conway Barsetti didn't move from his seat. Everyone was rigid around him, waiting for whatever would come next.

Was I supposed to do something?

The woman who was telling us what to do a second ago had disappeared with the other girls, so there was no one to give me any direction. I kept my posture as long as I could, feeling my shoulders ache from pulling them back so tightly. It was difficult to tell exactly what Conway was doing because the audience was a haze when the bright lights hit my face so hard.

Then he spoke again. "Leave us."

He'd dismissed the others, but now, he seemed to be dismissing me.

Everyone seated in the audience rose to their feet and started to leave.

I turned away and did the same.

"Not you." His voice rose slightly. "Stay."

Somehow, I knew he was talking to me. I slowly turned back around, watching everyone else walk out the double doors. They shut behind them, and after that loud clank, it was silent again.

Now it was even more silent than before.

Conway rose to his feet, buttoning the front of his suit at the same time with elegant grace. He moved to the center of the wide aisle, his hands sliding into his pockets. Now that he moved away from the shadows of the seating area, his whole face was on display.

His eyes never looked so green.

His wide shoulders hinted at the power underneath his suit. He was in the audience and I was the one on stage, but he seemed to be the center of focus. For a man like Conway Barsetti, he didn't need a stage. He was always the star.

I crossed my arms over my chest, hiding my bare stomach from view. Now that it was just the two of us, I felt even more on vulnerable. I was aware of the way the lingerie pushed my boobs tightly together to form a dramatic cleavage line. I was aware of how revealing my thong was. My bare skin pebbled just from a single look from him.

"Don't slouch."

It took me a moment to process the order. I was used to firing back with smartass comments, but he was potentially my new employer. So I dropped my hands to my sides and stuck out my chest.

"Good." He took the stairs and slowly reached the

stage, his heavy footfalls echoing from the acoustics of the auditorium. He approached me from behind, making me feel like a small fish while he circled me like a shark.

Now I was even more aware of my bare ass.

I could feel him stare at it.

He slowly circled around me, coming around my left until he was directly in front of me. His hands remained in his pockets and his eyes combed over my body, examining the roundness of my shoulders and the hollow in my throat. He moved farther south, taking in the sight of my cleavage then progressed downward.

I wanted to cross my arms over my chest again. I felt fire all over my skin, the heat in his gaze. I felt defenseless against this man—like I had no power whatsoever. That was a recurring theme of my life lately. Everything had been taken from me, but now this man was about to take whatever was left.

Once his examination was over, his eyes met mine. "Name?"

I didn't want to have a name. I wanted to leave my old identity behind and start fresh. I didn't want anyone to trace me back here. I was running from the American authorities and the mob at the same time. My odds of success weren't great. "Does it matter?"

He must have expected me to answer him obediently because he couldn't control the slight rise of his right eyebrow. He was nearly a foot taller than me even in the five inch heels I wore, but I could still see his reactions easily. "You'd rather I called you Ten?" The baritone of his voice was mesmerizing. It had a hypnotic ability to stop me from thinking about anything. It was like a spell.

"Call me whatever you want. I don't care."

"If you don't care, why don't you just give me your name?"

Not only was he handsome and authoritative, but he was smart too. No wonder why he was a billionaire and the most respected lingerie model on the planet. "Ten, it is."

His eyes narrowed this time. "The only reason a woman won't give her real name is because she's running from something—or someone."

"I won't bore you with my baggage, Mr. Barsetti. But yes, you're right."

"It's Conway Barsetti."

"My mistake..."

"Fine, Ten." He stepped away, his cologne lingering in my nose once he passed. "Walk."

"Where?"

He never answered me again. He only snapped his fingers.

My eyes immediately narrowed at the action.

"Don't waste my time, Ten. There and back."

He wanted me to walk the runway like the other models. I sucked in my stomach and then did as he asked, mimicking their movements the best I could. When I saw fashion shows on TV, I never understood just how difficult it really was until I tried to strut in insanely tall heels.

I walked to the edge, posed, and then turned around and walked back to him.

His eyes didn't linger on my face. He watched all of my movements, from my arms to my legs. He brushed his thumb along his bottom lip and furrowed his brow, as if he was really thinking about what he was seeing.

I returned to the spot where I started.

"Poor mechanism. Loose control. Not enough confidence. Shoulders back farther...widen your steps." He circled around me, eyeing my legs and my hips. "You need a lot of work."

"I need a lot of work?" I snapped. "Then why don't you pick one of the other nine? They were flawless."

He circled behind me then came back around. "Don't question me."

"Don't question you?" I asked incredulously. "You just insulted me."

"I critiqued you." He stopped in front of me again. "And you're going to have to get used to it if you want to be a Barsetti model."

"So that means you've chosen me?"

"Would I be here otherwise?" He stepped toward me and placed his hands around my rib cage just below my breasts.

It took me a second to understand he was touching me because it happened so quickly. It was one thing to stare at my nakedness, but another to touch me like he had every right to do whatever he wanted. "Uh, do you mind?" I slapped his hands away.

His face was just inches from my face, and he stared at me with arctic coldness. "Do you always interview for a job like this?"

"Do you always assault your employees like this?"

He dropped his hands and stepped back, his eyes touching me even more than his hands did. "I need to understand your body. I need to feel it, to measure it. If you can't handle being touched, then this isn't going to work."

"You could have asked permission first."

"I don't ask for permission," he snapped. "Every model who wears my lingerie belongs to me. I can do whatever I damn well please. Now, if you want to work for me, your attitude is going to have to change."

"Asking me to change my attitude is like asking me to change my personality."

"Then control it." He slid his hands into his pockets and headed to the stairs. "We have a lot of work to do. Be in my dressing room at six tomorrow morning—and expect to be touched." He took the stairs until he was back in the aisle.

"Six in the morning?" I asked incredulously. I usually wasn't up until eight.

"Yes." He adjusted his cuff link then looked at his watch. "I start my day at four."

Jesus Christ. If I were a billionaire, I'd allow myself the luxury of sleeping in every day. "I know this is a weird request, but I need to be paid under the table. If that can't happen...then I can't do this."

Once he was finished with his sleeves, he looked up at me again. His bright green eyes cut into me like they were knives. He watched me with distinct coldness, the ice reaching every corner of the room. He could replace me with another beautiful woman at any moment. People didn't make requests like mine unless they were hiding something illegal. I definitely was, and he may not want to help a fugitive. "I accept your terms. But that means you better accept mine."

Order Muse in Lingerie

CPSIA information can be obtained
at www.ICGtesting.com
Printed in the USA
LVHW02s0044280818
588281LV00001B/195/P